The
Truchas Light

The
Truchas Light

A Novel

R. M. Lienau

SUNSTONE
PRESS

SANTA FE

Sunstone books may be purchased for educational, business, or sales promotional use.
For information please write: Special Markets Department, Sunstone Press,
P.O. Box 2321, Santa Fe, New Mexico 87504-2321.

Cover artwork by Leslie Lienau
Book and Cover design › Vicki Ahl
Body typeface › Vani
Printed on acid-free paper
∞

Library of Congress Cataloging-in-Publication Data

Lienau, R. M. (Richard M.) author.
The Truchas Light : a novel / by Richard Lienau.
   pages cm
ISBN 978-0-86534-974-2 (softcover : alk. paper)
1. Scientists--Fiction. 2. Kidnapping--Fiction. 3. Murder--Fiction. 4. New Mexico-
-Fiction. 5. Mystery fiction. I. Title.
PS3562.I4533T78 2013
813'.54--dc23

                      2013035244

WWW.SUNSTONEPRESS.COM
SUNSTONE PRESS / POST OFFICE BOX 2321 / SANTA FE, NM 87504-2321 /USA
(505) 988-4418 / ORDERS ONLY (800) 243-5644 / FAX (505) 988-1025

*T*o the memory of Paul Robinson, a friend.

1

*D*r. Abe Bartle leaned forward, anxiously staring at a rectangle of rapidly changing, lurid red LEDs. Both his hands squeezed the arms of his chair. The light emitting diodes were part of a vast array of numbers, dials and screens scattered across an electronic test control panel that angled away from a long, narrow console.

The room with concrete floor, walls, and ceiling where he sat was cramped. Its only window was a tilted, double-glass observation panel that looked out onto an immense test bay half a floor below. Seated next to him were Virginia Montaño to his left and James Ransom on his right.

Bartle's stomach knotted up and his heart rate rose dramatically as the value of the numbers he focused on climbed rapidly. He glanced in turn at the color video monitor to the left of the meter panel, then at the technicians next to him.

They returned his gaze briefly, their faces betraying stark terror.

Bartle looked at the video monitor again as the fuzzy red dot on the monitor grew and pulsated. He stood abruptly, freeing his swivel chair to roll back across the narrow room and leaned forward to peer into the deep area below. He focused on the flanged, circular viewing port that jutted out from the shiny horizontal cylinder in the bay. He saw the light captured in the monitor with his own eyes. Increasing in size, it glowed orange, then went white.

He angled his head down to look at the monitor. The light on the screen turned blue, then blue-white. His jaw slack, he watched, incredulously, as over a three second period its colors ranged across the visible spectrum. Bartle looked down into the bay again. The general lighting in the cavernous, two-story room was overwhelmed by the fierce beam emanating from the thick crystal glass of the viewing port. He brought his right arm up to cover his eyes at the same time he lurched for the red, palm-sized emergency button on the control panel, but it was too late.

The huge metal cylinder, which lay on concrete pedestals parallel to the grey concrete floor, burst along its length, spewing blinding, blue-white plasma into the huge test bay. Test gear next to the viewing port of the big tube vaporized, while that in the blast path farther away was either blown apart or smashed into the concrete wall separating the confined chamber from the control room above it.

Pieces of cylinder flew in every direction. Three penetrated the concrete ceiling and the roof above. A large, ragged piece of the tube's center, along with the viewing port, arced across the test bay and smashed through the double safety panes of the control room observation window. As it did, it took pieces of glass with it and struck Dr. Bartle in the head and chest, blowing him across the narrow control room and smashing him against the back wall. He died instantly.

Another piece of steel debris, more than two feet long, sharp and spinning like an airplane propeller, scythed through the now glassless window and decapitated Jerry Ransom at the far right of the console.

Virginia Montaño dived under the console desk, but not before a foot-long splinter of steel lanced through her upper-right chest, spewing blood onto the console.

The opposite ends of the cylinder, four feet in diameter, dislodged from their moorings. Like a battering ram, one end broke into the staging bay, throwing chunks of concrete across the immense room, killing test technicians Joe Chavez, Penny Markus, and Phil James as they sat drinking coffee at a work table. The other end of the tube smashed into the empty cafeteria. Three seconds later all AC electrical power died and the emergency battery-driven system came on line.

Virginia Montaño, groaning in pain with the steel shard sticking out of her bloody chest, consciousness ebbing and flowing, lay on the hard, tiled floor in the half dark. With great effort, she pulled herself up and grabbed the lip of the console with her bloody left hand. With her right hand, she felt frantically for the cradled red telephone handset with its coiled lead. When she found it, she jerked it away from the console and sank back onto the floor, moaning.

Her shallow breath was now coming in gasps. She held the handset covered with slick, dark blood to her face and pressed the button on the mouthpiece. With the handset still close to her mouth and her eyes staring blankly ahead, her head dropped to the floor.

If Montaño had been alive, she would have heard the male voice on the phone say, "Security! Security! Security!"

Jason Thompson, at the wheel of a grey government sedan, raced south along the two-lane macadam road, ignoring the 25 MPH speed limit signs. He squinted against the first rays of sunlight that arced across the cold New Mexico sky, distorted and shaped by the black, ragged outline of the Manzano Mountains to his left. On either side of the lonely road the dark green cedar and piñon trees cast long, dark shadows against the browns and beiges of the dry land.

He managed the car through a screeching left turn, then steered it down another paved road, past a sign with large, red block letters that read:

"AREA 7, RESTRICTED, AUTHORIZED PERSONNEL ONLY"

Five minutes later, after being cleared by the nervous sentry through the lonely Post M, he drove around a huge berm overgrown with sage, grama grass, and prickly pear.

As he rounded the bend into the parking lot, Thompson was confronted with a jumble of vehicles. A rank of Navy-grey carryalls with U.S. Government numbers painted on their flank were parked next to the huge building, close to a steel personnel door with a flashing red light over it. More grey carryalls, along with two grey sedans, a red sedan, and two red and white ambulances, were parked at odd angles behind the first row and near an opening large enough to allow a semi-trailer rig to pass. A yellow fire truck was parked in the big opening. Beyond was a scattered, regimentally arranged row of private cars and pickup trucks. He parked close to the windowless grey concrete structure under the mound of earth.

The building was more than a hundred feet long. Large, camouflaged air-exchange ducts, pointing at the cloudless sky, pushed through the dirt that covered the roof.

Jason fished for the badge in his shirt pocket, pushed out of the car, slammed the door shut, and ran for the truck bay as he clipped the badge to his shirt collar. One of two harried armed, uniformed guards who stood next to the entrance, touched his picture ID and nodded.

He slowed as he entered and made his way around a fire truck blinking crimson emergency lights. Once into the staging bay, he stopped and looked around, panting with excitement and distress. The two-story high room was strewn with concrete chunks, metal shards, wire tubing, and a thick film of grey dust, some of which hung in the acrid air. To his left, paramedics and firemen worked over shrouded bodies. To his right, a photographer took pictures. He turned as Dave Manning came up behind him and stopped at his side. Manning then looked away.

"God. This is awful." Manning, two inches shorter than Jason Thompson's six feet, shook his head slowly as he breathed his statement. His face was deeply lined. He looked older than Jason, though he was younger.

Without answering, Jason moved away to walk slowly across the wide expanse of the staging bay to the small group of medical and fire-rescue people filling out forms or preparing bodies for removal. Debris crunched loudly under his shoes. Manning followed several feet behind.

Jason, his face drawn and white, looked at the smashed table where coffee cups and playing cards had rested, strewn ten feet from the gaping hole in the concrete demesne wall that separated it from the test bay. Chunks of grey debris and tangled pieces of steel from the huge test cylinder lay next to the ragged hole in the concrete wall. A reinforcing bar waved grotesquely in a tangled web from the jagged opening.

Tears welled up as he watched draped bodies being wheeled away one by one. "Jesus, how the hell—" He turned away as he pulled a handkerchief from his pants pocket and applied it to the areas around his eyes.

With Manning beside him again, he stood in silence until Hank Peppers approached them from across the staging bay. Peppers stopped and looked intently from man to man. "Dave. Jason. This is a god-awful mess. Thanks for getting here pronto." Mildly out of breath, he spoke slightly above a whisper as he worked his hands.

Manning said, "Jesus God, Hank! What the hell happened here?" He ran a tense hand through his white hair and glanced at Jason.

Peppers's eyes were wide. "You tell me. This is a war zone." He pointed vaguely. "Six dead. Three here and three in the control room. Fortunately, there was no one else in the building."

Jason Thompson ran his hand over his unshaven face and sighed as his eyes, red from lack of sleep, darted around the big room. "Bartle thought he was onto something. They were working overtime. Supposed to be here all night." He paused to rub his eyes. "There must have been a miscalculation." He turned to Peppers. "What time did it happen?"

Peppers looked at his watch. "Post M got the call at 3:16."

"AM?" Jason asked.

"AM," Peppers nodded. "Yes."

"Who called?" Jason insisted, his voice low.

"Virginia," Peppers answered.

"Is she alive?!" Jason's eyes were wide with anticipation.

Peppers bit his lip and shook his head.

Jason shook his head slowly. "Jesus—"

Manning strolled away as he looked at the floor, both his hands working in anguish. "We've got to keep a lid on this." He shot Peppers an anxious look.

Peppers scowled. His voice barely above a whisper, he said, "I'll run the Disaster Team through a special briefing. We'll secure the building and everything in it. Put an extra twenty-four hour guard on the place. Perimeter watch on the east side. Nobody past Post M without clearance from your office." He paused. "But we have to say something. The official statement has to come from your people." He looked at the two men in turn, his brow furrowed, his head in a negative gesture, both palms out.

Manning turned to Jason. "What're we going to say? This is your project."

Jason heaved a sigh, pinched his nose, and closed his eyes. "We'll come up with something. I'll talk with Los Alamos and our guys in Washington first."

Strength returned to his voice as he opened his eyes and dropped his hand. "The project has to continue. We'll put an analysis team together to find out what went wrong; then we can move on." He stepped away, then wheeled back.

Manning stared. "Isn't that a bit callous? These people—"

Jason fixed his gaze on Manning, his mouth firm. "What would these people say, Dave?" He gestured. "What would Abe Bartle say? What would you say if it were you?" He paused. "We owe it to them."

Manning looked away, then back. "You're right. Okay. You don't have much time, though." His eyes displayed fatigue.

"I know—I know." Jason paced away, then stopped and turned. "Rodriguez and Simpson are up to speed. I'll put them on it. Los Alamos has started research on the concept, so I'll get them to consult and check our data. Maybe we can find the problem. We need peer review."

They looked up as two men in orange coveralls moved awkwardly down the stairs from the control room. They carried a body on a litter.

Jason touched Manning's arm. "Better go look."

Manning held back. "Where do we do the test? Look at this place!"

Jason thought a moment. "We'll set something up out in Area Three. Smaller footprint. This was too big."

Manning nodded. "Okay." He started off, then stopped to look at Peppers. "Thanks, Hank. Get back to me ASAP. Okay?"

Peppers nodded. "Will do." He strode away.

After the two men mounted the rubble-strewn concrete stairs to the Control Room, they were intensely aware of the odor of concrete dust, burning plastics, ozone, and something else not immediately identifiable. They entered the room gingerly, as their shoes crunched on pieces of concrete wall and shards of glass and steel. A pall of smoke and dust hung in the air. The electronic gear along the console back was silent and dark. Two covered bodies lay on the floor in crazy attitudes. One lay next to the back wall; the other, under the console, lacked a head.

"Jesus," Manning wheezed under his breath.

Jason moved farther into the room, past a security officer and two medics preparing to move a body. At the other end of the narrow room, a photographer snapped away, the flash from his camera blinding. He looked down at the shrouded, decapitated remains of Jerry Ransom. He stiffened, turned away, and ran both hands alongside his face and over his mouth. He recovered and turned to look at the rack of reel-to-reel tape recorders as Manning came up to him.

"Looks like these made it," Jason said. His voice was low and cracked as he spoke. He took a deep breath and exhaled, opening and closing his hands tensely at his sides.

Manning, in a daze, nodded silently.

"I'll get Rodriguez started immediately." Jason's voice was so low that Manning barely heard him. "They should be able to analyze what happened up to the point of detonation. From the data tapes." He gestured, then forced himself to look around, taking in the details of the disaster. He glanced up at one of the video cameras in a corner under the ceiling. "Video tapes. Might help."

"Good God; look at that thing." Manning stared out through the gaping hole where the observation window had been.

Jason followed Manning's gaze. "Should be rebuilt."

"You really think it's worth it?" Manning screwed up his face.

The older man nodded slowly. "Once we have verification. Absolutely. This is proof, Dave. It works." He looked at Manning and nodded emphatically. "Yes."

Manning looked hard at Jason. "These people—they—"

Jason waited until the EMTs had exited, leaving only the security officer. He spoke with an intense whisper and jabbed his finger at Manning. "These people were dedicated. They were excited about this. You believe they'd want us to stop? No. The success of this project will be their monument."

Jason Thompson, Dave Manning, Hank Peppers, Manny Rodriguez, and Lloyd Simpson sat in a darkened room staring at a television monitor. In five-minute segments, they watched the seven tapes which had been removed from video monitors in the Area M main bunker and select parts of the building.

The tapes showed the neat, clean, antiseptic two-story building, its interior lighted by fluorescent ceiling lamps and strategically placed, high-intensity focus lamps. Long halls and floors of grey-painted concrete ran the length of the building on both sides. The immense staging bay, two stories high, abutted the reinforced steel truck door. Overhead was a high-tonnage traveling crane on an I-beam that ran the length of the test bay.

At the opposite end of the building were rest rooms, a cafeteria, a little gymnasium, and four diminutive sleeping rooms with cots. On the west side of the building, centered, was the control room with a long, thick, tinted safety-glass window which looked down into the huge, high-ceilinged test bay.

The test bay was dominated by exotic equipment, the centerpiece of which was a long, silver-shiny metallic cylinder, four feet in diameter and forty feet long, twenty feet short of the length of the room. Welded on top of it at the ends were tubes of the same girth, sealed off at the tops with thick, bolted flanges. Identically shaped circular plates closed off opposite ends of the main test cylinder. On shelving along the length of the horizontal pipe were hundreds of instruments and thousands of small chromed tubes, copper pipes, and electrical cables with supporting guy wires extending in every direction. Near the center of the main cylinder was a thick, round window surrounded by a heavy, bolted, chromed flange, eighteen inches in diameter. It appeared opaque, and faced out into the huge room. Television cameras, fixed and panning, stared from strategic points.

The control room featured a long electronics console. Two video monitors displayed motionless scenes; oscilloscopes with green traces, counters with numbers rolling up or down, and meters, both analog and digital. Communications gear was mounted for operation from rolling swivel chairs along the console. At both ends, racked from floor to ceiling, stood four sixteen-inch, reel-to-reel, high-band instrumentation tape recorders. All of the reels turned slowly.

They watched the images of two men, Joe Chavez and Phil James, both in white jump-suits, orange hard hats and clear plastic facial protection gear, work on electronic equipment next to the horizontal cylinder in the test bay. Penny Markus, also in protective gear, turned valves on a pair of shiny pipes high on one end of the test device.

On one of the tapes, Dr. Abe Bartle, Jerry Ransom and Virginia Montaño, all wearing headsets with pencil mikes, sat at the control room console. Virginia entered data at a computer keyboard. On the wall over the observation window in front of the seated people were five large clocks with sweep-second hands, one of which was labeled "Zebra Time." Below the clocks was a large, red digital display designated "Range Timing," with eight positions which ticked away the seconds and fractions of seconds.

In the test bay, the technicians finished their tasks, then grouped together to talk. Joe Chavez looked toward the control room, spoke into a handheld portable radio and waved. Dr. Bartle, seated in the center at the console, pushed a switch and said "okay" into his mike, nodded his head, and waved at Chavez through the observation window. The technicians then left the bay. Once the door to the staging bay closed and the test cell was cleared, Dr. Bartle flicked a switch on the console. Red emergency lights in the bay flashed, and the sound of a siren echoed throughout the cavernous concrete building for five seconds.

Bartle raised a red switch safety cover on the console and pressed a button. Counters which had been at zero counted up, while others counted down. Oscilloscopes changed, showing wild, green patterns across their screens, and meter pointers moved. A slight shudder rumbled across the test-bay floor and into the control room, and the glass in the window vibrated slightly. Something in the test cell whined as though a huge electric motor was increasing speed. A small, fuzzy red spot glowed in the otherwise opaque window on the main cylinder. It appeared on three of the control room video monitors. Two of the instrumentation tape recorders increased rotational speed.

Dr. Bartle, in a flat, monotonous voice, recited the events into his mike, his ballpoint pen poised over a note pad. From time to time, Virginia, on his left, and Jerry Ransom, to his right, spoke into their mikes as they moved their hands from one switch or knob to another to observe test instruments. All glanced up often to watch the test through the observation window.

Then Dr. Bartle made frantic motions before the blue-white explosion. The video monitor went blank.

Hank Peppers got up and turned on the lights in the screening room.

Manning emitted a long sigh. "Sabotage?" He looked at Jason Thompson.

Jason stared into space and shook his head. "The data tapes will tell us what happened."

"How soon?" Manning asked.

Jason looked at Manny Rodriguez.

Rodriguez sat up straight and sighed. "Tomorrow. By end of the day. We have the tapes, and my guys have started breakdown and analysis. They'll cross-load the data into the computer tomorrow. Algorithms 've been checked out. Shouldn't take long."

"Good," Manning said. He turned to Peppers. "What about the Feds?"

"We notified the FBI. Special agent and a forensics team are on the way." He looked at Rodriguez. "They may complain about you removing the data tapes."

Jason shrugged as he rose from his chair. "Sure. And they'll probably be upset with us for looking at the videos."

2

*J*ason Thompson and Dave Manning each thought the other looked tired and haggard in spite of sleep and fresh clothes. More than twenty-four hours had passed since the disaster in Area 7. They shared a windowless room with one grey rectangular table and four matching padded steel chairs.

Jason's eyes strayed over the room's steel door and rested on its code lock and hidden deadbolt. His attention turned to the red-and-white striped, classified-materials binder which lay on the table between them. He looked down at the file and spoke in a low tone. "We recovered what we could. All but one of the tapes had uninterrupted data. Simpson's group worked until they reduced everything possible." He looked up at Manning. "I stayed until eleven-thirty last night, when it was clear they had everything under control. I went over the first full set of data runs with them before I left. They finished about two this morning."

"So, what happened?" Manning's eyes bore into Jason's.

"Too early to tell the whole story, but the findings indicate I was right about Bartle's expectations. His notes and the test data for the seventy-two-hour period leading up to the accident show he was within 5 percent of predicted results. Apparently the last test went well beyond them. Climed up the curve. Vertically asymptotic. The knee of the bottom curve is pretty sharp. They'll have more on paper soon." He sighed as he drummed the tabletop nervously.

"Hadn't you done calculations yourself?"

"Yes." Jason untied the closure string on the security folder, opened it, and put a piece of paper in front of Manning. "That graph and table pretty well sum up our predictions." He pointed. "Look along this line here. This next one shows how close the tests actually came to a plateau."

"You can't tell from this? Why it blew up?" Manning's face wrinkled in stress.

Jason shook his head. "It's going to take more analysis, Dave. But I believe the power ramp was exponential beyond previous test data, something Bartle apparently didn't know before the last test run. I hate to say it, especially since it tends to implicate Abe, but the problem should have been predicted with the calculations. We'll have to look at the instrumentation figures in smaller increments, maybe as short as microsecond or even nanosecond intervals. If we run a series of curves, we should be able to draw some good conclusions. I think Abe just brought the test up too quickly."

"Damn." Manning shook his head and rubbed his face roughly with his hand. "If those materials are that sensitive to control, how can we ever make it work?"

"More in-depth computer analysis, tighter controls, better electronics interfacing, and finer chambering could be parts of the solution."

Manning stared at Jason with bloodshot, questioning eyes.

Jason tilted his head and continued. "I think once we get control of the central core, we've got a winner."

Manning shook his head. His voice was hoarse. "I don't want that project restarted until you're absolutely sure where it will lead. Christ, this is an impossible situation with you ready to retire." He slapped the table with the palm of his hand.

"I have every confidence in the team. I'm quite sure of Simpson and Rodriguez. They won't repeat Bartle's mistake. For one thing, we'll change observation and containment safety policy. Remote the test cell. Take a page from the nuclear test boys. That will delay the project as much as anything but protect everyone involved. We know more now."

"I sure as hell hope so." Manning shook his head and looked at the ceiling.

"We've got an advantage."

"What's that?" Manning frowned at Jason.

"The word on the street is that Geronimo Queen has been winding down ever since we secretly found it had merit. All we have to say is we had an accident with an unrelated project and take our lumps."

Manning ruminated. "I suppose you're right. That's the unofficial leak so far. It can stay that way."

Jason nodded. "No need to mention Geronimo Queen was even involved."

"Okay." Manning got up and went to the door. He turned. "How does this affect your presentation this morning?"

"Nothing's really changed. If anything, it reinforces it."

Jason strode down the wide hall and through the door into his secretary's office. He was trim and athletic, a man who, although greying and in his sixties, still had a youthful attractiveness. The bounce in his walk was helped by regular tennis games.

Angie, his secretary, looked up from her keyboard. "Oh, Mr. T, they're all assembled."

Jason stopped in front of her desk and checked his watch. "Okay. Would you buzz and tell 'em I'll be there in another minute or two?" He moved on, then stopped and turned. "Do you have my presentation file?"

"You'll need that, won't you?" Angie smiled and unlocked a steel drawer in her desk to take out a manila folder. She handed it to her boss.

He continued into his office, went around the back of his desk, and opened the center drawer. He pulled out a collapsible pointer which he clipped into his shirt pocket.

Jason's office was larger than his secretary's, but furnished in the same government grey. His desk faced the door to her office, and his window looked onto an exterior courtyard. A small conference table with two chairs, one on either side, stood at a right angle to, and in front of, his desk. A fire-proof file cabinet stood in one corner with a portable green "Secured" sign inserted into the top drawer handle, immediately above the combination lock dial. The credenza behind his desk held a photograph of his wife, Sarah, and another of their three children when they were small. The desk top was clear except for a desktop computer, a single, black multi-buttoned telephone, a vertical in-and-out tray, and a yellow legal pad.

He removed the "Secure" sign and unlocked the file cabinet by carefully rotating the safe dial on the top drawer three times. He opened it and dropped the folder with the red and white stripes into one of the hanging files, then slammed it shut and secured it by spinning the dial. He replaced the sign.

Presentation folder in hand, he walked past his secretary and into the hall, turning in the opposite direction from which he had come. He stopped at a closed door along the hall. He unclipped his badge from his collar, and held it against a grey box next to the frame on the latch side. A recessed light on the box changed from red to green, and with a loud click, the door unlocked. He pushed into the room.

He looked around. The large, plain room was taken up with a long, narrow table around which sat a dozen men and women. Recessed fluorescent ceiling lamps lighted the windowless chamber. A viewgraph projector which faced a pull-down screen on the wall, sat on one end of the table.

Jason walked to the projector at the opposite end of the room and glanced at each person. His demeanor was pleasantly business-like, but with a cast of sadness. "Good morning. I think most of you know me. I'm Jason Thompson, Technical Director of Project GQ. I think most of you know—although some would rather not—Dave Manning." He smiled and gestured toward Manning, who sat next to where he stood.

Most in the room chuckled while Manning flushed and smiled. He was also a scientist, but with more of an administrative bent. Jason was happy to have Dave Manning handle the people and all the attendant administrative headaches.

Jason, still standing, opened the presentation folder and straightened its contents on the table. "We're here to review our progress. I have pictures to show you, and Carol will fill you in with the numbers so far." He nodded to a plump, blond woman seated toward the center of the table on his left. "Before I proceed, I want to say a few words about what happened yesterday morning in Area 7." He lowered his head and paused. "There was a serious accident in the main test bunker. An explosion. The investigation isn't complete, but it looks as though there was a fuel leak. A welding spark may have set it off. Unfortunately, Abe Bartle and five others died. That includes Virginia Montaño, Jerry Ransom, Phil James, Penny Markus, and Joe Chavez." He looked around the room as people glanced at each other uncomfortably. "All of the families have asked that, rather than flowers, you donate to a favorite charity in the names of the deceased. In Abe's case, he gave support to the Santa Fé Area Non-Denominational Children's Home. We have no word on the others yet, but should soon. Angie's preparing a list. Please check with her."

He continued after he paused to study each face in the room. "It's very important we stifle any rumors, so if anyone, even Lab personnel, but especially outsiders, ask about the accident, we tell them to check with the Lab's Information Officer." He sighed and surveyed the room once more. "Okay, we need to get going. Manny Escobar, who I see hasn't arrived yet, will take you through the first-phase technical explanations. I need to comment on security restrictions for GQ. In fact, they were tightened this past week to Top Secret." He watched the stunned reactions to his announcement.

"Will the reason be explained in the report?" The question was asked by George Rudman who sat at the opposite end of the long table, wearing a goatee over an American Indian bolo tie and a red plaid shirt.

"I was about to say that the reasons would come out in my talk." He smiled as muted chuckles made the rounds of the table. "Incidentally, I think the reason Manny hasn't made it yet is because his wife's having a baby."

This information elicited "oohs" and "aahs" and relieved the tension in the room.

"So, let's get started." Jason turned on the projector, placed the first view-graph on it, and turned back to his audience. "For those of you unaware of how the project started, we received a proposal from GE two years ago, and a feasibility study was ordered. Staff decided, since we had surplus equipment which fit the bill and people with the right background coming off other projects, it might be worth looking into, especially since major funding was coming from GE and DOE. Well, it's worked far better than anyone could have reasonably predicted."

He pulled the collapsible pointer from his shirt pocket, extended it, and faced the screen. "Note the graph at this point. We began here, thought we would get here, but came here instead. I'll put the next chart up and you can see more clearly why."

Jason went through all the charts, fielded questions, gave opinions, and took notes. Manny Escobar, flushed and happy, came in during his talk, and took a seat at the other end of the table. A man next to him slapped him on the back, then returned his attention to Jason.

"So security has been increased on this project basically for economic reasons," one man said after Jason made his closing remarks.

"Essentially true," Jason answered. "I see national security, but I think I'll defer to Dave for a more rounded explanation."

Manning shifted in his chair. "The conference in Washington centered around the energy ramifications surrounding Geronimo Queen. The results, as Jason has pointed out, are outstanding. So outstanding, in fact, that we were forced to re-classify, primarily because of the potentially positive impact on our economy as a prime user of foreign oil, and because of the potentially negative impact on OPEC and other petroleum vendor states. Another reason is the patents aren't clear, and there's going to be a scramble to get on the technological bandwagon, not only by U.S. companies, but by foreign companies and governments. CIA and FBI—even the Defense Intelligence Agency—DIA—look at the possibility of attempts to subvert this technology, not only to foreign powers, but the potential for abuse within our own borders until the dust settles." He paused. "There's another, more important reason. This technology may have weapons implications."

A buzz of voices filled the room, but attention strayed for a mere few seconds.

"You'll notice Jason didn't cover that aspect; nor are we going to right now. It's too fresh and the directions aren't clear. So DNA—Defense Nuclear Agency—along with the other security agencies, have asked us to beef up our security, and place this on the same footing we have with nuclear weapons." Manning stopped and toyed with a fingernail. "All of you in this room are privy to this. Those who work on the GQ project under Jason and those with a need to know are being briefed. That includes secretaries with file access."

"What about work done before the classification change?" Carol asked.

Manning turned to Jason. "Want to handle that?"

"Sure," the older man answered. He cleared his throat. "Most of the work to the point of departure was of such a nature that it was easy to keep. The monitors, once it looked like we had a winner, put an administrative hold on all reporting until a classification council could be held. I'm confident we're covered. I think it appropriate for me to say, off the record, that part of the reason there's been a cap on this is because we're all used to keeping security utmost in our minds." Jason looked at the faces around the room once again. "Now, unless there are more questions, I'm going to hand the meeting over to the new father." He held out his hand toward the beaming Escobar. Laughter filled the room as Jason picked up his folder full of view graphs and Manny Escobar moved to the front of the room.

As Jason walked into Angie's office, Mel Vaslovic, who stood in front of her reading a magazine, turned to greet him. "Hey, you ready?"

Vaslovic was about 25 pounds overweight, swarthy, with dark hair thinning on top, but with very little grey. His face was a contradiction of lines, some of which displayed cynicism, some concern, while others crinkled with good humor. His dark eyes had a light of intelligence in them.

"Be right with you, Mel." Jason handed the folder to Angie, who was seated behind her desk, in front of her computer keyboard, fingers poised. "Angie, get hold of Vicky after lunch and have her secure that stuff for me, will you?"

"Sure, Mr. T."

"Thanks."

Jason went into his office to get his jacket and called from the other side of the door, "I forgot it was Friday and time for our burrito."

Vaslovic continued to flip through the magazine without looking up. "Yep. Just another burrito day."

Jason Thompson and Mel Vaslovic walked out of Rio Grande Labs building 800 to the parking lot across the narrow access road in front. They got into Jason's restored 1963 Ford pickup and drove away.

"So what's going on?" Vaslovic asked, looking out his side window.

"Wrapping things up. How about you?"

"A boring end to a boring job. I'll be glad to get out of here."

"Yeah, I'm ready." Jason tugged on the wheel and the Ford took a corner.

"Anything new about that explosion out in Area M?" Vaslovic frowned at Jason.

"Bad scene, Mel. Good people died. Very upsetting. Haven't slept much."

"What the hell happened?"

Jason shrugged, keeping his eyes on the road. "Not really sure. Looks like some unstable test fuel exploded."

Vaslovic grimaced at Jason. "Not sure? You manage that area, don't you?"

Jason shrugged again, looking out his side window at people on the sidewalk as the old truck moved along. "It was an accident. There's a team on it. They'll report back as soon as they figure out what happened. May have been a welding spark." He turned to look squarely at Vaslovic.

Vaslovic wanted to say something about Jason's testy answer, but decided to ignore it. "I hear there was a lot of damage."

"Some replaceable equipment was destroyed, but other than that, nothing too serious. To projects, that is."

"Those poor families." Vaslovic, talking to the glass, looked out his side window again. "You have anything more for me?"

Jason looked severely at his companion. "God damn it, Mel!"

Vaslovic faced forward, a bored expression on his face. "Okay. Okay."

Jason shook his head and drove.

Mel Vaslovic's sad, intelligent eyes darted around continually. He often nervously worked his hands—played with whatever was handy. Those who didn't know him found his personality immediately trying. He wanted to bore into the other person; to take them apart, as though testing them. Once someone gained his confidence, they discovered his charm and subtle wit. He was a complex man, a scientist like Jason, but unlike Manning, not as technical. He was well thought of by his peers, but had made no outstanding contribution to his profession during his career. He was passed over for management time after time. Meticulous but impatient, he left his job at the office. He preferred hobbies that rarely resembled his work. Vaslovic was not unathletic. Jason coaxed him into playing tennis with him from time to time, but Mel Vaslovic exhibited no real enthusiasm. His two passions were reading and movies, and he wrote poetry when the mood suited him.

Jason Thompson, on the other hand, was deeply interested in the technical side of his work. Although he had art hobbies, he worked on electronic projects at home. He had a darkroom, took care of his own cars, and rebuilt the 1963 pickup truck with care and pride. He had contributed to patentable ideas at the Labs, and worked on technical ideas in his spare time. Approached for management titles, he tried one stint, but gave it up as too stressful and went back to simple, technical project leadership. He loved tennis. His high blood pressure forced him to slow down, but he took the change gracefully.

The two men had known each other since childhood, and were opposite enough to get on well. Vaslovic felt isolated and lonely as a child due to conditions compounded by chubbiness. In grammar school, Jason befriended him, even championing him at times.

The two old friends sat in a corner booth in the back room of Baca's Restaurant, Jason with a bottle of Bohemia beer in front of him, Vaslovic with a bottle of Corona.

The light in the room was muted, and candles flickered in blood-red glass holders on each table. The huge, mirrored Italian back bar gave the room a Nineteenth Century flavor. Five other people sat in the room; two at the bar nursing Margaritas.

"How's Betty?" Jason asked.

"Feeling better." Vaslovic took a swig from his bottle. "Listen, I feel terrible about what happened to those people out there. Is it true Abe Bartle was one of them?"

Jason closed his eyes and nodded. "Yes. Virginia Montaño and Jerry Ransom were with him when it happened. Three techs—Chavez, James, and Penny Markus—were also killed."

"Christ, Jase, that's awful." Vaslovic studied Jason's eyes. "And they still don't know what happened?"

"As I said, Mel, the Disaster Team is trying to put all the pieces together. It tears me up." He sipped his beer.

"Sorry. I shouldn't have brought it up."

Jason shook his head. "It's okay. We have to talk it out. It was so senseless. It's a personal loss." He pointed to his chest.

Both men were silent while they let their feelings normalize.

"Will you answer my question now?" Vaslovic asked.

Jason scanned the room, then focused on Vaslovic. He shook his head. "I don't have anything for you." He kept his voice low.

"Nothing on GQ?" Vaslovic's voice was muted.

"I told you—that project is flat right now. We've got funding for another nine or ten months—which we're going to spend whether we need it or not. It may be dead." He drank again, then checked the room.

Vaslovic took in a deep breath. "Okay. I'm tired anyway. It'll be good to relax." He glanced around. "But why do you get so upset when I try to talk in the truck?"

"Mel, damn it, you know it's bad procedure." Jason's voice was a husky whisper. "I've had that Ford for years. It's not secure. I don't understand why you fight me on that issue." He leaned forward to emphasize his point.

Vaslovic shrugged and avoided his companion's eyes. A waitress appeared with two plates and set one before each of them.

Vaslovic picked up his fork and dug in. "Don't forget Sunday." With his mouth half full, his mood had changed.

Jason chewed, then swallowed. "Wouldn't miss it for anything." He cast a smile.

"Been awhile."

"Long time, Mel." He held his beer up in salute.

Vaslovic put his fork down and drank. "You know, the only regret I have is I couldn't work on the same projects you have since we've been at the Labs."

"Yeah." Jason took another bite, was silent for three seconds, then said, "But I think it worked out for the best." He moved his head in a negative gesture. "It could have been risky for us to be too close. Damn tense at times. I'm glad it's coming to a close, too."

Vaslovic nodded. "You're the one who's taken the risks."

"I don't know about that. Sometimes I wonder if we've accomplished anything." He looked up abruptly, then jerked his chin to indicate that Vaslovic should look behind him.

Vaslovic turned his head enough to see a man and a woman being seated in the next booth. Both men fell silent and finished their lunch.

The Thompson house sat on a corner lot in one of the older, leafier sections of Albuquerque. It was a split-level with short, round beams—so-called *vigas*—extending from the walls under the flat rooftops. Two ladders of stripped cedar ran from one roof level to another in imitation of a Pueblo Indian structure. A low, uneven wall separated the narrow front and side yards from the sidewalk. The front of the house was dominated by a long porch and more *vigas* protruding. In the rear, two large trees provided shade. Beneath one was a detached, two car garage.

Jason Thompson parked his Ford pickup in front of the garage, got out, and loped up the stairs to the room above it.

The landing at the top of the stairs was long and narrow, parallel to the street. A stuccoed half-wall hid the landing and half the door from view. At the end of the landing, next to the solid-paneled door, was a crockery "sleeping Mexican," with a large sombrero dominating the two-foot high figure.

Jason opened the door and went in. "Hi, honey."

Sarah Thompson sat on a stool, throwing a large pot on a spinning potter's wheel, her hands covered in light tan clay. She looked up at him and smiled. "Hello, dear." She returned her attention to the wheel.

Jason walked around a large work table, put his hands on her shoulders and leaned over to kiss her lightly on her bare neck below her upswept hair. "What are you working on?"

Sarah stopped the wheel and looked up at him as she wiped her hands with a towel tucked behind a sash at her waist. She was prettier and more petite than most women her age. Well-developed laugh lines creased the fine skin of her intelligent face. She turned away and looked at her creation, raising a clay-stained hand to her forehead, which left a light tan smudge. "A silly pot. One of the watercolor ladies mentioned she'd like one. It's her birthday next week, so I thought I'd make her one. I hope she likes it." She smiled and returned to the wheel. Then she drew in her breath, turned away from the potter's wheel, and looked up at her husband with worried eyes. "Jason! What about the accident? Those poor people!" She studied his face, her hands in her lap.

Jason heaved a sigh and told her what he'd told Vaslovic, about the fuel leak and the welder. He walked across the room and threw his jacket over the chair back in front of the desk against the wall.

The room held an odd assortment of chairs—mostly ladder back. There was a pot-bellied stove, an old wood desk, a worn sofa, and a small kiln on steel legs. A row of windows on the north side admitted strong light. Behind the desk, a large, multi-colored *Ojo de Dios* hung from the wall. Another smaller "god's eye" sporting tassels decorated the wall to the left of the desk. On the work table was a small bundle of wood dowels, a basket of multi-colored yarn, and another basket containing strings of large, colored beads. The potter's wheel was at the end of the table.

Across the big room from the desk and in the far corner were two small add-on rooms—a bathroom and a darkroom. Past that was a bench that featured electronic equipment, parts and tools.

"I'm sure she'll like the pot. What's for dinner?" Jason turned to watch his wife with the spinning clay.

"Jason! You forgot!?" Sarah swivelled on her stool and stared at her husband in amazement.

Jason's eyes went wide, his mouth dropped open, and he slapped his forehead. "God! I've been so busy with the disaster I completely forgot tonight!"

"How could you forget an awards dinner?" She looked at him as though he were a little boy.

He shook his head in mock disgust. "Oh, boy." He paused. "I don't feel good about it, though."

Sarah cocked her head. "I'm sorry. These past few days have been very rough on you, but you deserve the award."

Jason lowered his head and stared at the floor.

"Sally Randall called today and asked us over for dinner tomorrow night."

Jason winced and strolled away. "I guess we can't get out of it."

"They've been very helpful during the campaigns." She turned her head this way and that, admiring the shape of the pot.

"I suppose. I get a little tired of Randall's right-wing rhetoric, though."

"Did you have lunch with Mel today?" Sarah shut the wheel off, carefully draped a wet cloth over the unfinished pot, then went to the sink to wash her hands.

"Like clockwork."

"Mexican?" She walked to the bathroom and washed her hands.

"What else? You know I need my weekly fix of Baca's best." He smiled as he looked out the north windows.

"It's about time to pick up some more green chile. I think we should try Soccorro this year." Sarah spoke from inside the bathroom. She dried her hands, now free of clay, and came out.

"Alright." He turned to look at her as she walked toward the door. "Remember, we have that retirement party Sunday."

"Yes, dear. I talked to Betty today."

"She's feeling better, I take it."

"Yes." She paused, then asked, "Anything else new at work?"

"Nope. Cleaning up bits and pieces."

They went through the door onto the landing, and Jason locked the door behind him with the key from under the sleeping Mexican's hat.

"Where's the GQ project now that you're leaving?" Sarah was at the bottom of the stairs.

"In limbo. Sometimes I think they kept the thing going just for me. How's that for ego?" He smiled wryly.

"It's odd they've kept that thing going for so long if it isn't producing anything." She stopped and turned to look up into his face.

He shrugged and opened the gate to the back yard. "You know the government. They love to waste money. That's why we support the people we do."

He walked ahead and opened the kitchen door for his wife, then stepped in behind her.

3

*I*t was on a clear, warm Sunday afternoon that the Thompson's blue-grey Mercedes sedan pulled to a stop on a street near Albuquerque's eastern edge, close to the upper reaches of the Sandia piedmont.

Jason got out, walked around to the passenger side, and opened the door for Sarah. She wore a pleated dirndl with a western-style blouse and a small Navajo Indian squash blossom necklace of silver and turquoise. Jason wore slacks, a plaid shirt, and a cord jacket with elbow patches. His turquoise-and-silver bolo was of excellent quality.

They crossed the street and went up a flagstone path to a house that sat well back from the tree-lined street. Jason rang the door bell.

After a brief wait Betty Vaslovic opened the door. She was five years younger than Sarah, but her short, stout stature caused her to appear older. "Sarah! Jason! Come in! We've been wondering what happened to you! You're late for your own retirement party, Jason!" She held a fluted glass up in salute.

"Sorry we're late, but Jason got busy in the studio after church, and I ran an errand," Sarah beamed. "But here we are!" She leaned forward and pecked Betty's cheek.

Jason said, "Really apologize."

"Mel's in there talking his fool head off as usual." She indicated the innards of the house with a thumb gesture. "C'mon in, the drinks are fine!" Betty laughed and led them inside.

The three moved from the tiled entrance hall onto thick pile carpet and stepped down into the living room. Opposite the front of the house a large functional fireplace blistered out from a papered wall, its red brick bracketed on both sides by four-inch-square mirror tiles. Across the room, a large bay window framed with white lace curtains looked out over the front lawn.

Two women sat on a padded window seat. One was drinking bourbon and water, while the other, without a drink, was chatting with someone across the room, her bespangled arm gesticulating broadly.

The room was filled with convivial banter from an assortment of casually dressed people. Most were middle-aged, with a sprinkling in their twenties to mid-thirties. A few, men and women alike, wore turquoise and silver Indian jewelry. One of the men wore a heishi choker. One woman had on a concha belt, and another wore a bear fetish necklace. In one corner a girl sat looking at a photo-essay book by herself. Several of the guests stood around a curved bar near the hallway; others clustered near a table covered with a variety of hors d'oeuvres. More chatted at the other end of the room near open French doors which led to a patio.

"Jase! Sarry! Where the hell you been!?"

"Hi, Mel. Sorry. Hey look. We already said our 'sorries' to your old lady, so just shut up and fetch booze. Okay?" Jason chuckled as he walked over to his friend to shake his hand.

"God, you're something, Jase. You always manage to manage, don't you," Vaslovic laughed as he slapped Jason on his shoulder. "You're forgiven. So'er you, Sarry!" He bussed Sarah on her cheek as she offered it to him, her eyes closed. Vaslovic was an inch taller than Sarah. He stood back and looked at them both. "What'll you have?"

"Listen to him, will you? Wants to know what we'll have after more than forty years." Sarah smiled up at her husband.

"Yes, well, he never was any good at details," Jason replied.

The four of them laughed and moved toward the bar as Betty lead the way.

"Hi there, Thompsons." Jack Perry, middle-aged with short greying hair and lines in his weathered face that betrayed his age, got up from the long couch in the center of the big room.

"Hello, Jack." Jason extended his hand.

Sarah greeted Perry in the same way, crinkling up her handsome face as she held out her hand. He took her hand and bussed it in a perfunctory manner.

"Hello, you two." A middle-aged woman, her face lined from smoking, purred gutturally as she came up behind Jack. Her long cigarette rained ashes.

"Hi, Laura. Good to see you." Sarah reached out and squeezed Laura's hand.

"Laura. How are you?" Jason asked.

"God, Jase, that was some deal out in Area 7," Perry said. A frown creased his forehead.

Jason took in a deep breath and released it. "Yes. They were all friends." He looked around the room, and tried to think of a way to steer the conversation in another direction.

"Jason hasn't been sleeping well," Sarah said.

"How awful," Laura put in. She shook her head slowly aand squinted through her cigarette smoke. "What happened, Jason?"

Jason compressed his lips, shrugged, and shook his head. "Industrial accident. Sorry to say, those things happen. Even to us." He looked away again, hoping the topic would die.

"I mean, what happened?" Laura pressed.

"Laura, look, I don't have all the facts. I defer to the Labs Information Office. We speak with one voice." Jason awarded her another sympathetic shrug.

"Hm," she murmured. She took a drag from her cigarette and studied his face.

Betty brought white wine to Sarah and a scotch-and-water to her husband. Jack Perry, who understood Jason's anguished body signals, steered the subject away from the accident by opening a new subject line. Sarah and Jason joined in while Betty listened and three other people made their way over until a small crowd gathered around the Thompsons. Mel Vaslovic got himself another vodka tonic, then ambled over and stood at the periphery of the group. They and clusters of other people around the room made small talk for some time.

"So, Sarah," Laura asked, her cigarette nearly burned down to the filter, "are you and Jason going to travel?" She stood next to Perry.

"No, I don't think so," Sarah replied. She turned to face Laura. "Jason and I are looking forward to that little house of ours—the adobe—in Truchas. It needs work, and we enjoy that."

"That's certainly out of the way." Laura leaned over to snuff her cigarette out in a nearby ashtray.

Sarah looked up at her husband, then back at Laura. She smiled sweetly, her eyes wide and innocent, but with knowing behind them. There was more she wanted to say but didn't.

"We're going to leave touring the country to the Vaslovics," Jason put in, rocking back on his heels. He took a sip of his drink.

Everyone in the little cluster smiled and laughed.

A woman at the edge of the group said, "Truchas. What does that mean?"

Jason turned to her. "Trout. Plural for trout." He smiled.

A man wondered out loud, "Fish? Up there? I suppose . . ."

Jason raised his eyebrows and looked in the man's direction as he continued to slowly sip his drink.

"I just wish to hell I could look forward to doing anything like that, soon," Jack Perry said.

"Don't be impatient," Vaslovic said. He rotated his glass causing the ice to spin around and clink. "But you can do it your way."

Another man from the edge of the circle added, "Well, congratulations to you both. You deserve your rest."

"Yes," someone else said, "here's to Mel and Jason. May they enjoy!"

Most held their glasses up high as the mood swept to the rest of the room.

"Just think of all the time you can spend down at the club," Perry, wearing a silly grin enhanced by alcohol, said. He looked first at Jason, then at Mel Vaslovic.

Vaslovic started to choke, coughed, then said, "I don't know, Jack. You think I should be seen half-naked in public with a figure like this?" He laughed, patted his middle, then coughed again.

"Right," Jason said, looking at Vaslovic, then back at Perry, "Swim, tennis—"

"And spend more time in Truchas," Sarah said. She looped her arm through his and squeezed.

"And spend more time in Truchas," Jason said, as scattered laughter ensued.

"And spend more time at cards," Vaslovic said.

"Cards! Oh!" Sarah exclaimed. She raised her hand in approval.

Betty snickered and Jack Perry chuckled and swirled his drink.

Betty said, "I think Jason should stay away from card games—with his memory!"

"Don't pick on him, now, Betty," Sarah chided. She smiled and frowned at the same time, and waved a limp hand at her friend.

Betty went on, "Well, it's true! For such a scientific mind, he can't even remember the cards or where he is! How can you stand him as a partner?!" She grinned broadly.

"He has his ways!" Sarah leaned against her husband again and squeezed his arm. She brightened. "He's a scientist, and he remembers what he needs to remember." She pointed at Betty in triumph. "So there!"

"That's for sure!" Vaslovic commented. He tipped his glass up. "Hell, he can fly a plane, can't he?"

"Not lately, and not again," Sarah purred. She rolled her eyes up at Jason.

"I didn't know you flew," someone said.

Jason studied the ice in his glass. "Well, it's been a couple of years, and Sarah and I have an agreement on that score." He looked up.

The man who had asked the question, Roland Gurule, moved into Jason's circle. "Single-engine, or multi—?" He frowned in deep interest.

Jason swallowed and looked at the floor. "Single engine. Got started years ago back east. One of my goals as a kid. You know how that goes."

Gurule lost his frown and smiled. "Yeah. But you gave it up? Is it true it's like riding a bicycle?"

Jason raised his eyes to the ceiling. "I suppose. Yes, probably." He returned the smile and clenched his glass to feel the cold. "I soloed and did a cross-country."

"So you could fly now, if you—"

"But he isn't. Are you, dear?" Sarah looked up at Jason, then directed a smiling, but severe gaze at Roland Gurule, who retreated.

"Well, now, I think you're all being unfair to Jason, by God," Jack Perry put in. "I think he's really more of an artist than a scientist, anyway."

"Yes, those beautiful god's eyes he makes," Laura said.

A surprisingly deep and sonorous female voice came from across the room. The girl looking at the photo book spoke up, "What's a god's eye?"

Laura, a fresh cigarette held high, turned and took a step toward the questioner, and in a patronizing manner, said, "They're a couple of sticks crossed together, honey. Then they string colored yarn over them in bands until you have a sort of square of different colors. Simple. Indian thing." She sipped her drink and looked at Jason suggestively.

The girl's cheeks flushed pink and she looked away, as she forced her clasped hands between her knees.

"Yeah, those are great, Jason," Perry said. "You ever sell them?"

"Heaven's sakes, no! I—"

"He gives them away, don't you dear?" Sarah said.

"And hangs them in his office," Perry said.

"Selfish, selfish," Laura said.

"Well, I like the colors!" Jason shrugged and shook his head. "It's fun. I need a hobby, you know." He grinned.

"Boy, I'll say, so much so that he keeps putting new ones in his own office!" Perry turned to look at the others. "He puts different ones in there all the time. Different color combinations." He looked at Jason with a smirk.

"What do you do with the old ones, Jase?" Jack queried.

"Now, look, good friends and all, me thinks you've worn this subject out! I'm for the bar and another toot!" With that, Jason looked at everyone around him, made a face, and turned in the direction of the bar as he waved his empty glass high.

Someone across the room asked, "Jason, your kids are in California, aren't they?"

Sarah turned and answered, "Flo is. Justin's in Chicago. In computers. Charles is down at the University of Arizona."

"Teaches bi-o-phy-sics!" Mel Vaslovic spoke, stretching the word out between his teeth.

Sarah turned and looked at him with faked disdain. Vaslovic moved sideways and awarded her a hug.

"What's Roy doing these days?" Jack Perry asked.

"He's gone into business for himself," Betty answered. "He imports car parts—or something—from Europe and the Far East."

Jason, who poured at the bar, looked over at her, puzzled by her pathetic, defensive tone. "Our older two were pretty close to Roy," he said. He raised his glass, sipped, and moved back toward the group.

"Roy inherited the same bad trait I had as a kid," Vaslovic said with a smile. "He spent a lot of time at the Thompson's."

A chuckle rippled through the group.

Vaslovic held up both hands, and slopped his drink onto his jacket sleeve. "Listen, everyone. Listen. This is true. This lady here, this fine lady, Sarah, was like a block mother. I mean, she was always taking in stray cats, dogs, and kids!"

Laughter.

"Mel, you are such a silly!" Sarah spoke and made a face at Vaslovic.

Jason watched her move across the room as she returned her empty wine glass to the bar.

Roland Gurule stepped back toward the circle of people. "Jason got a Civitan award Friday night."

Some nodded; all murmured approval.

"For his work with the Boy Scouts and Big Brother," Gurule added.

Jason shifted uncomfortably. "You're getting pretty personal. This is embarrassing." He looked at Vaslovic and Gurule.

"You should be proud," Laura said.

Betty walked over to Sarah and looped her arm through hers, then looked at Jason. "She's right, Jason. You've done a lot for young people and raised three fine children, plus Roy." She smiled at Sarah.

Laughter danced through the room again.

"We were like one family from the time Mel and I got married. These two helped us a lot. Why, there were times—" Betty started to choke up, and tears welled in her eyes as her voice faded away.

Sarah moved to hug her while others in the room, embarrassed, disbursed.

Vaslovic looked away, rolled his eyes, and took a long draft from his glass. He walked to the bay window and looked out longingly before he returned to the sofa where he sat with a puff. He slopped his drink again. "At least we didn't raise a bunch of criminals," he said.

Jack Perry followed half way, then turned back to refill his glass at the bar near Sarah and Betty. "That's for damned sure," he said. "Considering all the crime today."

Laura started another cigarette and strolled over to Jason. She stared at him. "Criminals and druggies. Druggies and criminals," she said. She toook a deep drag on her cigarette and raked his body with her eyes.

"You gonna stay active in the Party, Mel?" someone asked.

"Damn right," Vaslovic answered, his voice rising a decibel. "We need a conservative majority in congress."

From a man standing near the mirrored wall next to the fireplace came "We're losing our freedoms, that's for sure."

"If the Democrats have their way, they'll tax and spend us into slavery," Perry said.

Bob Parsons, a young man with sandy-brown hair and a mustache of the same shade, pushed away from the fireplace mantle where he had been leaning. He took two steps toward the sofa where Vaslovic sat. His shirt front was open two buttons below the collar, and a heishi string hung around his neck. He held a can of beer in his hand. "Why blame the Democrats, Mel? Reagan brought us the biggest deficit in history."

Vaslovic looked up at Parsons with a frown. "Bullshit, Bob! It was the Democrat congress."

"Reagan was president." Bob smiled and drank his beer.

Sarah moved closer to Jason's side. "Who is that?" She whispered.

"Bob Parsons. A division supervisor," Jason whispered.

"Well, what's his problem?" She glowered at Bob.

"Problem? Bob doesn't have a problem. He's got a right to his opinion. He's a very bright fellow." He cocked his eyebrow at her.

"Well—" Sarah turned away, her arms folded across her chest.

"As I was saying before I was so rudely interrupted—" Vaslovic scowled at the group of people who had gathered in front of the sofa, then at those who were seated, scatter-shot, across from it.

"You weren't saying anything—at least nothing important," Jason said loudly. He smiled broadly at his old friend, drained his glass, and made for the bar.

Sarah frowned at Jason, then at the empty glass her husband carried.

"Yes, Mel. Don't get upset." Betty's voice was chiding as she approached her husband stiffly, nervous over his outburst.

"Damn it, Betty," Vaslovic flared, "I know how Bob thinks! The government is giving away everything to every goddamned, snot-nosed welfare chiseler that comes along with his hand out! Somebody has to protect the middle class! Why shouldn't it be me? This country's been pretty good to us! I've had a job ever since college!"

Parsons backed away, his head down, embarrassed.

"You were involved with the Manhattan Project, weren't you?" someone asked, directing the question at Mel Vaslovic.

"Jason there and I were drafted into that effort after the fun part." Vaslovic frowned into his glass, pointed it at Jason, then drank.

"Did you help make the bomb?" A young woman asked.

"The big boys got to play with the matches," Vaslovic answered. He looked up at Jason, who had returned from the bar without a glass.

Jason returned his gaze for a moment, then sidled away to look out the bay window. He was silent.

"Good hard work never hurt anyone," Vaslovic continued, swirling the ice in his glass again.

"That's right!" Perry stared at Bob Parsons with a pinched smile.

Parsons, with mock hurt on his face, caught Jack's look and pointed his thumb at his chest. "Moi?"

"Jack isn't saying you don't work, Bob, but I'll bet you're all worried about those who won't," Vaslovic said. He looked away with a hint of disgust.

Parsons shook his head. "Hey, I believe everybody should pay his own way." He felt under attack from Vaslovic, so he lowered his voice in an attempt to ameliorate the situation. "I'm sorry I said anything. Congratulations! Again." He held up his nearly empty beer can in salute.

Perry, feeling his liquor, moved closer to Parsons and looked him in the eye. "Well, I do think we need an energy policy." He winked.

Parsons smiled. "Good thinking, Jack." He winked and twisted his mouth.

Mel Vaslovic, tipsy, scowled up at Jack Perry from the sofa. "What's that got to do with anything?"

"We need new sources. Thought I'd bring it up," Perry said flippantly. "Up, I say!" He raised his nearly empty glass and strolled away.

"It is a problem," Laura said gutturally. She flicked ashes from her cigarette, but missed the tray intended for them.

Parsons turned to look at Laura. "Maybe not for long. With Geronimo Queen on line—" He stopped and whipped around to look at Jason, his face scarlet.

"Bob!" someone shouted, "This isn't a secured meeting!"

The room went quiet as Bob Parsons, his face ashen, stood frozen in place. He first stared at Jason, who had turned to look at him, then the carpet at his feet. Betty and Sarah, who had left the room together, returned and stood near the entrance from the hallway as Parsons spoke. Jack, near the fireplace, watched Parsons and Jason. Jason, near the bay window, after having had his eyes fixed on the hapless Parsons, looked at Vaslovic, who also watched Parsons.

Vaslovic moved his head slowly to meet Jason's gaze. Jason stared back, his face expressionless.

Vaslovic got up and muttered, "I need another drink." He walked stiffly to the bar.

Jason went to Parsons, put a hand on his shoulder and looked directly at him. In a low tone he said, "I don't think there's too much harm done, Bob. We're all friends here. But you should be a lot more careful about what you say and where."

"I'm sorry, Jason." Parson's face had turned scarlet.

Betty went to her husband at the bar. She pleaded in close to a whisper, "You've had enough, dear. Please. Remember, you have to take me to the airport."

Vaslovic ignored her. A deep frown extended down over his face.

Sarah watched Vaslovic intently as he stood stiffly. His hands shook as he mixed a drink. He looked at her briefly, then away again, as he poured vodka from a decanter.

Sarah looked closely at her husband and furrowed her brow as she took a step toward Betty. "The airport? Today?" Strain underlay the pleasantness in her voice.

"Yes," Betty said, "my mother's in the hospital."

"I'm sorry. If there's anything I can do."

"No. Thank you, Sarah. We'll be fine." Betty wrung her hands.

Sarah smiled and, preoccupied, walked over to her husband. "Jason, dear, I'm a bit weary, and we really should give Betty time to get ready for her trip."

Bob Parsons, completely chastised, nodded to Betty, moved to the bar, set his beer can on it and left the house without another word.

Jack Perry came across the room to Jason, pleased with the turn of events. "How's the old ticker?" He asked.

"Fine," Jason answered. "It's not so much my heart. Blood pressure. It's under control." He patted a small plastic vial in his jacket pocket and smiled wryly, but continued to look at Mel Vaslovic across the room.

Sarah watched her husband's face, then turned to looked at Vaslovic who was staring blindly at Jason.

Sarah's coaxing Jason to leave began an exodus as Vaslovic disappeared, leaving the job of seeing everyone off to Betty, who fretted to the Thompsons about her husband's sour behavior.

With the house quiet, Vaslovic reappeared and plopped down in the over-stuffed chair in the living room with another vodka. Betty, who had donned her apron and started dinner, could resist no longer and came into the living room.

She sat on a footstool beside him and touched his hand. "Dear, what's wrong? Is it because you're upset over retiring? Or me going to mother's?"

Vaslovic looked through bleary eyes at her hand on his, then at her sad countenance. "Why would I be upset over that? Over either one?"

"Then, what is it? Is it something I did?"

Vaslovic took a deep breath and exhaled slowly. He shook his head. "No, no. Nothing. Listen, what time is your flight?"

"Seven. We have time. I'm making you dinner."

He tried to work up a smile, closed his eyes, and patted her hand. "I'm alright. Guess I had a little too much to drink."

Betty smiled lovingly at him and stood up, her hands smoothing down the apron over her plump stomach. "You looked so angry at Jason."

"Oh?"

"Yes. Were you?"

Vaslovic hesitated, then stood and went to the French doors, now closed. "Yes, I was."

"Why?" Betty's heart beat faster.

"He lied to me."

"He lied to you?"

"He lied. I've known Jason since we were boys, and he's never lied to me before. That I know of." His words came in a rush.

"How, dear?"

"Something he said earlier." He stared into the back yard. "It doesn't matter."

"What did he say?"

Vaslovic arched his back, turned suddenly, glared at his startled wife and shouted, "It doesn't matter, goddamnit!"

"Mel?!" Tears welled up in Betty's eyes.

"Just finish fixing dinner and we'll go!" Vaslovic's fists were clenched at his sides.

Betty turned slowly and moved toward the hall.

"Betty!"

She stopped, and without returning her husband's gaze, looked at the wall, her chin as high as she could manage. Tears rolled down her cheeks.

Vaslovic's voice was hoarse. "Dear, I'm sorry. I'm just nervous. I—I'll just have to get used to staying home. Please forgive me."

Betty stood still, waiting for more, and when it didn't come, she moved toward the kitchen without a word.

Vaslovic watched her disappear into the hall, then turned to look into the yard again. The passive look he had conjured for his wife hardened into a scowl, then evolved into a feral look as he stared out into the gathering dusk at nothing, his jaws clenching.

4

At 10:33 on Monday morning, Angie looked up from her desk and smiled at Mel Vaslovic as he walked into her office.

Vaslovic held a magazine in one hand. "Jason in?"

She straightened and put both hands on the small of her back with a grimace. "Staff meeting. Until eleven." She glanced at the clock on the wall.

Vaslovic looked at his watch. "Right. Right. Forgot." He dropped his arm with the magazine, turned half way and stopped. "Okay if I leave this for him?" He waved the magazine at her, turned, and marched straight for Jason's office door and opened it.

"I can take that." She jumped up from her chair and followed Vaslovic as he entered her boss's office.

He turned and faced her with what she considered a "simpleton grin" as though he were insincere. "No problem, Angie. I know where he keeps things." He craned his neck to look around, as the magazine still flopped from his hand. "And while I'm here, I'll help myself to an article he told me about. Magazine there." He gestured with his magazine. "No need to bother yourself. Thanks."

Angie hesitated, frowned as she backed away, and pulled the door closed after her. "Okay, Mel." As the door neared the latch, she thought about what he was doing and left the door open six inches. She then went back to her desk as she shook her head in frustration, her mouth tight.

Two minutes later Vaslovic emerged. "Got it." He waved another magazine at her as he walked by. "Thanks. You'll let 'im know, okay?"

"Sure, Mel." She nodded and turned to her computer keyboard.

"Angie, where did this magazine come from?" Jason came out of his office with a puzzled look.

"Which one?"

"*Byte.*" "Where'd it come from?"

"Maybe it was the one Mel Vaslovic returned to you."

Jason wrinkled his forehead. "*Byte*?" He shook his head. "I don't remember having a *Byte Magazine*." He turned slowly and looked toward the hall door. "Maybe he wanted me to see it. Probably an article he wants me to read."

"That's probably it. I must have misunderstood him."

"When was that?"

"Little while ago. You were in your staff meeting. I forgot to tell you. I'm sorry." She cocked her head with a pained look.

"Hm. Okay." He raised his eyebrows in a shrug.

"He also looked for that article you wanted him to see."

"Really? Which one?"

"He didn't say. When he came out, he told me he'd found it and to tell you thanks."

"He was in my office?"

"I'm sorry, Mr. T. He just went in without asking. I didn't know what to say, and your office was secure."

Jason was silent , then, "It's okay. No harm done."

Angie went back to her work; and Jason, scowling at the magazine's cover, moved slowly back into his office.

Sergeant Willie Vargas was making his rounds on graveyard shift. He felt pretty good, considering the fact it was after three in the morning. Thoughts of his grandchildren occupied his mind. They had come down to Albuquerque this past weekend from Rodarte with their parents and great-grandmother Vargas, bringing crisp apples from the old orchards and fresh, green chile from the fields there.

The only negative was the slight pain he felt in his left leg, the one that caused him to limp. It had stopped a burst of shrapnel at Inchon Reservoir and felt arthritic from time to time. That had ended his fighting career with the Army. They gave him a Purple Heart and a job at the battalion aid station where they patched him up. His buddies said he looked a lot like Willie in the *Willie and Joe* cartoons drawn by his fellow New Mexican, Bill Mauldin, and the name stuck. His real name was Incarnación. He had been with Rio Grande Laboratories Security Division for more than twenty years.

He turned out the lights to Security Room 803A and started to close the door when he stopped and stared at the crack of light streaming into the room from the hall along the tiled floor, past the door's edge. Something was wrong. What was it? He knew it had to be something, something in the back of his mind, something about the room.

He re-entered the room, flicked on the lights, and walked slowly along the last row of cabinets as he re-traced his steps. As he moved along, he looked carefully at each cabinet, not knowing what he was looking for or what he would find. At the last one along the back wall, before he turned into the next row, he stopped. He looked hard at the file cabinet, then at the one next to it. Both were closed. Weren't they? Was there something different? he mused. He looked from one to the other. The only difference he noticed was that the cabinet to the left had the green, T-shaped "SECURED" sign dropped in between the top drawer handle, and the drawer front slanted differently from the one on the right. Was that it? He quickly walked along the rest of the route and back, looking at each cabinet, inspecting for the green sign. Each was square in the door. Except for that one. His mind reeled as he realized the sign was the difference, the thing that bothered him. He had toured these rooms on his shifts for years and had never given something like this, something so minor, a second thought.

He shook his greying head as he walked over to the cabinet and straightened the sign. Then he noticed that the big, round safe-dial on the top drawer rested in its open position, zero, a band of red paint over it, straight up, aligned with the dial pointer. He pushed down on the drawer-latch release lever. It gave with a click. He pushed again, and pulled the drawer open. Someone had forgotten to spin the cylinder after closing the drawer—or drawers. The green "secure" indicator was wrong—false. The cabinet was *not* secure.

His face turned red with the realization that he was supposed to look for those sorts of things. What was the procedure in a case such as this? Right. Report to the Watch Commander, who would write a report to the Division Head, who would write a reprimand to the Section Leader, who would chew on the monitor, scientist, or secretary responsible.

Willie Vargas reached for the two-way radio on his belt.

The Watch Commander, Captain Arkin, arrived in five minutes. Together, he and Vargas opened all the drawers in the cabinet, looking for anything unusual. Arkin saw nothing obvious, but decided to call the Division Head anyway. The call went through at 3:44 A.M.

It took David Manning twenty-five minutes to drive from his house in the hills near Tijeras Canyon, past the base gate to Building 800, and another two to make it past the building guard shack to Room 803A.

Manning looked at the file drawers, then reached in to finger the files; but Arkin admonished him from doing so, telling him that it should be done by the responsible monitor. He stared first at Arkin, then at Vargas, before going to his office to phone his secretary.

She was there in thirty minutes.

Vicky Torres was a small, tidy woman, who wore her hair pulled back in a bun and looked through a pair of half-frame glasses that she let fall to her chest from a beaded neck chain when unneeded. Her mouth betrayed conviction, determination, and self-confidence. Manning was awed by her secretarial and organizational talents and by the homemade *tamales* she brought in on Christmas and Easter. He was amazed at how unruffled she appeared after having been awakened in the middle of the night.

She frowned at the three men, all taller than she. "What have you found?"

Manning rubbed his eyes. "Officer Vargas found this safe open. It's one of ours. But the captain here told me you're the one to look."

"Impossible." Vicky put half-frame glasses up to her eyes and peered at the file cabinet, her head high to accomodate her spectacles.

"It was open," Officer Vargas said. He stood back three feet.

"Did you look at the log?" she asked.

"No," Vargas said. He reached for the aluminum-covered book lying on the top of the cabinet and handed it to her.

Vicky opened the metal book. "There. I closed and signed at 5:03." She ran her finger along a line of notes. "The last file re-deposited, D-404, a drawing file checked out by Madison at zero eight thirty, was returned to me complete before 4:45." She looked around at Manning and Arkin with one eyebrow raised.

"But it was open. Look. It still is." Vargas unlatched and opened the top drawer.

Vicky stiffened, took in a deep breath, exhaled, and peered at the drawer full of neatly arranged hanging files, color-coded by chronology and purpose. Barely tall enough to see along the tops of the typed tabs stuck into each folder, she turned and looked at Manning with a pained expression.

"Vicky, I know you locked up. Don't worry. There's probably a logical explanation for this." Manning nodded at her reassuringly.

Captain Arkin glanced at officer Vargas who frowned at Vicky Torres.

She shook her head. "I did. I did. I locked up." She waved her arms, returned the log to the cabinet top, and gestured with both hands. "Madison must have goofed."

"What's next, Arkin?" Manning asked, his eyes puffy.

Arkin shrugged one shoulder and said, "We don't have much choice. We have to go through the drawers."

Vicky looked up at the officer in the brown uniform with the .38 holstered at his belt. "You mean *I* have to go through them!" She tapped her chest with her finger, then looked from man to man.

"I guess so, Vicky. You're the monitor, and you know what's supposed to be in there." Arkin grimaced an apology.

David Manning helped Vicky remove and carry each drawer to a six-foot-long table in the center of the big file room where she went through each file methodically, referring to a master list in the front of each drawer and a sub-list in each folder.

She removed each folder, examined each page, checked it against the list, then returned it in order. She had gone through the second drawer with Manning yawning next to her, reeling from lack of sleep. Arkin and Vargas were standing next to the door or pacing outside in the hall. She whispered to herself in Spanish.

"What?" Manning asked.

"There's something puzzling about this file. Look." She picked up an orange folder with red and white tape across the front and back in an "X" pattern.

Manning jerked awake and moved closer. "What is it?"

"Geronimo Queen."

"Pages missing?"

"Pages? There's an entire four-page document missing!"

Manning looked pained. "Are you sure?" He croaked.

"Look. See this? Look at the list and compare it with the doc numbers." She looked up at him as though she thought him stupid.

Vargas and Arkin, both curious after hearing her exclamation, moved closer to watch and listen.

"Yeah," Manning said.

"And I never fold these over. This has been folded over. It's almost torn."

Manning paled.

"Vicky, when was the last time that folder was checked out?" Arkin asked.

She turned and looked up at the senior guard. "Never. This is a file copy—an archive, not a library file. It hasn't gone to the archive room yet because there's still an action item on it. This's never been checked out. It's here in the log." She tapped the log page fiercely.

Arkin frowned. "I guess I don't understand the significance of the tear next to the staple, but if we really have a document missing, this is serious!"

Vicky sighed, "I'm trying to explain! I typed this. I stapled it. I put it in the file and put it in here. It's on the log. No one was to touch it. No one has signed it out. But it's been tampered with. Somebody folded it over. I would never do that! There's definitely a document missing."

Arkin put his finger on one corner of the file cover and moved in closer. "Anything else?"

Vicky looked at each part of the 115-page file. "Yes. This page has been folded over and resmoothed. And here. See? Corners folded over the staple." She looked at each of the three men in turn, her lips compressed.

Arkin eyed Manning. "If you're correct, someone's been in here and helped himself to these files in the past seven or eight hours."

Manning turned white and stared at Vicky, who stared back.

5

*J*ason awoke from a flurry of dreams, lifted his head off his pillow, and peered at the bedside clock. It was 6:05 in the morning. He closed his eyes, sensed something was different, and rolled over to see if Sarah was there. She was not.

Odd, he thought. She wasn't an early riser, and he nearly always preceded her on weekday mornings. His habit was to rise around six, shave, shower, and fix his own quick breakfast. Sometimes Sarah would pad downstairs in her robe just as he was about to leave and pour herself a cup of coffee, her eyes still heavy with sleep. He felt her side of the king-sized bed. It was cold. He lay on his back for ten more seconds, then looked in the direction of the bathroom. The door was open.

He heard a door shut gently downstairs with the click of a latch going home against a steel striker plate. He reckoned it came from the kitchen. He frowned, rubbed his sleepy face, glanced at the clock again, and forced himself out of bed.

"Is that green chile I smell?" Jason asked as he walked into the kitchen-dining alcove. He adjusted his Indian-made bolo, a piece of apparel almost obligatory amongst upper echelon Labs employees.

Sarah, dressed in baggy pants and a sweater, turned and smiled. "I thought you might like some on a couple of eggs this morning. It's Mrs. Abeyta's."

"Great," He beamed. "You're up early." He reached for a cup to fill with coffee as he frowned at her, curious.

"Couldn't sleep. Bit of indigestion. I drank some camomile, then decided to take a walk and treat you to a decent breakfast."

"How nice! Tummy better?" He set his coffe cup on the rustic trestle-table, sat and picked up his cloth napkin.

"You deserve a little pampering." She reached for a pot holder. "Only five days left. Yes, I feel better."

"Four. Four days." Jason raised his eyebrows. "I'm going to miss those people. And my work."

"Right. Four. You've plenty to do here." She turned, opened the oven door and, using a pot holder, pulled out a big plate. "It's ready."

"Watercolor today?"

"Yes. We're going to Jemez."

Jason looked up from his plate as she set it down in front of him. "That's a long way."

"We'll be back by four or so."

On his way to work, something gnawed at Jason's subconscious. Thoughts and ideas reeled through his mind as they usually did at this hour of the day—normally about work-related things, but he kept returning to the irritant. Then it dawned on him. Sarah had been especially sweet this morning. What was going on?   She rarely walked out to the garage-side drive to see him off. Usually, if at all, she made it to the kitchen door in a sleep-induced fog. Sometimes she didn't even speak.

Something had changed between them in the last few years. It was nothing in particular, but a distance seemed to have had crept into their relationship. Maybe she was tired of him. The idea didn't frighten him, but maybe he was too used to their marriage. Perhaps he was the one who was remote, and she was getting back at him. She was affectionate at the retirement party. He didn't believe she was as interested in the house up north as she had intimated to all those people. He would have to talk to her about getting away—out of the country perhaps.

He drove the Ford quarter-ton pickup into the parking lot and entered Building 800. He carried a carved leather briefcase Sarah had found for him in Mexico years before.

The red quarry tile under his feet gleamed to perfection much in the way the lawn in front of the big building was trimmed, an anomaly in a place where green grass is reluctant to grow. Ahead of him, a large, windowless hall was blocked by a precisely set barrier of steel bars. A door, also of steel bars, part of the fence, was open. Just inside the door a uniformed, armed guard sat on a high stool. Jason showed his picture badge, which the guard touched with his finger. Two halls later, he turned and entered Angie's space, effectively his outer office.

"Morning, Mr. T."

"Morning, Angie." Jason returned her smile.

She straightened a sheaf of papers. "Coffee?"

"You don't have to do that, but thanks. Better make it de-caf."

She rose from her chair. "How are you today? Any symptoms?" She sobered and looked at him with concern.

"I'm okay. Thanks." He stopped and tapped his lower jacket pocket, causing a rattle from the plastic vial inside. "That reminds me. Need to get this prescription refilled. Down to the last two or three."

"I'll be right back." Angie disappeared into the hall.

He opened the door to his office and went behind his desk. He raised his briefcase to the top of the credenza and pulled out the roll-around chair from under the desk. He sat down slowly and opened a desk drawer, one without a lock.

Angie reappeared in front of his desk. "Your coffee, Mr. T. Mark is down the hall with some security types and Mr. Manning. They want to see you right away. Said it's urgent." She set a mug down on Jason's desk. She looked at him with concern.

He looked up at her quizzically and spoke more to himself than to her. "Okay. Wonder what they want? Thanks, Angie."

Dave Manning, Division Chief Mark Thurston, Tech Liaison Peppers, and Security Chief and graveyard shift Watch Commander Arkin, the latter two in brown uniforms, stood in the half lighted, energy-efficient hallway just outside Manning's office. Peppers and Arkin had their arms folded across their chests and were studying the patterns in the floor tile. Manning, his collar open, no tie and unshaven, looked up as Jason approached.

"Morning, Dave. Mark. What's up?" Jason furrowed his brow at Manning's appearance before looking at the two security people.

"Morning, Jason," Manning said. "You know Peppers, here. This is Arkin, graveyard shift commander. Let's convene in the conference room." Manning was haggard from lack of sleep. His voice reflected his fatigue.

Jason frowned at Manning and nodded at the other men, his mouth pinched with curiosity.

Manning was the last one into the room and closed the door. Peppers had taken a seat, but others were slower to sit down. They waited for Manning to get seated, then everyone focused on Jason.

Manning, with his eyes tired, sat rigidly in his chair. "For now, what we are about to discuss must remain in this room." He paused. "There's been a security breach—the first in more than fifteen years."

Jason didn't speak for five seconds, but his mouth opened reflexively. "A security leak?" He looked at each of the other men in turn, scanning their faces for meaning, his brow deeply furrowed.

"No, Jason, a breach," Manning said. He sighed and ran his fingers through his thinning, greying hair.

"I don't get it."

"The guard making third-shift rounds found a safe open. One of ours, in 803A."

"An open safe?"

"Yes. Open safe."

Jason shook his head. "Well—was the door open? The room door?" His mind reeled.

"No. Apparently they had the combination to that as well."

"But left the safe open?" His face was pinched.

Manning nodded, his eyes closed. "Yes. The drawer wasn't physically open, but the cabinet was unsecured."

"Something's missing?"

Manning sighed heavily. "A classified document. It looks as though they pawed through the entire file."

Jason tried to fathom the importance of his words, so kept his eyes on Manning.

"Vicky Torres, the monitor, went over it. You know how meticulous she is. It was part of Geronimo Queen, Jason." He nodded sagely.

Jason stared at Manning, then finally let his gaze drift away. "Geronimo Queen?!" His eyes returned to bore in on Manning. His mouth dropped open.

"Afraid so. Officer Arkin here decided to go around regs and call me as soon as they discovered the breach." He nodded in Arkin's direction. "Good call."

Arkin shifted his weight self-consciously.

Jason drew in a deep breath and exhaled. He glanced at Arkin. "Were there fingerprints, anything at all to—?"

Peppers broke in. "FBI team has been here since 5:30. Nothing so far, but they don't tell us much."

Manning leaned toward Jason. "They're going to want to talk to everyone. They may even interview people at home."

Jason, his breathing deep, asked, "Are they going to seal the base?"

"No indication. They'd have done it by now. Too much elapsed time. It's not like a nuclear material disappearance."

"And they figure whoever's responsible is probably long-gone by now," Peppers said.

Manning faced Peppers. "More than likely they don't understand the significance of the loss." He turned to Jason. "How could this have happened? You have the combinations, right?"

"Yes." Jason paused and shooked his head. He paled as he looked at Arkin, then Peppers. "The room door was closed and locked?"

"Correct. No sign of tampering," Arkin said. "Officer Vargas discovered the breach on his shift. He was pretty upset, so we let him go home after his report.

Jason winced, looked away and pressed his forehead with his hand. He lowered his head and leaned forward, his face in a grimace. Mark Thurston and Arkin were up and at his side in an instant.

Manning jerked out of his chair. "Jason! What's wrong?!"

Jason caught his breath. "I—bit of pain—I"

"I'll get some water," Thurston said as he ran out the door.

Manning pointed at Peppers. "Call an ambulance!"

"No. Don't! Water's fine," Jason croaked. He held his hand high.

Mark returned with a paper cup of water and gave it to Jason, who downed it quickly.

"Jesus, Jason, are you okay?" Mark asked.

"Thanks." Jason's face was ashen. "Sudden headache. I get dizzy, and my stomach sometimes goes nuts."

"Heart?" Peppers asked.

"Hypertension. Sometimes excitement'll bring it on." He looked up at Peppers and forced a wan smile.

"You should go home. I'll take you," Manning said.

"I'll be okay." He paused. "Listen, I'll go back to my office and rest awhile. That's the best thing to do. I'll be fine." He waved, then stood and braced himself against the table.

"Okay, Jason, but—" Manning cut in.

"When are they going to talk to me?" Jason turned at the door, ignoring Manning and looking at Peppers. His face exhibited pain.

Peppers shook his head. "I don't know. Last I knew, they were with Vicky." He looked around the room. "Remember, they want a lid on this. No one outside this room for now."

"Of course," Jason said.

"Mr. T, are you all right?! You look terrible!" Angie frowned up at her boss.

He smiled. "I'm okay, Angie. Thanks. Listen, did you use your key to unlock the offices this morning?"

"Yes." She renewed her frown.

"Both doors? The hall door and my office?"

"Both doors. Why?"

He waved his hand. "Part of the reason for the meeting. Checking up on security."

"Mr. T, you don't look well at all. "

"I'm fine, Angie. Really. Please don't worry. I'm a lot healthier than I look." His frown turned to a reassuring half-smile.

Jason walked into his office and closed the door. He sat behind his desk, peaked his hands against his mouth, and stared at the colorful six-inch god's eye that hung on the wall behind the door.

He rose slowly, walked over to have a closer look, then turned and looked at the credenza. A short stack of magazines, mostly technical and scientific journals, rested on the left end nearest the window. On top was a copy of *Byte Magazine*. He picked it up and flipped through the first half, then put it down and went to the door.

"Angie, what time did you say Mel was here?"

"Mel Vaslovic?"

"Yes. Yesterday."

She looked up from her keyboard and studied the ceiling. "Uh, about 10:30."

"How long was he here?"

"It couldn't have been more than a couple of minutes. He said there was an article in one of your journals he wanted to look at."

"Right. Thanks."

Angie looked at Jason curiously, then returned to her work.

Jason took several phone calls and reviewed some papers before meeting with two subordinates. He closeted with Dave Manning twice over the breach crisis and discussed details of his parting with Angie, until noon. Angie left with another secretary for the cafeteria, and Jason called Mel's office again with no success.

Frustrated, he looked at his watch, put on his jacket, and headed for the front of the building. As he walked down the last section of hall toward the main guard gate, he saw Mel, who stopped to show his badge to the guard, then come toward him.

Jason took Mel aside and grabbed his arm. "Where have you been?!"

Mel frowned up at the taller Jason. "What?! Why?!"

"I've been trying to reach you all morning."

"I've been to the doctor, for crying out loud. What's the matter?" He looked down at Jason's hand on his arm.

Jason removed his hand, sighed, and looked away for a moment. "Hell, I don't know. Just an anxiety attack, I guess." He shifted his feet and refocused on Vaslovic's face. "Listen, are you upset with me?"

"Upset? Why would I be upset with you?" Vaslovic frowned anew.

"Well, it's just that you've seemed strange to me lately. Since Sunday."

"Oh, come on now, Jason." Vaslovic stopped and relaxed his face into a smile. "Hey, maybe so. Look, it's because Betty's gone. I hate it when she's gone. You know I'm spoiled. That's probably what you're seeing." He brushed his hand against Jason's shoulder.

Jason looked hard at him, then relaxed. "Yeah. Okay—sorry. Sorry. I should have known. Well, hey! How about lunch even though it's not Friday?"

"Okay. I could stand some food. Haven't been eating right. Let me check in before we go."

"Sure." Jason fell into step alongside Vaslovic as they headed for his office. "But you know, Betty's only been gone two days, Mel."

"Yes, and it feels like two weeks."

"So why'd you see a doctor?"

"Oh, you know how Betty's been after me to get my cholesterol down; and if I expect to keep the Labs' insurance policy, I have to do something."

"Right. Of course."

"Say, what *is* the problem? You don't look well yourself."

"Nothing!" Jason snapped his answer, then softened. "Oh, hell, that's not true. Christ, I've been under a strain lately. It's not bad enough, with trying to complete last minute business, and then the accident happens. Every time I turn around somebody wants another report or a meeting. I can't get anything done, and I'm losing interest." He hesitated. "Got one of my headaches earlier."

"Hm. Sorry," Vaslovic said.

The two friends smiled at each other as they entered Vaslovic's front office.

Jason parked the old pickup in the garage drive and entered the house through the kitchen. Sarah was at the sink washing her hands. He put his briefcase down on the kitchen trestle table. "Well, what have you been doing? Your hands are black."

Sarah turned and smiled. "Digging. Setting out some plants in the back yard."

"I thought you went to Jemez."

"We did. It started to rain and we left early. Got back early, so I decided to root around in the garden."

"Aha." Jason picked up his briefcase and began to walk out of the room.

"Dear?"

"Yes." Jason stopped and turned to look at Sarah as she wiped her hands on a towel.

"You're pale. Did you have an attack?"

"'Fraid so."

"Why? What happened?" Sarah's face clouded with concern.

Jason tossed his head to one side. "Oh, just the bureaucratic log jamb, I guess."

"Did you eat lunch today?"

"Yes. Why?"

"Just wondered. You know how the wrong foods can bother you. Alone?" She turned away to hang up the towel.

"No. I ran into Mel. We went together."

"That's nice."

Jason scratched his cheek. "This is new. You checking up on me?" He cast her a wry smile.

She faced him, her head tilted with concern. "No, of course not; but I care about your health. You need to eat right, but you don't always, especially when you go out with Mel to get those greasy tacos and burritos that have too much salt." She continued to fuss while she straightened the towel.

Jason nodded and smiled.

"How is he?"

"Who, Mel?"

"Yes."

"He's fine. You just saw him Sunday."

Sarah, busy at the sink with a bunch of carrots, turned away again. "I was curious. He behaved so strangely Sunday, and with Betty away at her mother's—" She let the sentence hang.

"You know Mel. He's acting like a spoiled kid with his mama gone."

"Mm. Did he get to work at the regular time this morning, then?" Sarah looked out the window as she scraped a carrot.

Jason was halfway through the door from the kitchen to the dining room. He stopped, looked frontwards before turning his head with puzzlement on his face. "I have no idea, Sarah. Why are you suddenly so curious about Mel?" His tone was tainted with irritation. He looked away at nothing, his mind in turmoil.

Sarah worked her hands faster. "No reason. I just get concerned about him. You know how I am. Earth mother." She turned, gave him a quick smile, then looked away.

It was dark and cool out when they finished dinner. Sarah had merely played with her food. They moved into the living room where Jason sat on the edge of the comfortable chair nearest the television and flipped through a copy of *TV Guide*. Sarah went to the sofa opposite the television and picked up a book she'd been reading.

Sarah was independent, cool, and self-confident, able to find abundant resources within herself. This showed in her face and in her carriage. Although there was a spark of something resembling unspoken rebellion in her eyes, they showed wisdom and kindness. She was fair and level headed and rarely raised her voice. Her demeanor was of one who seemed to know precisely where she was, had been, and was going. Even death seemed to hold no threat. To most she endeared herself, especially those who were basically honest and naïve. To those who were competitive, devious, or needy, she was often impatient and sometimes cutting. She provided a sort of quiet, matronly leadership that pacified people.

Sarah read voraciously, a trait she passed on to two of her three children. She could do so under most circumstances and would often, while Jason watched television in the same room. Novels were her favorites, but she would read almost anything at hand.

Food preparation was not her strong suit, but she told herself to work past the drudgery it imposed upon her. The result was a consensus that she was good at it. Dinner was the meal she felt should be well-rounded when the children were being raised, something to end the day with a sense of satisfaction, both nutritionally and psychologically, especially if the day had been taxing. Although she tried, she had difficulty making the same effort for the two of them; she and her husband. Jason was pleased and surprised when she did and always let her know.

Jason read, too, but his curiosity and interests were wide. He was compelled to experience everything at hand. If he missed a good piece on PBS, he became anxious and felt cheated.

When the Thompsons fought, they did so with a certain dignity and grace. Whenever one raised his or her voice, it was usually followed by embarrassed silence, as though courtroom decorum had been sullied. As likely as not, during a period when both understood the unspoken fact that they were "not speaking," they would speak—as a practical matter. Such conversations were necessary to routine, but perfunctory.

The automatic dishwasher roared in the kitchen.

"What's on? You don't normally watch television on Tuesdays." Sarah looked at her husband over a pair of reading half-frames.

"PBS is airing a special I want to see." He grabbed the remote control and powered the set on. The sound was immediate with the picture ten seconds behind it. Jason moved to the sofa where Sarah sat occupying the opposite end and settled back to check the time on the big clock near the stair.

The news was on. "And this just handed me," the newsman said. "An anonymous source has informed this station that the FBI is investigating a report of a breach of Rio Grande Labs security. Let's go to Ned Chambers out at the Labs."

Jason blanched and sat forward as the picture shifted to a grey-haired field man.

The reporter blinked away the late afternoon sun while standing in front of a large, wooden sign emblazoned with the stylized American Indian logo of the Laboratories. He held a microphone to his mouth. "Late, unofficial word has it that, behind these closely-guarded fences and walls of the sprawling Rio Grande Base and Laboratories, security agencies of the United States Government, led by agents of the FBI, are searching for reasons behind, and persons responsible for, the theft of classified government property."

A panoramic shot of a portion of the Labs appeared with the reporter's voice-over as Jason leaned forward and jolted.

"We tried to get onto the base to interview people close to the situation, Andy, but were turned back by guards here."

The picture cut to a military policeman holding an automatic weapon, standing outside a guardhouse, then back to the newsman, whose hair was blowing out of place because of a sudden gust of wind.

"When this reporter called to talk to Dr. Arthur Bledsoe, the man who, for more than ten years, has run the Labs for the the Department of Energy, we were told by a spokesperson that Dr. Bledsoe would not appear on camera and had no comment, other than to say that these reports were pure rumor and speculation." The newsman, looking harried and busy, attempted to control his hair for the camera. "Unfortunately, we have so far been unable to identify the individual who reported this story. What we can tell you is that there has been a great deal of FBI activity which tends to verify that *something* is happening out here."

The picture cut to a frontal view of the Federal Building in downtown Albuquerque and the bronze letters on the marble walls that read "Federal Bureau of Investigation." There was a scene with two plain sedans pulling out of the building's driveway and being waved on base by armed military sentries.

"Andy, these are FBI vehicles; and, as we have seen, a lot of them have been coming and going today. Reliable sources tell us these specially -trained and armed sentries do not appear unless there is a serious problem on the base."

Once again, the picture was of the field man, who was again managing his thinning hair. "Back to you, Andy."

The anchorrman reappeared. "Ned, how do you see this report? Is this reliable, or just a crank?"

Then came a shoulder shot of Chambers holding the microphone to his mouth. "Well, Andy, it's hard to tell without an official admission. Our source, who happens to be an insider, was very insistent; but we have been unable to verify anything at all."

"This was a man or a woman, Ned?"

"Someone who wishes to remain anonymous."

"Well, Ned, we're anxious to see and hear any further developments on this report. Thanks."

The picture switched to another angle of the anchorman. "And now, let's see what the weatherman has in store for us. Peter?"

Jason killed the power to the TV, put the remote control aside, and stood up slowly, whispering, "Jesus Christ!"

Sarah had lowered her book to watch and listen to the news report. She watched Jason as he moved past her like a wraith. "Jason? What's wrong?"

"That's ridiculous! Why do they let them get away with that sort of thing!?" He slapped his leg.

"What? It's not true?" She put her book down, tensed and turned toward him. "What's happened?"

He shook his head and went to stare out a window. "Nothing. Just irritates me. Makes us look bad."

"Jason, have you heard about this?"

"Hm?" He turned to look at her with a look of preoccupation, then back out the window. "No. Of course not. Just somebody trying to make trouble." He waved a hand irritably.

Sarah chewed her lip and watched him a for few seconds. She closed the book carefully, making sure the bookmark was on her page, and looked down at the petite watch on her wrist, then at her husband's back.

6

$\mathcal{J}$ason walked into Angie's office the following morning, and was surprised as she blocked his way when she jumped up from her chair and came around her desk.

"Mr. T, there's an FBI agent in your office. He's been there since I came in." She spoke in a harried, hushed tone and looked furtively behind Jason at the hall doorway, then at her watch.

Jason sighed as he moved his briefcase from one hand to the other. "Okay, Angie, thanks."

"I wanted to catch you before you went in so you could get a cup of coffee or something." Her hands worked against each other. "You know—catch your breath."

"Angie, you're too good to me. I'll be fine." He smiled down at her and continued into his office.

The man standing near the window was of average height and weight. He had sandy brown hair and wore a dark, conservative sport jacket over dark grey pants. A special security badge was clipped to his jacket.

"Good morning," Jason said as he swung his briefcase onto the credenza.

"Good morning," the man said. "Special agent Grayson. Albuquerque office." He pulled a thin leather wallet from his inside jacket pocket and flipped it open for Jason to inspect. His face was intelligent and pleasant, punctuated with dark, steady eyes. In his late thirties, his hair was longer than Jason would expect for a man in his job. "Hope you don't mind my waiting for you here."

"No; fine." Jason indicated a chair for Grayson.

"I'll get right to the point of my visit, Mr. Thompson. I'm sure you know what it is." Grayson shifted in his chair, which Jason took as a sign he was about to get down to business.

"I'm sure."

The FBI agent pulled a notebook from the opposite side of his jacket interior. "Mr. Manning explained the importance of the missing classified file. He said it's a document from a project you've been involved with since its inception." Grayson turned his head to make sure the door was closed.

"That's true." Jason peaked his hands together, his elbows on his desk.

"Understand—we're required to interview everybody connected with the project. And you've been Acting Director for, uh—" Grayson leafed through his notes.

"Geronimo Queen."

"Yes, right. Geronimo Queen." Grayson wrote in his notebook and looked up. "In the briefing, Manning said Geronimo Queen is an energy project." He looked at Jason expectantly.

"Yes it is." Jason's answer was clipped.

"Mr. Thompson, I can understand your hesitation at discussing a classified project with outsiders. That's been your training. I can assure you I am cleared to hear any and all information, especially under the circumstances."

Jason took in a deep breath. "Right. Okay. It *is* an energy project—no weapons involved. Geronimo Queen started as a doctoral thesis—I don't recall the writer or the school—and turned out to be far more important than anyone could have reasonably expected. The start-up budget came out of general funding, based on the government's off-and-on interest in alternative fuel sources; but it ended up with a special budget of its own when it proved to be a possible answer to some of our energy problems. A secrecy lid was clamped on it. Normally only weapons systems get classified. Now energy's included." Jason sat back in his chair. "And, with the kind of energy it looks like this technology could provide, it might not only mean a stop to importing foreign oil, but also have implications for upsetting trade balances. There are some who could profit if they got their hands on this thing before we can get it fully developed. My one regret is that I won't be able to be involved in bringing it to fruition."

"So there's strong motivation for interested parties to get their hands on the data."

"Absolutely. I said it wasn't a weapons technology, but that's only partially true. As it turns out, this project has implications for that realm as well. The data are inconclusive, but it looks as though, if research were carried out in that direction, certain aspects of it could be used for weapons. The energy application alone would be well worth stealing."

Grayson finished writing, then looked up. "Who would be most likely to benefit?"

"Who?"

"Countries, industries, individuals? Like that?"

"Well, almost any foreign country with energy deficiencies. There's the distinct possibility that oil-rich countries wouldn't like it because of what it would do to exports. It could easily affect the price of petroleum, natural gas and coal. It could be ideal for the generation of electrical energy such as fuel cells. We might be able to do away with long power transmission lines. It's possible the automobile industry, as we know it today, could be deeply affected. Any vehicle using the internal combustion-engine might be affected. Cars, buses, and planes would require redesign to accommodate new engines using this technology. The economic impact would be global—Wall Street—bond and futures markets." Jason shrugged, his eyes going wide. "And there's more discussion about global warming and its effect on climate change. Still an open question, but there it is."

"Hm."

"Industrial espionage could possibly have an impact on industries here and abroad. Who knows—if someone with money got a crack at this technology before all the domestic and foreign patent applications are run or someone who's aware of the military possibilities?"

"Do you have any idea of anybody in the labs who might have done this?"

Jason sat forward and shook his head broadly. "No. The scary thing is that very few people know this project even exists. What do *you* think?"

"So far, I'm just fact-finding. I'm not at liberty to discuss the case progress-wise beyond the investigation side such as this interview. "

"Sure. But you certainly would suspect an insider?"

Grayson breathed deeply and raised his eyebrows. "It appears that way. There was no break-and-enter, and this facility has good security." Grayson was silent, searching for meaning in Jason's face. "What can you tell me about the explosion at the Geronimo Queen test site in Area 7?"

"Only that two of my best people and their teams are working at tracking down the cause. Personally? I think that—without good confirmation—the test got out of control."

"Would you say there was a connection between the accident and the disappearance of the file?"

Jason shook his head slowly, frowning. "I fail to see how. I suppose it's possible, but—" he shrugged.

"Of course." Grayson looked down at his notepad. "You have the combinations to the file room and the cabinets. 803A. True?"

"Yes. I'm one of four people who do." Jason marveled at the man's ability to leap abruptly from one subject to another. It made him nervous.

"To both the security room and the files?"

Jason changed positions in his chair. "The monitor and I have the codes to the room and our file cabinets."

"Vicky Torres?"

"Vicky? Yes."

"Is there a backup?"

"Vicky is division monitor. That file cabinet is one of five belonging to my projects. If anyone else should need the codes in an emergency, they have to go through Security. It's not simple."

"Where do you keep the combinations?"

"Keep them?"

"Are they written down? Do you keep them under lock and key?"

Jason shook his head before Grayson had finished. "No. They're not written down. We commit them to memory. If we forget, we have to go to Security, and they use the double-key system. It's not easy, so we remember." He smiled at the FBI man briefly, then sobered.

"So far as you're concerned, there's no way for someone to take the codes from this office or the next?" He waved his hand vaguely at the door.

"Correct. Breaking in here would be fruitless for someone wanting to find the combinations."

Grayson stared. "Did you leave at the regular time Monday?"

Jason's head began to throb. "Yes. I was home all evening. I left for work at approximately 7:45 a.m. yesterday—and today."

Grayson smiled. "Thanks. I have to ask." He shifted his weight and took in a breath. "Mr. Thompson, you have been friends with Mel Vaslovic is it? For a long time?"

Jason jolted and wanted to swallow but resisted the temptation, for fear it would give something away. "Vaslovic. Yes. Why?"

"It's our understanding that both you and Mr. Vaslovic are retiring after this week." Grayson studied Jason' s face.

"That's true. I don't understand. He works in another division."

Grayson's demeanor stiffened. "I'm aware of that. But we're required to chase down every lead in a case like this, and our information is that he was expected at work this morning but hasn't shown up."

"Has anyone called his house?" Jason frowned as his headache worsened and the dizziness started.

"I understand you and your wife attended a retirement party at the Vaslovic residence this past Sunday."

Jason, annoyed with the FBI man's intimate knowledge, squirmed in his chair but forced his facial expression to remain unaffected. "Yes. There were a number of people from the Labs there. Sarah and I were there. Sarah's my wife." The instant Jason added this bit of information, he realized it was unnecessary.

"Did Mr. Vaslovic indicate anything to you that might lead you to believe he would not be in today?"

"No."

"Mrs. Vaslovic's name is Betty?" Grayson consulted his notes. "Did she indicate that anything would be different today?"

Jason, hoping his stomach would behave, took in a deep breath. "She didn't tell me, but she told my wife she was going to see her mother."

"Out of town?"

"Out of town."

"Mr. Vaslovic's secretary's recollection is that he left his office at the regular time yesterday. Did you see him last night?"

"No. I went home. I was home all evening. I spoke to no one, other than to my wife, of course." For some odd reason, he thought his headache was backing off; but he was still dizzy.

"Okay."

"Why all these questions about Vaslovic? He's in another division, as I've already told you. Is he a suspect?" Jason shook his head, impatience welling.

Grayson waved his hand. "No. Please understand that, in order to complete our investigation, we must have a complete picture of everybody, their associations, and their movements. Neither you nor Mr. Vaslovic is a suspect—but sometimes things innocent people say and do can lead us to those we're after. Now, I know this is stressful for you, but I have to inform you that, until our investigation is closed, we may have to talk to you again."

"I understand." Jason closed his eyes in an effort to relieve the tension and his symptoms.

Grayson stood up. "I've been wondering about something."

"What's that?"

"The god's eye. Very nice. Where did you get it?"

Jason smiled. "I make them. They add a bit of color." He turned to glance at it on the wall behind his desk, then swiveled back.

"Thanks for your time, Mr. Thompson."

They both stood, and Grayson reached across the desk to shake Jason's hand.

Jason watched Grayson leave and close the door. He then sat down and closed his eyes again. He opened them, then turned again to stare at the god's eye with its colorful bands of yarn. He lifted the telephone handset, keyed four numbers and waited. "Jason Thompson. Is Mel in? Has he been—? Not yet this morning? Has he called in? I see. Thank you."

He thought for a moment, then keyed a series of eight digits into the telephone and listened. A full minute later, he put the receiver down slowly.

Briefcase in hand, he left his office, then stopped in front of Angie's desk. "Angie, anybody looking for me, tell 'em I'll be back later."

Two miles north of the Interstate bridge, the traffic thinned out but was still heavy enough to annoy Jason considerably. He found it easier going in the residential sections. There were no cars at all on the street where the Vaslovics lived.

As he drove past the house, he noticed the empty driveway and the closed garage doors. He turned left at the next street, left once more, then pulled over and parked in the shade of a tree. He sat for a minute to study the street through the windows of the car and the rearview mirrors. He got out, crossed to the opposite sidewalk, and walked back in the direction of the Vaslovic house, now a block away. As he approached it, he watched for people along the street or in houses on either side. He saw nothing obvious as he walked quickly to the front door of the house.

He knocked, looked around the empty street again, then tried the door. It was unlocked. He let himself in quickly and stood still for a few seconds just inside the door. He listened as his heart pounded and his head ached. He put his arm out, steadied himself against the wall, and fought the dizziness. "Mel? Betty?" He called out as he stared out through the open door into the street, then closed it carefully until it latched.

The house was cool and still, the only sound that of the slow tick-tock of the antique grandfather clock that stood in the foyer. He took each step carefully as he moved into the innards of the house. The living room, where the party had been only three days before on Sunday afternoon, was neat and empty. The French doors to the patio were closed and curtained. He turned and walked down the carpeted hall toward the bedrooms.

The first door on the right was closed; but the second, on the left, was open. Beige, deep pile carpet came out to meet the brown of the hall carpet at the doorframe. Across the room, the curtains over the window behind the bed were open enough to let in the morning sunlight. To his right and next to the closet doors stood a huge, antique dresser, mirror atop. On the floor at the foot of the big four-poster bed, stretched out on his right side, suspenders over his white shirt, was Mel Vaslovic.

Jason's dizziness increased with the pounding in his head. He became nauseous. He stood with one hand supporting himself against the door frame and the other pressed against his head. After he regained his composure, he crossed the room and bent over the still figure.

Vaslovic's left arm was alongside his body with the palm of his hand cupped. His right arm pointed under the bed. In that hand was a small-caliber semiautomatic pistol, index finger inside the trigger guard. As he fought his nausea and headache, Jason moved around so he could see his friend's face. Dull, partially open eyes stared at the ceiling. Dry blood encircled a small hole in Mel Vaslovic's right temple.

Jason stood up, shaking, and took one step backward. He froze in place and listened. The house seemed alive—watching. He moved only his head to look quickly around the big room. Nothing appeared to be out of place. The bed was made. He noticed that one of Vaslovic's feet was tangled in the bedspread that draped to the floor. To the right of the dead man's foot was a small object, dark against the light carpet.

He resisted a desire to flee as he knelt near the still body to reach under the bed and retrieve the marble-sized object. He recognized it as a crude clay bead, a replica of those made by Indians in central Mexico, with streaks of vibrantly colored paint and a string-hole through its center.

Still in a crouch, he looked down at each of Vaslovic's dead hands and felt around the pockets in his pants and shirt. He stared at nothing, chasing some related thought through his shocked and confused mind, then stood up. He put the bead into his pants pocket, then froze in place to listened again before he made for the front door. As he came to the entry hall, he stopped and looked around as his breath came in short gasps. With a handkerchief from his pants pocket, he wiped the inside of the front-door handle, as well as above and below it. He then opened the door, just enough to wipe the outside hardware as he scanned the street.

He shut the door and locked it. He walked back to the master bedroom where Vaslovic lay and wiped the doorframe where he had put his hands. He then made for the garage through the kitchen. With his handkerchief wrapped around his hand, he felt the hood of the car parked there. It was cold.

He made sure the handles were clean as he let himself out the side door. He studied the backyard briefly and looked up along the roof lines and at the windows and doors of neighboring houses. He made sure the street was empty before leaving through the side gate.

As Jason turned the corner to walk up the next street, he heard a car behind him. He maintained a normal pace, and glanced to his right. A small Japanese car with a woman at the wheel moved by him and drove on down the cross-street after slowing at the corner. He heaved a sigh and walked on.

The Mercedes was gone from in front of the garage where Jason parked his pickup. He got out and moved quickly up the stairs to the studio.

He lifted the colorful clay hat from the sleeping Mexican and retrieved the two keys that lay on the dished-in head. When he inserted the Schlage key in the dead bolt and turned it, he realized it was unbolted. He got the same result with the second key in the door latch. He stopped, stared at the door, put the keys back, then briefly looked up and down the street. Oddly, he felt his symptoms abate.

He removed his dark glasses and went inside. He stood for a few seconds to allow his eyes to adjust to the change in light, then looked around the room carefully. He laid his jacket over the back of a chair and went to the potter's wheel. Sarah's clay pot was still on the wheel at the end of the large worktable, but the dampened cloth used to keep the clay supple against the high, dry air was not on it. Instead, it lay on the floor near the wheel. He peered intently and closely at the surface of the pot, then ran a finger over its drying surface. He knelt down, picked up the cloth and fingered it. It was dry. Jason opened the kiln door and peered inside. He closed the door quietly.

He flicked the light on as he moved into the darkroom. He felt the surface of the sink, smelled his finger, then opened the cabinet over the sink. It was lined with large, yellow film boxes. He scanned the row of boxes and pulled out the leftmost one. He opened it and looked inside. After closing the box, he returned it, shut the cabinet, and turned and stared at the enlarger that sat on the combination work surface drainboard in the tiny room. He knelt down to remove a big, plastic clamshell box from the cabinet under the sink. He then opened up the inner boxes one by one.

Each box contained a lens or filter set. After inspecting each item, he closed and returned the boxes, snapped the light off, and left.

He went to the sculpture work table, took the bead from his pants pocket and reached for a wood clay roller. He smashed the bead against the table with the roller and rummaged through the remains with his finger. After a thorough inspection, he scraped the residue into his hand, dumped it into a wastebasket, and brushed his hands clean.

He again turned his attention to Sarah's pot on the wheel. He examined it closely, then turned it slowly. His dizziness almost gone, he leaned close to the surface of the clay and fingered a small area along the top bulge underneath the lip. Then he took the drape cloth, wet it in the bathroom sink, and covered the pot.

Jason parked his pickup in one of the marked spaces across from a mall supermarket. He got out and moved quickly to one of the three pay phones near the newspaper racks. He stopped to adjust his dark glasses. He then turned around to look up and down the sidewalk and over the parking lot before digging for a coin.

"Collect, operator." He waited. "Is Mr. Adams in? Okay, please take a message. This is Benjamin. Correct. I have engine problems. He needs to look at it right away. Tell him it's urgent. I'm having a hard time driving to work. That's all."

When Jason returned to his office, Dave Manning, who paced, was waiting for him in Angie's office. "Jason—where have you been? This thing is heating up!"

Jason looked at Manning, then down at Angie who was fretful. "Another headache. I was out of meds. Come on in, Dave." Jason continued into his office.

Manning followed and closed the door. "Jason, these FBI guys are driving us nuts!"

Jason turned to face Manning with the sudden realization that he didn't want to talk to anyone, not even Dave Manning. "How do you mean?" He furrowed his brow.

"They're not only interviewing everyone inside the division, but outside. Over into Peck's outfit."

"Well, they have a job to do." Jason turned away to avoid Manning's eyes as he pretended to do something with his briefcase on the credenza. His head throbbed for an instant.

"Jason, they've sealed all the files. Poor Vicky has hardly gotten any rest. They're making her go over them again and again." Manning walked a tight circle. "They're ransacking the labs and offices one by one."

Jason turned around. "Do they have a suspect?"

"I don't think so. But according to Peppers, they think it's someone right here inside the division." He jabbed his finger toward the floor.

Jason shoved his hands into his rear pants pockets and stared at Manning. "Do they give a reason?"

Manning shook his head, "No. Our security has been tight. They've looked at our methods and don't see how anyone who wasn't inside could possibly get in without inside help." He looked harried.

"They suspect me?"

Manning's eyes went wide. He threw up his hand defensively and cocked his head to one side as though blocking a blow. "I didn't say that, Jason. I didn't say that."

Jason drove around the front of the house and turned left to pull onto the driveway next to the Mercedes. Sarah was upstairs; he heard the shower running. He looked up the steps toward the familiar noise, then walked slowly to the front door to set his briefcase on the floor as always. He pushed open the screen, stepped out onto the porch, and looked at the street and up into the trees. Ten minutes later he heard the squeak of the screen-door hinges behind his back. He turned.

"Jason, what are you doing out here?" Sarah wore a terrycloth robe, and ran a comb through her damp hair.

"Oh, just out catching some air, I guess." His facial muscles were tight.

She backed up as he came inside. "You're distracted, aren't you? By what's going on out at the base."

He frowned at her. "Sarah, you can't put any store in that stuff you hear on the news. You know how reporters are."

She walked past him toward the kitchen. "What would you like for dinner, dear?"

He stopped, folded his arms across his chest and stared at the living-room floor. "I don't really care. I'm not very hungry."

She came back through the dining room to look at him. "Did you eat a big lunch with Mel again?"

He looked at her abruptly. "Mel? No. No, I didn't. Uh, I just don't—I had lunch. I'm just not very hungry."

"Well—"

"I'm sorry. I'll eat anything."

"Leftovers okay?"

"Sure." He managed a quick smile as Sarah turned and padded back into the kitchen.

"Sarah?"

"Yes?"

Jason, his face dark, turned toward his wife. "I—"

"Yes, Jason? What is it?"

He pinched his lips tight, lowered his eyes to look at the floor, then up at her. "Nothing."

"Jason, are you feeling alright? Did you have another attack today?" She took a step toward him. "It's something at work, isn't it?"

He sighed heavily and nodded. "Yeah. Work. I'm sorry. I'm okay." He turned away.

Sarah stared at him with a sad face and returned to the kitchen.

Jason stopped. Without turning around, he asked, "Isn't it a bit unusual for you to take a shower in the afternoon?"

"I went to see Maggie and got involved with her dogs. You know how stinky they can be." The sound of a pan banged against the sink came from the kitchen. "I just couldn't stand smelling myself anymore. I had to put all my clothes in the washer, too."

Jason nodded silently and walked slowly into the living room on the verge of tears.

7

*J*ason arrived at work a little before 8:00 a.m. on Thursday. Angie had not arrived, and the halls were quiet in the division wing. He was grateful for both these facts, since he was very distracted by events of the past two days and forced himself to behave normally. As the morning wore on, there was little increased activity. Even phone calls and messages for him dried up. At one point, he poked his head out of his office and asked Angie jokingly if it was a holiday the two of them had missed.

Jason returned to his office after lunch at a little past 1:00 p.m. He had been outside to walk and think. Angie jumped up from her desk to intercept him as he came in.

"Mr. T, that FBI man is waiting for you in your office." Her demeanor begged for answers. Her voice was barely above a whisper.

Jason took off the dark glasses he had worn into the building and looked beyond her toward his closed office door. "Okay, Angie. Thanks. Don't worry. It's routine. I'll fill you in later." He touched her lightly on her shoulder.

Grayson, in a matching suit this time, stood next to the window and looked out. He turned to look at Jason as he entered. "Sorry to break up your day like this, Mr. Thompson."

"Not at all." Jason hoped it didn't show when his face began to tighten. He smiled briefly.

"I need to ask some more questions."

Jason seated himself at his desk. "Ask away." He busied his hands with unnecessary rearrangements of objects on the desk top.

Grayson remained standing. Jason felt the agent was attempting to hide nervousness. It was at that moment the telephone on his desk rang.

"Excuse me," he said, and picked up the phone. "Thompson."

"Is Benjamin there?" the male voice on the phone asked.

Jason looked at Grayson, then out the window. "You have a wrong number. I think you're looking for Division A."

"Sorry," the voice said.

Jason returned the handset to the cradle and looked at Grayson in a questioning manner.

"You told me you have the combinations to both room 803A and the project file cabinets. Correct?" Grayson asked.

"Yes." Jason frowned and tilted his head.

"You, Vicky Torres, and the two backups in the Security Division."

"I forgot—there's also a backup within the division, but once that person is authorized to open under emergency conditions, the codes are changed. Security Division people, using the double-key system under the authority of two division heads can get in. Those provisions haven't been used in years."

"That's been explained to me."

"Then, why—?"

"You could easily have taken that file."

"What?!" Jason glared at Grayson and leaned forward against the desk.

"Please calm down, Mr. Thompson. We—"

"What the hell are you saying?! If you're going to charge me with something, you'd better do it now or take another tack!"

"Calm down. Please calm down." Grayson moved forward and extended his hand in a placating gesture. "Please."

Jason sat back slowly. His eyes burned. The FBI agent sat down in one of the chairs across the desk from him.

"I'm speaking hypothetically. The problem is that there are too many windows of opportunity during which you or someone else with code access could have gotten into that room. Part of the difficulty is that we can find no way anyone could have taken the codes from your offices here or any other place we know of in this building."

"What are you talking about? I thought the theft took place between close of business and 3:00 a.m. Tuesday? I was home!"

"Well, that hasn't been established beyond a doubt." Grayson angled his head to one side.

"Good God, man! Are you saying that I burglarized my own files or that I gave the codes to someone who did?! If I had done that, I sure as hell could have done it at any time, and I sure as hell wouldn't have been sloppy enough to leave that damned drawer open!"

"Perhaps."

"Perhaps?! Perhaps what?!" Jason hesitated, breathing hard. "Your charge is even more preposterous in view of the fact that I have been intimately involved with Geronimo Queen since the beginning. If I wanted to pass information to someone, I could do it easily without stealing paperwork!" He writhed in his chair. "I could do it off the top of my head!"

"With all due respect, Mr. Thompson, you could pull something like this off with the express purpose of making it look as though someone else had done it."

"Jesus Christ, Grayson! That's a sick and slanderous suggestion!" With his mouth curled up with disgust and his hands ballled into fists at his side, he burst from his chair and turned to the window.

Grayson ignored the outburst and continued. "Perhaps you've been planning to augment your retirement fund."

Jason turned around. "You—! I'd appreciate it if you would leave. Right now!" He growled.

Grayson ignored Jason's demand. He stood and paced away, then turned to look at his quarry. "Mr. Thompson, when was the last time you spoke to Mel Vaslovic?"

"What? Why?" Jason shook his head in annoyance.

"Mel Vaslovic was found dead."

Jason stared at Grayson, his eyes widening as perspiration beaded up on his forehead. "What?! Mel?!"

"His body was discovered this morning."

Jason returned to the window, calmed, yet fitful. His head started to throb. "God! I warned him about his health. Heart attack?" Jason continued to face the window, his mind reeled. He hoped he wasn't giving anything away. "Where? When?"

"It seems Mrs. Vaslovic tried to call him from her mother's house in Minnesota last night, then again this morning. When she couldn't reach him at home or work, she tried your house, but apparently both you and Mrs. Thompson had left already, so she called the police." He stared at Jason's back.

"My God, I had lunch with him just yesterday—no—the day before. How did it happen? Does Betty know?" He shook his head, turned to look briefly at the federal agent, then continued to stare out the window.

"My source in the Albuquerque Police Department says they tried to get in touch with Mrs. Vaslovic after the discovery, but she had already left for Albuquerque. They didn't inform the mother. It appears to be suicide, but the coroner isn't sure."

"Suicide?!" Jason turned to look at the FBI man. He spoke under his breath, but loud enough for Grayson to hear. "No! How?!"

"Gunshot." Grayson paused and peered at Jason with penetrating eyes. "That's the obvious cause of death." His remark was heavy with insinuation.

Jason took a step toward Grayson. "What are you implying? Are you now accusing me of murder—on top of everything else?!"

Grayson bounced the tips of his fingers against his chin. "It wouldn't matter if I thought you guilty of Vaslovic's murder, Mr. Thompson, if that is what happened. It's not a federal crime in this case."

Jason hesitated and stared at the young agent. "Then what are you driving at?" His eyes slits, he drew his words out.

Grayson, a pained expression on his face, dropped his hands and paced away. "I'll be frank with you, Mr. Thompson, we consider the relationship between you and Mr. Vaslovic and what has happened here at the Labs oddly coincidental." He hesitated, turned, and searched Jason's face for any sign of wavering. "It would help a lot if you would tell us anything and everything you know."

Jason scowled in anger. "Now listen, goddamnit—!"

Grayson took a deep breath and released it, then interrupted. He stared at Jason. "I think it only fair to tell you, Mr. Thompson, that special agents of the Bureau are at your house now with a search warrant." He looked at his watch.

Jason hesitated and attempted to keep from hyper-ventilating. The throbbing came back, and he was certain the dizziness would follow. "On what grounds?!"

"We have general warrants. Title Eighteen. Again, if you know anything—"

"I resent the inquisitorial nature of your questions! Now I'd appreciate it if you would leave!" Jason's face reddened.

Grayson didn't budge. "I suggest you not leave the building without checking with me first, Mr. Thompson."

Jason leaned forward on his desk, his eyes boring into Grayson. "Are you threatening me with arrest?"

Grayson made a side gesture with his head, but didn't answer.

Jason was silent for a few seconds, then, in a stage whisper, said, "Get out of my office. Now." He pointed at the door.

Grayson turned and hesitated as though he were about to say something more, then left and closed the door quietly. He walked quickly through Angie's office and into the hall. A man in a suit and tie, younger than he, but wearing the same special type of picture badge, turned and looked at him expectantly.

Grayson stopped and looked around the hall briefly, then at the other agent. He moved closer and spoke in a low voice. "Hang around here until I say it's okay to leave, alright?"

"How did it go?"

"Oh, I pissed him off. That's for sure." Grayson tugged at his chin with his hand. "Made him think we suspect him. He's mad as hell." He took in a deep breath and released it as he rubbed his stomach. "Christ, we're batting zero here. We've got to do something." He looked around again, then focused on the other FBI man. "The Vaslovic thing was a perfect opener. Listen, I want you to make him think we're tailing him. If he leaves his office, fall in behind."

"Stay close?"

"Shadow. But let him know you're there." Grayson, ready to leave, turned on his heel, then spun back. "Gimme a shout if he leaves the building."

"Will do."

Grayson kept his voice low. "I'm gonna see if the others have come up with anything. Who knows? Maybe the damned file will turn up under somebody's lunch. Hell, it's not as if plans for a nuclear warhead were on their way to terrorists." Grayson wheeled once more and strode off down the hall, his voice trailing behind. "Bunch of idiots . . . " He threw his arm up in frustration.

Jason stood and looked at the door as he felt the rising effects of his confrontation with Grayson on his hypertension, then sat. He stared at the blotter on his desk. His head hurt so much he pushed at it with both hands. His breath came in deep surges.

Angie rapped on the door but came in without waiting. "Mr. T, your wife called while you were with that man. She asked me to tell you there are FBI agents at your house. She was pretty upset. Mr. T, what is going on?" She was close to tears as she wrung her hands.

Dave Manning barged in past her. "Jason, we need to talk. Okay if I close the door? Sorry, Angie." He made an apologetic tilt of his head toward her.

Angie smiled defensively, exited and dutifully closed the door.

Manning watched the door shut, then started. "Did you hear about Mel Vaslovic?!"

Jason nodded, awarding Manning only a glance.

"God, it's just awful. I'm really sorry. You were close." Manning attempted self-control as he watched Jason, then changed the subject. "Listen, Jason, this thing is out of control. Those FBI guys are threatening to shut down some of our operations here! Do you believe Geronimo Queen is really important enough for a 'secret' classification? Isn't there a possibility we could convince the director to scale the classification down?" He started pacing, keeping his eyes on Jason as he moved. "That might take the pressure off."

"What?" Jason's voice was nearly a whisper. In his state of mind, he could barely hear, let alone understand, what Manning was saying. He paused and tried to recall the other man's words. "How, Dave? De-classify it after the fact? The classification is correct. And, hell, you know the director isn't going to change it, especially now." He hesitated as he searched for words. "Look, I read a microfiche copy of the stolen file. The data is too narrow to help someone develop the Geronimo Queen technology to the point we've taken it. There"s time." He waved his hand impatiently and paced toward the window. "I know that's not the answer you're looking for. You want the FBI off our backs. The cat's out of the bag. It's too late." He rubbed his eyes.

Manning stopped and faced Jason, then released his pent-up breath. "You're right. But who the hell did it? It just has to be some son-of-a-bitch here in the Labs!"

Jason, unable to look at Mannimg, stared out the window. He spoke tightly. "There has to be a problem with our internal need-to-know procedures."

Manning walked in a tight circle on the other side of the conference table. He ignored Jason and talked to himself as he flapped his hands. "We're all suspects, you know. Poor Vicky is not taking this well. She blames herself. She's one of the calmest people I know, and she's a nervous wreck."

Jason turned and went to his desk. "Dave, I hate to be rude, but if you don't need me anymore, I have to get out to Area 7 before the end of the day. Final test procedure review." He glanced at his watch, then at Manning.

"You go on. Sorry to hold you up. Sleep well tonight if you can. I know I won't be able to relax much. I'm sorry about Mel." Manning held up his hand in a friendly gesture, turned and lurched out of the room.

Jason put on his jacket, closed his briefcase, and slowly opened the door to Angie's office. Angie was bent over a file drawer in a cabinet near her desk, her back to him. He saw no one near the outer door, since he hoped to avoid her, he moved quickly across the office. He peered into the hall and pulled back. One of the FBI agents he had seen earlier was hovering no more than ten feet away.

He returned to his office, closed the door part way, then stood for a short time. He worked his lower lip between his teeth and studied the floor, glad his symptoms were abated. Then he put the briefcase back on the credenza, opened it, removed his jacket and hung it behind the door. He reached into an inside jacket pocket and removed his wallet, which he stuffed down inside the front of his shirt. He took his keys out of the jacket side pocket, put them in his back pants pocket and rolled up his sleeves. He picked up a legal pad from the edge of his desk, opened the door, and strode out into the hall past Angie, headed for the men's room. Out of the corner of his eye, he saw the young federal agent with the special badge move in his direction.

The men's room was tiled from floor to ceiling an off-white. A man he didn't recognize was using one of the urinals to his right. Against an outside wall in front of him were four toilet stalls. On his immediate left was a row of four wash basins with mirrors above them. A quick check along the base of the toilet stalls told him they were all empty. He went into the one he wanted, closed and locked the door.

Jason looked up and studied the frosted glass window above the toilet. He stood precariously on the bowl, pulled himself up to the window, and discovered it was permanently closed. Back on the floor, he pondered for a moment before he flushed the toilet and left the stall. He washed his hands and re-entered the hall. Instead of turning right and going back to his office, he turned left and headed along the hall to the next junction, then right. As he hurried on, he turned his head just enough to see the agent follow him.

He walked to a door at the end of the hall, entered an empty room and halted to wait for his government shadow. When he saw that the agent tail was close, he came back out into the hall, then turned to look back into the empty room. He said, loudly, "Yeah, thanks. I'll get that and be right back." He made a simple wave of his hand to his non-existant listener, then almost collided with the young FBI agent as he lowered his head to scribble on the legal pad. He mumbled an apology with a wan, preoccupied smile from under his eyebrows, then headed back in the direction from which he had come.

Jason walked as fast as he could for his office, feigned entry, then made a gesture with his hand against his head as though he had forgotten something. He continued along the hall in the same direction. As he started off again, he noticed the agent had slowed, thinking he was going into his office, then had moved quickly to catch up. He turned the corner and sprinted for the main door. He counted off four seconds, then slowed to a walk as people in the hall looked strangely at him. He turned and pretended to wave at someone so he could check the hall behind him. The agent was just turning the corner. Jason cleared the security desk, then angled left to the news counter that was just outside the guard perimeter in the main lobby.

Behind him, the agent saw Jason stop and reach for coins in his pants pocket and buy something. Nearly out of breath from the sudden exertion, he stopped, looked around, then turned his back to Jason. Three seconds later he turned again, expecting to see Jason coming back toward him. He was nowhere to be seen.

Jason kept one eye on the agent as he bought a pack of lemon drops. When he saw that the FBI man was sure of him and had turned away, he slipped past the counter, moved for a door that was out of the line of sight of the entry hall, and raced through it onto the front patio. He watched for unfamiliar faces or anyone loitering near the old Ford, then slowed to a fast walk toward the pickup in the parking lot across the steeet. There was no one who expressed an interest in him.

His spine tingled with anxiety like a child escaping an angry parent, and his head began to throb again, as he forced himself not to look back. He got into the truck, threw the legal pad and the candy onto the bench seat, started the engine and backed away. Only then did he look back toward Building 800. He saw that the agent had just exited the doorway and was looking frantically in every direction, but made no move toward the parking lot.

He pulled out of the lot and drove south along the main base thorough-fare, and headed for the base open range. Half a mile later, he turned right onto a paved road lined with old barrack-like warehouses left over from the Second World War. Soon he was in open space and saw the beginnings of the wide concrete runway which served both civilian and military aircraft. Before that was a wire fence with an opening in it through which the road passed. There was no guard house and no one in sight. It was a way to move from the Labs area, through the lightly guarded military base and onto off-base civilian streets. He looked in the rearview mirror. The only traffic he saw behind him and coming in his direction was an old compact car, certainly not an FBI vehicle, moving slowly a good half-mile back.

Once past the fence and before the end of the runway, Jason pointed the pickup north and off the base through another unguarded gate. He drove north along a six-lane boulevard for a half mile, then turned west for several blocks. After turning north again and driving through two traffic lights, he pulled into a small shopping mall and parked in a marked space near a light pole embedded in a huge concrete cylinder. He turned off the engine and sat for a full minute to study the mall through the truck windows and rearview mirrors. Five stores were lined up along a covered concrete sidewalk. Second from the right was a large, well-lighted drug store. The sun, mid-afternoon high, reflected off its plate glass windows.

He reached behind the seat and retrieved his tan windbreaker, then pulled the visor down. As he got out, he put on the sunglasses he had taken from the pocket of his jacket and put them on. He moved his wallet from inside his shirt to an inside windbreaker pocket as he walked across the tarmac to enter the drug store.

Including the clerks, there were no more than a dozen people under the soft glare of the fluorescent lamps embedded in the ceiling of the huge, barn-like store. Once past the chromed entrance turnstile, Jason made his way to the magazine rack against the wall to his left. He stood and looked at the vertical stacks of magazines. He finally chose one, flipped through it, then did the same with another. Finally, he reached up and removed the rearmost *Time Magazine* from its stack, looked inside briefly, then took it to the nearest register and paid for it.

As he walked across the nearly deserted lot in the late afternoon sun, he noticed a small green sedan parked by itself near the street entrance. Something about it sparked an interest, but he couldn't figure out what it was. To Jason, the car appeared to be empty.

He got in the pickup, put the magazine on the seat, and drove off. He turned south, then west to take a wide boulevard that slanted down the piedmont to meet the streets that spread out over the flat river valley. When he reached the first major boulevard in the valley, he turned the truck north and drove beyond the city's curbs and sidewalks into an area which featured patches of old farms and orchards. A mile on, he drove the truck into the parking lot of a bar which occupied the corner of the intersection of two paved roads. A red and white plastic sign which sat atop a steel pole at the corner nearest the intersection advertised beer.

Several cars and pickups were parked against the building. He looked around, then opened the magazine in the shade of the cab, and flipped through the pages. Near the center of the periodical, a gummed note paper was stuck to a page near the binding. He turned the magazine sideways. The note read, "T-house. Now." He closed the magazine and went to the pay phone with its clear plastic sound bubble near the bar entrance.

He heard two rings. "Sarah? Jason. Are you alright? Still? Please stay calm. Of course, I know you are. There's really nothing to worry about. It's just routine. Sarah, there's a problem at the base I can't discuss right now. They're just doing their jobs. They are? They—When?" He rubbed his face and the back of his neck with his hand. "Sarah, I have some terrible news. Yes. No. It's Mel. He's dead. Yes, that's right. The police—She's on her way back, but she doesn't know yet. No. They don't know. I heard it from the FBI. I'll be there as soon as I can, but I may be a little late. Yes. I have to run an errand. I should be home in a couple of hours. Don't hold dinner. No. I'll grab something. I'm fine. I'll call you before I leave. They did? Don't worry, it's routine. I know, it's awful. Yes, yes. I have to go now. Please don't worry."

He hung up the phone and stood for several seconds. His eyes were closed behind his dark glasses, his face toward the phone. He rubbed his forehead with his palm. As he opened his eyes and turned toward the parking lot and the highway, the small green sedan moved slowly by and turned onto the main north-bound road before noving slowly away.

8

*J*ason glanced at his watch and waited until the green sedan was out of sight before he turned the pickup north. The road ran straight for a couple of miles, then curved in a westerly direction where it met up with the old highway leading north to Bernalillo and Santa Fé. Orchards and farms in the rich river bottom were being abandoned for tracts of new frame houses designed to favor local architecture, but remnants of the past remained, such as fruit trees in side and backyards. The cottonwood population increased as the highways and the river closed on each other in this northern reach of the county.

He stopped at a traffic light that seemed to have been erected in the middle of nowhere and turned left toward the late afternoon sun. He had watched for the green sedan. Traffic was light in the last hour before the rush, and he could have spotted it easily. He saw no sign of it, but he realized why it had piqued his interest at the drug store. It had to be the car he had seen behind him when he left the Labs area for the military side. He realized he was looking into the rearview mirrors every few seconds.

He kept his speed down along Alameda Road, across the Rio Grande bridge, and into the ancient town of Corrales, a rural patchwork of big houses and old adobes amid alfalfa fields and orchards. Cars began to pile up in front and behind as people, mindful of the narrow old road, the speed limit, and the local police, made their way home at the end of the day.

The huge, dirt parking lot of the "Territorial House Restaurant and Bar" was all but empty. As Jason drove slowly into the lot, he looked around carefully, noting the workers' cars in the rear, near the remnants of a fine orchard, just short of the ancient irrigation ditch that used to feed it brown river water. It had sold out years before. He studied two shiny new cars, one a BMW, parked near the front of what had been an old adobe farmhouse, now the modern business.

Jason parked his pickup so it would not be seen from the paved road whose edge was only a few feet from the high, stuccoed adobe wall that fronted the road. He made his way to the restaurant entrance, set deep into the old earthen wall of the building, and walked under the deep, slant-roof porch which followed the crooked-S pattern along the front of the building. The entire structure was dominated by an immense old mulberry tree that grew out of the porch floor and through a special hole in the roof.

He was greeted at the cash register by a young woman who led him to the brick-floored dining area. He heard guitar music drifting from speakers hidden in the ceiling and the sound of splashing water coming from a small grotto near the entrance to the dining area as he followed her to the rear.

Jason stopped in the doorway to the main room and looked around, his tan windbreaker thrown over his shoulder. The large dining area, with its open-beamed ceiling and continuation of polished red brick floor, was filled with empty, linen-draped tables, save for one in the corner to his left where a young man and woman sat close to each other, deep in conversation. His female escort stood in the center of the room, a large plastic-covered menu cradled in her arms. She looked back at him expectantly. He signaled to her that he would like to look in the alcove farther to the right, and walked that way.

Victor Nantes, who wore a dark blue sports jacket with a white shirt open at the throat, sat at a corner table. He watched the opening with his hands folded on the table top. His face betrayed the fact that he spent a lot of time in the sun. With a sense of humor in the lines around them, his green eyes revealed a hard-cast intelligence. The skin on his high cheekbones shone in the light from a lamp that hung from the ceiling. Jason thought he detected a hint of American Indian or Slav in his features.

Jason turned to the girl behind him. "I recognize a friend. I'll sit with him. Thank you." He pulled a Mexican ladder-back chair out from the table, turned his head to look back at the opening to the alcove, then sat down. He looked at the man across the table. "You're quick, Victor."

"Caught the next flight." Nantes stood up and shot Jason a crooked smile as the two of them shook hands perfunctorily across the table. "What's going on?" He regained his seat.

"You haven't heard?"

"Nothing. Fill me in."

"Someone breached one of my files in the wee hours Tuesday. A document's missing. Looks like an insider."

Nantes narrowed his eyes at Jason. He folded his hands on the table. "What'd they get?"

"Nothing earth-shaking, but classified, as though it were. They're looking closely at everyone. It's a real problem. I'm worried."

"Hm." Nantes studied his still-folded hands.

Jason glanced over his shoulder. "My old friend is dead."

"What?! Mel? That is bad." Nantes's voice was a near whisper. He hesitated a moment, as he darted his eyes around the room. "How?"

Jason ignored his question. "I have a sinking feeling I've been exposed. That's when I decided to contact you. The FBI is hassling me. They went through our house and studio today."

Nantes forced his eyes into narrow slits. "What about Mel?"

"I was there. I saw him. Looked like suicide. The FBI didn't say it out loud, but implied the police suspect murder. It doesn't make sense." He shook his head and looked down at his paper place mat.

"Jesus. No, it doesn't." Nantes unfolded his hands, picked up his fork and tracedd a pattern in the tablecloth.

"Unless there's a connection."

Nantes stared hard at Jason. "You think?"

"I have bad feelings about it. Everything's coming unhinged, Victor." He paused. "You haven't had any traffic?"

"Nothing. But who? And why are the Feds pointing at you?"

"Someone in private business?"

"Inside?" Nantes made a face.

Jason shook his head. "Who? With Mel dead—"

"Anything to do with that accident out there last week?"

"If it does, I can't figure the connection."

Nantes furrowed his brow. "What was the situation when you left?" He stopped abruptly, and his eyes widened as he looked up and smiled at the approaching waitress.

The conversation halted as they ordered *carne adovada burritos* and beer. They made small talk as the wait-people came and went to serve them.

Jason continued after the food was served and they were left alone. He maintained a low voice. "The FBI has been all over us like ticks on a southern dog, tearing through all our files at the Labs. They've effectively halted work in our division. They're shot-gunning, trying to uncover anything—desperate. Sarah said they removed things from our studio. I talked to her just before coming out here."

Nantes watched customers move about in the main room, then focused on Jason. "What could they find? Are you vulnerable?" He frowned.

"Damned if I know." Jason shrugged, his eyes wide. "Fishing trip. Maybe they think they'll panic me."

"Time for you to drop out of sight?"

"I don't know." Jason sighed and shook his head. "I don't know. I hate to think that. I know one thing. I need help." He looked at Nantes closely and pointed his finger. "I gotta go home tonight. I'll look guilty as hell if I don't. I can't leave Sarah holding the bag."

"I came as soon as I got your message. Haven't had time to make any contacts. I'll get on it." Nantes nodded.

"We've got to find this free-booter and stop him before the FBI does."

"Tall order." Nantes sipped his beer and glanced around the room again.

"Can you protect me if I take the fall?"

Nantes looked at Jason from under his eyebrows as he chewed. "We'll take care of you."

"I wish that made me feel better." Jason looked around again as he heard voices coming near. "Where will you be?"

"Close. We'll stay in contact, but our friends in Washington and their local yokels wouldn't like it if they knew a company man was nosing around." He laid his fork aside and reached inside his jacket pocket to retrieved a calling card. He slid it across the table as he checked for watchers. "Commit this number. Contact me by 9:00 a.m. tomorrow. Use tradecraft. "

"How about eight?"

"Okay. Fine." Nantes took another bite of his *burrito*. "This is good."

"Their specialty. Not too hot for you?"

"I like hot stuff."

Jason kept the table after Victor Nantes left, toyed with *natias* for dessert and peeked at his watch. He studied the card, let ten minutes pass, then, with nervousness driving him, he got up, left a tip, and took the bill up front to the cash register. From there he went into the rest room area and found the pay phones.

"Oh, Jason! It's terrible! They've come back looking for you! I asked them why and they won't say, just that it's important they talk to you!" Sarah's voice was strained and emotional. "And Betty called. Jason, she's hysterical. I've got to go to her!"

"Okay. Stay with her. I'll come over later." He pinched his nose between his closed eyes. "The FBI wouldn't say why they want to see me or why they took stuff?"

"No—they wouldn't."

Jason began to go cold and dizzy, His head throbbed on one side, and his knees felt weak. He looked to his right, into the bar, then back at the chrome and black telephone.

"Jason, the things they took from the studio and the house—they even took that pot I was spinning. Why are they doing this?!"

"They took—?! What else did they take? Never mind. Sarah, listen to me. Listen. I'm going to tell you. No. No, sorry. Listen, Sarah, I—" His right hand went up to his forehead where he pinched at the skin until it hurt. Shit! he thought. They've probably got the damned phone tapped.

"Jason, what is it? What?! Please, tell me why this is happening to us!"

"Tell them I'll be there soon. And Sarah, I ate."

"They left, Jason. They're not here." She hesitated. "Where are you?"

"Okay. Good. Talk to you when I get home. Please stay calm, Sarah."

Jason's head began to pound in earnest, and he thought of taking one of the last pills in his pocket. He looked back into the bar, with its muted lights glinting through glasses and bottles. People sat at tables and the bar, enjoying themselves, and he considered having another beer, or something stronger. He took the card Nantes gave him, looked at the number again, tore it into small pieces, and dropped it into the sand-filled ash tray next to the telephone carrel.

He walked back through the foyer, past the cash register and out onto the porch, and pulled his windbreaker on as he went. As he passed the trunk of the ancient mulberry that shoved its way past the turned-up bricks in the porch floor, a man walked toward him in the half-light cast by the deep-set windows and widely-spaced porch lamps.

"Thompson? Jason Thompson?" He was thin, wiry, and shorter than Jason by half a head.

Jason stopped, startled. "What—?!"

"Am I right? Jason Thompson?" His accent was Spanish, but not the slow, lilting accent of New Mexico.

"Who are you? FBI?" Jason instinctively took a step backwards as the man came closer.

"FBI? No. Don't be afraid, Mr. Thompson. I am a friend. My name is Cuzco. Antonio Cuzco. People call me Andy." He grinned briefly, then returned his visage to nervous watchfulness as he looked about to check his surroundings.

Jason made out his facial expressions despite the shadow of the tree trunk. "What do you want? How did you know I was here?" Jason looked past the man, then back toward the deep-set bar entrance. They were alone on the porch.

"I'm here to help you. Please come with me." Cuzco looked around, then focused on Jason again.

"I don't know what you're talking about, Mr. Cuzco—Andy. I don't need any help." He started to move past Cuzco. His heart rate was up and he felt close to panic.

Cuzco put out a hard, bony hand and pressed it against Jason's stomach. He tilted his head and shrugged in a typically Hispanic, negative gesture. "Please. You need my help. Come with me."

"Out of my way!" Jason's heart pounded as he pushed Cuzco's hand aside.

Cuzco stepped back, stuck his hand inside his jacket pocket and cameout with a .32 caliber Beretta semiautomatic. "Mr. Thompson, you have to come with me! Now move! That way!" His voice became a growl as he pointed toward the parking lot with the pistol, then looked toward the twin entrances to the restaurant and bar.

"Jesus! What the—who the hell are you?!" Jason's voice rose an octave as he stumbled toward the edge of the porch.

A car with its headlights on bright pulled into the lot in the impending dusk. The beams swept across Jason and Cuzco as they moved off the porch and onto the dirt. Cuzco came around into the shadow on Jason's left side and jammed the muzzle of the semiautomatic into his side. They walked to the passenger side of the small green sedan Jason had seen earlier. In the car, Cuzco bound Jason's wrists together with a plastic tie-wrap, then placed a wide-brimmed western hat on his head.

With Jason in the passenger seat, Cuzco headed north along the winding road through Corrales and onto the highway to the Jemez-Farmington Road, then east toward Bernalillo. They had traveled a half mile when Cuzco pulled off the pavement across from the Coronado Monument gate. Straight ahead and to their right, the lights of Bernalillo and Albuquerque glowed like a swath of white foam along the river. The aircraft warning lights on the antennae atop Sandia mountain blinked red.

Cuzco reached around to the back seat and came up with a bandanna. He folded it over and tied it around Jason's eyes. Then he had Jason lean forward while he tied a thin rope around his waist and arms. He then looped it through the tie wrap, making it impossible for Jason to remove the blindfold.

The car pulled away, and Jason found his senses begin to sharpen. At first, he felt every bump, sway, and change of direction and speed. He tried to trace the route they were taking. He knew they were headed down toward old Highway 85 and Bernalillo, that the Interstate connecting Santa Fé and Denver to Albuquerque and El Paso was only a half mile east of the junction, a mile beyond the river. His mind reeled at what was happening, and soon he began to lose track of time and the motions of the car. He wasn't sure if they had turned at the junction or had gone straight through; whether they were climbing or on level ground. Oddly, the speed of the car seemed to be the same, even when Cuzco stopped or slowed before driving on.

Jason thought about Sunday and the party; an eternity ago. Mel's death was unreal, and the FBI's tactics draconian. And Sarah; what must she think and feel? In an effort to turn his mind to more pleasant things, he tried to recall Saturday tennis games at the club or dinners out with Sarah and friends. Then the car hit a bump or strained against a curve, and reality returned.

Jason sensed they had driven for almost an hour when Cuzco slowed and turned the car onto dirt or gravel. Of that he was sure. He knew the turn was to the right, because he was forced to lean toward Cuzco in the driver's seat. He counted from the turn, each count for a second, sixty for a minute, thinking that later he could determine his location. Then the car braked to a stop and the engine was silent. He heard Cuzco get out, and a moment later his door opened and Cuzco helped him leave the car.

The air was cool, and Jason smelled sage and pine. They must be up high, he thought. He staggered in front of Cuzco for several yards with the other man holding his arm before he was halted. At that point, he was aware of light through the dark cloth of the bandanna, and a rush of warm air washed over him as he heard a door open. Cuzco then guided him to a chair with a hard seat.

"Okay, my friend, now we are going to make you more comfortable." Cuzco pulled the big hat off Jason's head and removed the bandanna.

Jason blinked to get accustomed to the light as Cuzco removed the rope, but not the tie wrap, from his wrists. The room was large, but sparsely and cheaply furnished. He decided it doubled as a bedroom, since it had a couch used as a bed. At one end was a small, crude kitchen. Near that was another door. The walls were of mud-plastered adobe, and the ceiling had open beams of rough-hewn logs. The weak light was from two kerosene-burning storm lanterns. An old house, it had not been remodeled into modernity.

Different odors came to him. He sensed kerosene residue, burning *piñon* wood, cooked red chile, pork fat, and flour tortillas; even the smell of the old, dirt walls. Another smell assailed him:; dainty, subtle. He turned and looked to his left. Leaning against the wall, wearing blue jeans and a sweater, was a dark-haired woman, arms crossed over her chest, whom he reckoned to be in her thirties. A blue steel Colt .38 revolver, a western model, rested comfortably in her right hand.

9

Sarah Thompson left a note for Jason and went to see Betty Vaslovic. When she pulled into the driveway in the Mercedes, Betty stood in the open doorway. Light from inside the house streamed around her.

Betty's face was tear-streaked, her hair unkempt, and her clothing disheveled. She sobbed uncontrollably with both arms wrapped around Sarah, as her friend patted and rubbed her back. They stood in the foyer, the front door open wide.

Sarah forced her to eat, then waited while Betty talked to her son Roy for more than forty-five minutes on the telephone. Then she followed Betty, alternately crying and calming as she moved frantically about the house, looking for something she thought she had lost. Sarah knew it was merely a way for the distraught woman to avoid coming to grips with the truth of her husband's death. Finally, they sat on the living room couch and talked, cried and even laughed until nearly midnight. It was then that Sarah openly realized Jason Thompson had not shown up or called, so she informed Betty.

She phoned the house, but there was no answer. Betty wanted to know what was going on, but Sarah decided not to tell her about the FBI and her concerns for her husband. She had enough troubles without that. Betty insisted Sarah go home, but Sarah made up the bed in a spare bedroom and spent the night.

Sarah did not sleep well, and awoke well before dawn on Friday. She got up and checked on Betty who had slept miserably, gave her a hug and a kiss while she still lay in bed, and told her she was going to go home to check on Jason.

When Sarah arrived at the house, the first thing she noticed was the absence of the pickup truck. Just to make sure, she raised the garage door. It was empty.

She took a shower and changed into a baggy grey sweat shirt covered here and there with dabs of paint. It had a small tear in one sleeve just above the pinch cuffs where it had torn on a nail at an old house on a watercolor club field trip. She wore blue jeans and hole-scarred sneakers. She held a cup of coffee as she stood in front of the kitchen sink, both arms pressed against her stomach to offset the cold she felt. Through the window and to her left, the first rays of the sun rose over the Manzano Mountains.

To her right, she saw three cars parked across the street; a black-and white APD car and two plain sedans in subdued colors. Two uniformed policemen sat in the patrol car. In one of the other cars were two men in civilian clothes, and in the third a man and woman similarly dressed.

She looked around the kitchen and reflected on how it had been in better times, before her children had left—all of the good smells coming from the meals being prepared and the talks with her sons and daughter about their problems and triumphs. She conjured up the days when she and Jason had met. They were so happy and so naïve. How careful she had to be not to bruise his feelings with the money available to her. It had been difficult to give him up to his work—Mel, and the travel and meetings that dominated so much of his time. But it had been worth it—hadn't it?

Her thoughts were crowded with concern about him. Was he well, and not under too much stress? She shifted to musing about her work with the church and the watercolor club trips as she sat down at the trestle table where her coffee cup rested.

The sound of the door chimes made her jump, and lukewarm coffee spilled on the table. She stood and looked out through the living room, then turned and stared at the little puddle of spilled coffee before going to the door.

She peered through the screen as she gripped the brass handle of the big front door.

"Mrs. Thompson? Special agent Grayson, Albuquerque office of the Federal Bureau of Investigation. I think you met agent Lucero yesterday. Sorry to bother you so early. May we come in?" He opened the screen door. He wore a sport shirt without a tie under a dark blue windbreaker. At his side, in a suit and tie, was a tall young man with dark hair, whom Sarah recognized as Lucero.

Sarah, her face flushed, said, "Alright, come in."

Grayson studied the interior of the house as he walked halfway across the living room. He turned to Sarah as she faced him, her hands working across her midriff. "Have you heard from your husband, Mrs. Thompson?"

"What do you mean? Why would you ask that?" She backed up a step.

"We're pretty sure he's not come home, Mrs. Thompson, unless he left his vehicle somewhere else and walked. Did he?" Grayson cocked his head as he shot a glance at his partner.

Sarah turned and paced away a step. She shook her head. "No. I can't imagine what's happened to him. I'm so worried." She moved to the sofa and sat down, placed both her hands between her knees and clamped her legs against them.

Grayson noticed the grey in her hair. Without makeup, the wrinkles in her face made her age apparent to him.

Lucero moved toward the dining room, which adjoined the kitchen beyond, and looked in.

Sarah turned to look at Lucero and snapped, "He's not in there, Mr. Lucero!"

Lucero turned and faced her. "Sorry, Mrs. Thompson. I know." He lowered his head, chastened.

Grayson ignored the incident. "I realize it's early, Mrs. Thompson, but this is urgent. It's very important we talk to your husband as soon as possible. Do you know where he is? Are you sure he didn't tell you where he was last night?" Grayson helped himself to a chair.

Sarah shook her head with slow deliberation, her eyes closed. She produced a wad of tissues from her sweat shirt pocket and dabbed at her eyes. "He told me he would talk to me when he got home. I spent the night with a dear friend who lost her husband. He wasn't here when I got home. I called his office, but there was no answer. I haven't heard from him since last night. I left him a note." She pointed vaguely.

Grayson breathed deeply. He stroked his hair with his hand, a gesture of frustration. "What time did you talk to him? Remind me."

"Around six. Maybe five-thirty."

"Last night."

"Yes, last night."

"Mrs. Thompson, your husband has worked at Rio Grande Labs for many years. Now there is a serious problem in his division, and he disappears. You're aware of Mr. Vaslovic's death? That's where you were last night?"

"Yes. It's just awful. Betty is so dear. She's devastated. Yes." She nodded emphatically.

"May I call you Sarah?" Grayson asked. His voice smoothed and lowered.

She looked at him and nodded, her eyes red with tears.

"We have unfortunate news, Sarah. The original APD theory was that Mel Vaslovic committed suicide, but that has changed. The preliminary coroner's report indicates that he was dead before the gunshot. It looks like homicide. Mrs. Thompson—Sarah—this will leak out eventually anyway, so I'm going to tell you but ask you not to talk about it to anyone. The problem we have at the Labs is theft of government property. It's called a breach. It means that someone took important classified information—"

Sarah interrupted him. "Is that why you have all those cars out there, because you suspect Jason? Is that why that police car is there, because you think he killed his old friend?" She swept her arm toward the street, then stared at Grayson, tissue to her nose, eyes wide.

Grayson lowered his head and eyes, then looked up at her. "Sarah, we have evidence of your husband's involvement in this case."

"What evidence?!" With her eyes still wide, she sat up straight.

"I'm not at liberty to say, but it's strong. I'm sorry."

Sarah rose slowly from the sofa, turned and looked out the window. "I won't tell you where my husband is if I find out. I won't help you ruin our lives."

Grayson hesitated, then spoke in a soft voice. "I'm afraid your lives are close to that already, Mrs. Thompson, unless we can get some cooperation." He paused. "Interference in a federal case is a federal offense, Sarah. Just so you know."

Grayson and Lucero left, with more admonitions to Sarah about interfering with the legal process. One of the plain sedans remained, and the APD squad car was replaced by another.

Sarah cleaned up the spilled coffee and dumped the rest from the cup into the sink. As she walked toward the dining room door, the phone rang. She picked up the wall phone handset. "Hello? Who? Benjamin? I'm sorry, you have the wrong number. Yes. Bye."

She went upstairs and started getting clothes ready for the laundry, when she was overwhelmed with sleepiness and lay down on the bed. She fell into an immediate, dreamless sleep.

The door chimes awakened her. She sat up groggily, looked at the bedside clock and realized she had slept more than two hours. The bell rang again as she went to the head of the stairs and peered over the railing, where she could see a man through the glass of the front door. With strong trepidation, she went down and to the door.

"Yes?"

"Mrs. Thompson?" The man wore a dark blue sports jacket and an open shirt without a tie.

"Yes. What do you want?" Her voice was heavy with sleep.

Victor Nantes reached inside his jacket pocket quickly, retrieved his wallet and produced a plastic-covered card. "I'm Victor Nantes. With Reuters. The news agency."

Sarah stared at his penetrating green eyes and strong, confident face with its high, angular bones. A frown grew on her face. She shook her head. "What? Why are you here?"

"Mrs. Thompson, may I come in?"

"No! I want to know why you're here!"

Nantes took a step backward. "I know this must be a difficult time for you, but I'd like to speak to your husband. Jason Thompson, right?" He turned to glance at the street, then back.

"Why are you here?!"

"Mrs. Thompson, we at Reuters often get wind of news-worthy items before other news agencies. It happens I was privy to a wire story indicating there was a security problem at Rio Grande Labs. Mr. Thompson's name was mentioned. I'd like to talk to him—if I may. I tried to contact him at his office, but was told he's not in today." He smiled as his eyes darted around, looking over and past her into the house.

Sarah sighed heavily. "This is an outrage! Certainly not! Now I must ask you to leave . Or I'll call one of those policemen over there!" She pointed.

Nantes glanced at the two cars parked across the street. He lowered his head, then looked at her intimately. "Mrs. Thompson, is your husband here? Or is he missing? Please."

Sarah, who stood in the doorway, took a step backward and pushed the heavy wood door halfway closed. "I want you to leave. My husband has no interest in talking to the press. And I'm sure he knows nothing about any problems out at the base. Now, please go." With that, she shut the door and locked it, leaving Nantes holding the screen open.

Nantes let the screen close slowly. His face took on a firm, solemn set as he stepped off the porch and walked to the sidewalk as he watched the federal and city cars out of the corner of his eye. He hesitated at the sidewalk, started to turn right toward his car, then turned left and walked to the corner and along the side of the Thompson house. As he moved along the sidewalk at a quick pace, in an attempt to be unobtrusive, he studied the residence. Once past the rear of the house, he turned into the alley and made for his car parked down the street that fronted the house.

Sarah stood behind a curtain in her bedroom on the second floor and watched Nantes come from the right, out of the alley two houses down, and get into his car to leave. To her left, across the street, first the remaining FBI car, then the black-and-white left. Half a block north, partially blocked by a large elm, she spotted a grey van parked against the curb. She went to the bedroom closet, got Jason's seven-power binoculars and focused on the vehicle. A sign on the side advertised a carpet cleaning company. Dead center on the top of the van was a small square of what appeared to be flesh-colored fiberglass or plastic. Three thin, rigid wires of slightly different lengths stuck straight up from the square through small black rings. Along the side of the vehicle were two rectilinear areas that resembled darkened windows rather than steel.

She lowered the binoculars and set them on the dresser top. Her left arm was still pressed against her midriff, holding her right elbow, as she stroked her chin and studied the carpet near the window.

Jason awoke to the sounds of kitchen clatter and the smell of strong coffee. He lay on the couch which had been folded out into a bed, two tattered blankets over him. He blinked his eyes against the sleep, and stared at the crude ceiling with its round, rough-hewn *vigas*, or ceiling beams, over which were rough-hewn, unfinished pine boards. He looked to his left. The woman who had greeted him with a pistol the night before was busy with a spatula and skillet. She wore a black leather motorcycle jacket.

Soon the aroma of coffee was joined with the odors of meat and chile in his nostrils. A shaft of morning light streamed in through a cracked, cardboard-repaired window on the east side of the house, illuminating motes of dust that floated about the room. Jason shifted his weight and realized his hands were still strapped together.

The woman cut the plastic strap and Jason massaged his numb hands. Without speaking, she handed him his tan windbreaker, which he put on, then walked him out through a rear door to the outhouse, her pistol handy. The cold was enough to make him shiver as he looked up and around at the steep cliffs and verdant, mountainous terrain behind the house. Back inside, with her pistol obvious, she sat and watched him eat alone.

Cuzco arrived shortly after Jason finished breakfast, and without word or ceremony, he and the woman re-bound his hands and put the blindfold and hat on him. The woman got in the back seat of the car, and Cuzco helped Jason into the front. No words were exchanged between the three. Jason reasoned he would derive nothing from questioning his captors, who, to him, seemed to run the operation as professionals.

He made no attempt to remember sounds and motions of the car as it made what he assumed to be a return trip. He wanted desperately to ask his captors why they had kidnaped him, but remained quiet. He had managed to relax and sleep some during the night, and the breakfast made him feel good, but his anxiety rose as the car progressed. Somehow he knew they were not retracing the route Cuzco had driven the night before. He had not once heard the woman speak because Cuzco did all the talking, and mostly in a low voice, in Spanish.

After traveling for almost an hour, the car stopped. Cuzco relieved Jason of the blindfold, tie wrap, and hat.

"There, I'll bet that's better," Cuzco said.

Jason looked at the man. "Marvelous, Andy." His voice dripped with nervous sarcasm. "Where we headed?"

He glanced back at the woman who still held the pistol casually pointed at him through the seat back. He reckoned they were on a secondary road on the east side of the Sandia mountains, somewhere north of Interstate 40. He looked at the sky. Except for some high, thin cloudiness to the southwest, it was clear. He cast his gaze about and recognized the low, dark mesas that spread to Texas in the east and the green and black of the Sandia and Manzano ranges that hid Albuquerque and the Rio Grande valley from view to the west.

Cuzco threw the bandanna, hat, and broken cable tie into the back and started off again. "I think you'll enjoy the trip, Mr. Thompson. I know I will." He grinned.

Jason looked at Cuzco. He wore all khaki, including a shirt with military pockets. His left pocket was unbuttoned, with the flap tucked inside. A small, white envelope protruded. It had a label with red lettering which made him think suddenly about his pills, and he did a double take. Should he say something about his blood pressure? No; he would wait to see where they were taking him. The Beretta was not in evidence, but he knew it must be somewhere on Cuzco. He wondered again how Cuzco had managed to tail him to the restaurant in Corrales, given that he had not seen the car after his stop to phone Sarah.

"I know you don't believe me, Mr. Thompson. We're here to help you. Things are rough right now. I'm lucky to have someone like my friend here to assist me. We don't want to hurt you, but it's real important you be nice and stay calm. Know what I mean?" He drove the little car back onto the uneven asphalt and headed south, toward Moriarty.

In another fifteen minutes Cuzco pulled the car onto the grounds of a small airport. Jason took the place in quickly. Three large metal-clad buildings served as hangars. A fourth, of concrete block, to him looked as though it might serve as headquarters and flight lounge.

Cuzco drove past the graveled parking area and headed for the last hangar on the right, then around it to a tie-down ramp.

A dozen light planes, in two rows, were tethered to steel rings in the earth. Cuzco pulled up and stopped next to one of them. It was white with red trim. Jason recognized it immediately as a Piper Cherokee.

After stopping the car and killing the engine, Cuzco turned and looked intently at Jason. "There are people here, Mr. Thompson. That doesn't make you safe from us. If you try to escape, my friend will shoot you, and we will get away, so please do as we say and you will be safe." He looked at the woman silently, then back at Jason. Without another word, he got out and left the two of them behind in the car.

When he was finished with his pre-flight check, Cuzco waved to the woman, and Jason was directed to walk to the plane ahead of her with the pistol hidden in her jacket pocket. He tried to walk nonchalantly to hide his fear and nervousness, but felt increasingly anxious and weak. He moved his eyes from side to side as he took everything in. The airport seemed to be deserted, although he reasoned there must be other people in the hangars, offices, or the lounge.

Cuzco climbed into the pilot's seat, and Jason followed into the right-hand. As he settled in, he spotted the Beretta stuck in Cuzco's belt on his left side. The woman climbed up onto the wing-walk and closed the hatch. As the plane pulled away from the tie-down, its engine racing, she stood next to the driver's door of the car, her dark hair wind-blown from the prop wash. Cuzco looked down at her, but made no sign. Then, her face impassive, she got into the little green car and drove away in the direction from which they had come.

The Cherokee climbed out of the shallow valley and headed west over the Manzano Mountains. Soon they were flying over the Rio Puerco, headed due west. Cuzco competently dialed in the trim settings, set the omni frequencies, and checked in with Albuquerque Center, giving them an in-flight plan, and then referred to a map on his lap. From time to time he looked out his windows to scan the horizon on both sides and above.

Jason considered his predicament. This little man had captured him at gun point, held him overnight with the aid of a female accomplice, and now they were flying west toward some unknown destination. Why? None of it made any sense. He had never seen either one before, and they gave no reason for their actions. They hadn't harmed him, and seemed to wish him no injury. So far, he was without headache or dizziness.

Jason raised his voice over the rush of the air and growl of the engine as he looked at his captor and asked, "Cuzco—Andy—now that we're safely away from Albuquerque, can you tell me who you are and what this is all about?"

Cuzco wore a set of large headphones over his ears, but he heard the question. He pulled the right earpiece away, then said, "Soon. Be patient." He re-set the headphones on his head and resumed his sober study of the airplane's flight path and condition.

Jason looked at the little envelope in Cuzco's shirt pocket and tried to fathom its purpose.

The plane veered south of the east-west Interstate, and Jason thought he could identify the city of Grants off to their right. The sun was high as they passed over mesas with dark green stands of ponderosa. He thought he recognized Zuñi Pueblo on his right.

More than two hours passed and Cuzco set the plane into a descent. They had crossed over the deep green of forested regions and were flying over flatter, dun grass-covered land that stretched many miles to the west and south. To their left, Jason saw the smoke stack of a power plant.

Cuzco landed the Cherokee expertly despite a strong afternoon cross-wind.

Jason looked around. The airport was smaller than the one from which they had taken off. Two small hangars sat on either side of a stuccoed building that served as office and lounge. The legend, "East St. Johns," was painted over the door of the flight lounge. To the right of the entrance was a single, glass-walled phone booth. An orange windsock flew from a steel pipe attached to the side of the building. Two gas pumps stood near the door of the wide open hangar on the right. In the dark shade of the interior was a small plane. Its nose was truncated where the engine had been removed.

Cuzco taxied the Cherokee near the phone booth and killed the engine. He pulled off the headphones and looked at his reluctant passenger. "I know people here. They know me. Don't try anything, okay? We don't need fuel but I gotta make a call. You can go to the bathroom, but I'm going with you. Want a soda?"

"No." Jason looked away and studied the emptiness of the place. He looked at the grama grass and the way a stiff breeze whipped at it along the edges of the pitted asphalt runway.

"Hungry?"

"No." He was, but his nervousness made him reluctant to eat.

Cuzco struggled into a khaki windbreaker and zipped it closed. Jason reckoned it was to hide the semiautomatic in his belt.

Stiff after sitting for so long, Jason got out. Cuzco walked close to him. Both entered and crossed the empty lounge and crowded into the men's room. When they got inside, he realized why Cuzco insisted he go with him. A large window was open to the world in the rear of the room. Cuzco got a coke from the machine, then led his captive outside to wait while he phoned.

Jason hovered near the glass door to the lounge, then strolled past the phone booth toward the Navajo mechanic who was tightening bolts on an engine that Jason figured came from the plane in the hangar. He looked back at Cuzco, who watched him from the booth. Cuzco lowered his eyes to feign disinterest.

Jason looked at his watch, then strolled closer to the mechanic to look closely at what the man was doing. The disassembled engine block was bolted to a portable work frame near the open hangar door. Next to it was a steel tray with parts and tools.

"Lycoming?" Jason asked.

The mechanic looked up at him. "Yep. Outa that plane." He pointed with a wrench. He was tall and thin with coal-black hair.

For a minute Jason watched the Navajo, who then walked inside the hangar to get an engine part. Jason glanced back to check on Cuzco who was still talking and inspecting his shoes, then back inside at the mechanic who had his back to him. Without further hesitation and with his back to Cuzco, he picked up a large box-end wrench and stuffed it up his sleeve. He put his hand in his jacket pocket, checked the still distracted Cuzco, waited a few seconds, and walked slowly back toward the phone booth.

Cuzco hung up and burst out of the booth, motioned to Jason, and waited for him to precede him. Then they both strode off toward the Cherokee with Jason a few steps ahead. Jason kept the wrench hidden in his sleeve, one end palmed, as he climbed in behind Cuzco. As Cuzco maneuvered into the pilot's seat, his back to Jason, Jason dropped the wrench out of his sleeve, and grasped it in his fist. He drew back and hit Cuzco hard across the back of the head. Cuzco grunted and reacted by raising his right hand to his wounded head. At the same time, his right foot went out and hit the left bulkhead hard. He collapsed across both seats, face up, limbs in a tangle.

Jason turned to see if anyone had noticed the attack. Satisfied, he stuck the wrench in his rear pants pocket so he could grapple the unconscious man out of the cockpit and onto the wing root. He placed his arms underneath Cuzco's armpits and dragged him backward over the seats and through the open hatch. From there, he lowered him, feet first, to the ground. With Cuzco lying on his back, Jason pulled the white envelope from the unconscious man's shirt pocket, looked at it closely, turned it over once, then put it in his own shirt pocket. He removed the box-end wrench from his pants pocket and dropped it on the ground next to the unconscious Cuzco. Then he jumped onto the wing root, climbed in, pulled the hatch closed, cranked up the engine, and ran the flaps out.

The Navajo mechanic, who had come back outside to continue work on the Lycoming engine, looked up at the sound of the Cherokee engine starting. He spied Cuzco on the ground, stopped what he was doing, picked up a grease rag and wiped his hands as he walked slowly toward the downed man, unsure of what he saw. His eyes alternated between the man on his back and the red and white Piper on the blacktop with its engine racing, headed for the down-wind end of the runway.

Sarah's pleading about his interest in flying intruded on Jason's thoughts as he pushed the throttle forward which caused the plane to surge and bring the controls to life. The nose of the plane went down as he pushed forward on the wheel, then came up and climbed as he brought it back again. To his left, high on the instrument panel, the stall light flickered on and off.

Twice more he pulled back on the wheel, still too rapidly, and twice the stall light came on. In another moment the plane was off the ground. It rose quickly, and the ride was smoother. He pulled back gently on the wheel and shoved the throttle forward to gain altitude. The craft responded, and he felt the controls. Even in his state of terror, he remembered to pull the flaps back in. He wanted to arc the plane around to see what was happening on the ground, but kept the plane on a straight course. A thrill rippled through him as the craft responded to his touch. Maybe it was true, he thought, that flying was like riding a bicycle.

He studied the instruments to re-familiarize himself. He took particular notice of the fuel gauges, one for the right tank, the other for the left. The right gauge indicated full; the left, half. Unconsciously pointing around with a finger, he finally located the fuel tank transfer valve to his left, down near his feet. Jason stared at it. The handle was missing. Cuzco must have broken it off when his feet kicked out.

The mechanic, dumbfounded, walked to where Cuzco lay, as he continued to wipe his hands with the dark red cloth. He looked down at the prostrate man who was just beginning to awaken. The Beretta was on the ground next to him.

"Hey, I better call the sheriff," the Navajo said.

Cuzco peered at the mechanic through half-open eyes. "No, I'll take care of this." He struggled up on one elbow and smoothed his dirty, disheveled hair. "Don't do or say anything. This is a federal case. I'm a federal officer. I'll take care of everything." He held up his free hand and waved authoritatively.

The mechanic looked at Cuzco, then turned around to squint at the Piper Cherokee which had become a gleaming spot over the southern horizon.

10

*J*ason pushed the throttle toward the dash of the Piper Chero-kee to increase the power of the engine. He then nervously pulled on the steering gear to bring the plane to a higher altitude. To his right, through the scratched plastic of the copilot's side window, the sun was low and red over the horizon. On his left and ahead, he saw the ragged beginnings of the forests of the great Gila Wilderness. After checking all the instruments and wiping perspiration from his brow with his bare hand, he tried to relax against the seat back of the airplane as it settled into level flight.

He switched the radio on and tuned across the range of frequencies most likely to carry a call for him to land or broadcast further information pertaining to him. Other than a few conversations between light plane pilots near Gallup, Grants, El Paso and Tucson, the aircraft channels were quiet.

He looked behind the seat and found the maps Cuzco had stowed there. He pulled out two before he found one that referred to the area below him. He spread it out on the right seat. He was on a southerly heading. Where should he go? Turning to fly north would put him over the Navajo Nation and the can-yons of the High Plateau. In that direction were unknown up-and-down-drafts and, to him, uncharted landing strips. East or west would invite more scrutiny from the major flight control centers in Albuquerque and the west coast. Going directly back to the Albuquerque area would most certainly invite scrutiny and possibly arrest. He remembered a small airport near Silver City where he could land. Maybe they wouldn't ask questions.

Fuel was a problem. He looked again at the damaged transfer valve, then at the fuel gauge. The right tank was full, but of no use to him without a function-ing valve, and the left was getting lower with each passing minute. He peered hard at the flight chart in the gathering gloom, and he let the plane drift without control for several seconds at a time, grabbing the controls only when he felt the craft begin to nose down or up, or veer off to one side. Three omnidirectional transmitters were indicated on the chart. He tried unsuccessfully to tune into any of them. The only thing he knew for certain, with the setting sun on his right, was that he was headed south. He looked around and behind to see if there were any tools he could use to manipulate the transfer valve. He swore under his breath with the realization that he was committed to the fuel that remained in the left tank.

To the west, he saw roads and highways, strangely enhanced by the band of shadow created by advancing darkness. He compared them with the chart, then with his recollection of the area from his travels and study of highway maps. He dared the sometime violent up-and down-drafts, which he knew plagued light planes over rough terrain, as he brought the Piper down a thousand feet so he could see the ground more clearly. It was a risky maneuver,since he knew his fuel would go faster. He reasoned it would be easier to spot other aircraft from below, rather than from above as he scanned the sky in every direction. He leaned forward again to peer closely at the left tank fuel gauge to make sure there was as little parallax as possible to distort the reading.

His head ached. It was close to the time of day he should take his medicine. He reached into his shirt pocket, removed the little white envelope he had taken from Cuzco and stared at it. His eyes narrowed in thought. Then he worked up spittle to help swallow one of the pills dry. He reckoned he had about an hour until total darkness set in, and the notion of the impending setting of the sun served to depress him. He had two major problems. One was to find the airport near Silver City in the dark, while the second was to make it there on the available fuel. A third problem occurred to him. How would he bring the Piper down safely if there were no landing lights?

These panicky thoughts led him to turn his mind to the comforts of home and Sarah. She seemed so far away, almost as though she had never existed. Maybe she was just a figment of his imagination. The plane was his existence and he flew it forever, as though he were an airborne Flying Dutchman. Everything else was a dream, with a wistful hope of home.

How pretty Sarah had been when young. She had become even more beautiful to him after the arrival of Flo, Charles, and little Justin. She was such a good mother, and the children loved her dearly. Sarah was so artistic. Even while cheerfully raising the children, she had taken up watercolor to fill what little empty time she had. And how she had fussed at him and worried about his health in the early years. She had encouraged him to play tennis, but wanted him to do something more creative, and had insisted he try pottery, a talent with which he had toyed. His interest in photography and electronic experimentation she applauded as well.

And how she put up with the Vaslovics. Crazy Mel and long-suffering Betty. All those parties and family trips. The help and attention she gave them. Mel. What a strange friend he had been down through the years. And now he was gone.

The picture of that day when he and Mel graduated from their advanced studies grew in his mind. There was Mel's father, and how embarrassed Mel had been when he came to the ceremony, shouting at his son from across the green in his thickly-accented English.

Then there was that Saturday of the week following graduation when Dean Harvey Munson visited him. He had asked to be alone with him. Munson had politely refused breakfast, then dove into a discussion about his own politics, shifting eventually to Jason's position on economics and world affairs, concentrating on the Communists. Then he had turned the subject to Mel. Even now he could clearly see the intensity in Munson's face as he asked him to follow Mel into the Socialist Youth League.

Jason's reverie was broken when something caught his attention out the left side of the airplane. He turned his head sharply and looked into the darkening sky. Nothing. No, there it was: blinking lights; red, green and white, like bright dots against the void of the gathering darkness in the east. He pressed his forehead against the rattling plastic window to steady himself, but it didn't help. He blinked his eyes several times, then he stared again. There it was, very definitely, and the lights were attached to something like a dark blob.

The blob came closer. It moved at an angle toward him, at his same altitude, as though it were going to cross his path. Its speed surprised and excited him. There was enough light to discern that it had two engines. It was a turboprop—and fast. The plane approached at a ninety degree angle and flew over, headed west. Seeing it whip by made his heart pound and the perspiration pop out on his forehead. His head throbbed for a few seconds; then mercifully, the pain died down. He watched intently as the plane disappeared into the orange glow of the western sky.

The mountainous land gave way in spots to broad valleys with few trees. He made out a house or two, their lights on against the dusk, and to the south, the dun-colored beginnings of the great Chihuahuan Desert that stretched into Mexico. He banked to the left so he could get a better look below before he brought the Cherokee back on a straight and level course.

The plane shuddered as the engine missed a beat. The damned fuel gauge was lying to him, or something about the maneuver starved the carburetors! He swore under his breath and rapped on the fuel gauge in his frustration. It made no difference.

The plane began to lose altitude, and as it did, features on the ground were more prominent, even in the greying dusk that now covered the land. He saw individual trees, another house, even vehicles and fences. The engine coughed with conviction, and he turned the wheel violently. He kicked the rudder to bring the plane left. Down below, a broad, shallow valley lay with one house at its head. Sharp, rocky ridges defined the boundaries between the valley and the mesas that rose and stretched away on either side.

The Piper trembled and the stall light came on as he felt control slip away. He realized that the nose was too high, so he pushed the wheel forward. Then the engine conked out for good and the prop stuttered to a stop. The air made a whistling sound as it rushed by the rapidly slowing craft. Then it rose in an updraft, and the plane veered to the left. Jason fought hard to control the plane and keep it aligned with the ridge. He felt the cabin warm as he lost altitude. What remained of the sun was now to his left in the greying sky. He was moving due north. The ridge was coming up fast so, without thinking, he set full flaps.

Below, he saw what appeared to be a road along the edge of the mesa, so he steered the dead plane for it. Panic rose in him as he realized the open spot he had picked out was not a road at all, but a stretch of bare rock on top of the ridge. It was too late; no time or fuel to circle in search of a new place to land. There was obviously no reason to put the gear down. Strange, he thought, his fear evaporated, and he began to concentrate on the technical problem of bringing the power-dead aluminum thing down with minimal injury to himself. A weird feeling grew over him as he thought about how this must be the way people face death all the time. Nothing to it. Strictly business. Rational to the end.

The updrafts that streamed up the side of the mesa from the decaying warmth of the valley floor were severe now as he came close to the tops of the scraggly ponderosa competing for turf with other plant life. The stall light popped on and off as the rough air buffeted the wings and the Piper shuddered and bumped as though a land vehicle. The swath of rock was wider than he originally thought, but it was rough. He saw, even in the diminishing light, the lumps and boulders he was about to face. The prop whistled in the cold, rushing air; and like a dry twig, the first part to go, the lower half—snapped off with a metallic bang.

An instant later, the belly of the Piper Cherokee hit, and the plane slid along the rough, rocky surface like an immense aluminum can. He was instantly reminded of a bad carnival ride. He couldn't put his hands in one place, his head flopped around uncontrollably, and everything he saw was blurred out of existence. The right wing hit a tree, ripping away three feet of aluminum nearest the tip. The plane lost momentum, pirouetted over the side of the ridge and down, groaning like a beached whale. It came to a halt no more than ten feet below the ridge against a cushioning bramble of bushy evergreens and one adolescent ponderosa with a six-inch diameter trunk.

At first he was dazed, but as he recovered, surprised to be alive, he shook uncontrollably at the thought of how close he had come to death.

He gathered his senses and looked around. The wings were hanging at nearly 45 degrees to the valley floor some hundred feet below, with the fuselage about 10 feet below the line of the ridge. Jason sat still, with his head dangling between his shoulders, afraid to move, incongruously straining against the seat belt. Attacked by another headache, he felt sick and dizzy. He let the ringing in his ears die down and the shakes subside, but remained static for a full five minutes. An eerie silence crowded in on him after the ringing in his ears faded.

He angled his knees up and pushed on the instrument panel to support his weight, then carefully released the seat belt. As he slipped forward, the whole plane rocked; squeaking shiny aluminum against pine needles and branches, which made him feel as though it were about to drop. He froze, waiting for the plane to move again. After a full, tense minute, he stretched across to the hatch and tried the door above the right wing. It wouldn't budge. He pushed on the sliding section of the window on his side, and it moved, but the opening it created wasn't big enough for him to crawl through. He searched his memory and thought of the fire extinguisher behind the right seat. He strained to reach for the steel cylinder, but it was not there. Confused and in a mild panic, he craned around in the waning half-light for the extinguisher, and finally spotted it on the floor near the front bulkhead, where it came to rest after breaking loose upon impact. He wielded it awkwardly because of his extreme angle to the ground and banged it against the clear-plastic side window. After eight tries and extreme effort, the brittle plastic broke away with loud popping sounds, which gave him room to maneuver out of the cockpit.

Sharp pieces of broken plastic broke the skin on his hands, arms and face, and branches of trees and bramble stuck and whipped him as he inched his way out of the stricken craft. The rocks along the ridge were sharp and steep, and, in some places, loose. He nearly lost his footing as he jumped clumsily from the left wing. Sunlight was only a fond memory, and he was able to see no farther than six feet away. He realized he should have looked for a flashlight in the cockpit. It was too late and too dangerous to return to the plane.

He made his way, hand over foot, along the sharp rocks, to the top of the ridge. There, he rested against the trunk of a small, gnarled ponderosa pine whose red-barked roots stretched down the side of the ridge. In the distance, down on the valley floor, he saw the yellow lights of a ranch house.

Enough light was reflected from the twilight sky that he discerned the contrast between the dark foliage and the lighter rock and earth. Using the house lights as a beacon, he made his way painfully through the brush, along the edge of the ridge another five hundred feet, until he came to a place where he established a footing on a series of rocks and boulders leading down and away from the high mesa ridge. A section of the mesa's edge which was not so steep supported a trail which zig-zagged back and forth to the valley floor below. As he picked his way down, criss-crossing back and forth, he used all four limbs much of the way for fear of falling.

He fought loose rocks and sharp brambles all the way, such that it took him nearly an hour to reach the bottom. By this time, features on the land were little more than darker or lighter shadows. The warm, yellow-orange lights of the house were closer.

Several times he put his foot into an animal burrow or other depression as he stumbled toward the glow. He smelled alfalfa and animal ordure, and was sure that more than one shape out there was either a cow or a horse. A muffled stomp, like that of an animal hoof, came to him more than once. Something slimy got onto his shoe. Then he ran straight into a very thin, sharp object that crossed his mid-section, and bounced away, and nearly knocked him down. He nursed his wounded stomach briefly with his filthy hands, then felt around carefully for parallel strands of barbed wire to separate so he could crawl through what he percieved to be a fence. The ground beyond the fence was harder, but the house was close enough now to see detail through the windows on the porch. He reasoned that he had crossed a pasture.

At thirty feet from the house, Jason was aware of someone standing on the porch. A long, thin object protruded from the dark shadow.

He stopped. "Hello," he croaked, barely able to get the word out.

"You from the plane?" It was a woman's voice.

"Yes. I need help." He took a step.

"Stay right there, Mister." The voice was middle-aged, impassive, twangy, but definitely feminine.

"I—I mean no harm. Not—not armed. Plane crash. Cuts. Bruises. Please—"

"Come closer," she interrupted as she backed up a pace.

Jason moved slowly, haltingly, toward the porch until he saw her more clearly. He guessed she was younger than he by a few years. Ill-fitting pants, tucked into work boots, hung on her slight frame. She held an old Marlin .30-.30 lever-action rifle pointed vaguely at him from her hip.

She peered at him intently, glanced briefly at the sky, then watched him again. "You runnin' drugs or somethin'?"

Jason barely stood on his two feet with extreme effort. Conquered by the fatigue that swept over him, he stared at her, then looked down at the ground and wiped clumsily at his face with a grimy hand. "No, Ma'am. No drugs. Out of fuel. Crashed. May I—please sit—I—"

She shifted, reached for the screen door, then opened it and stood back. He stumbled past her into the house and went straight for an overstuffed chair, where he collapsed.

The woman looked out into the intensifying darkness again, and listened carefully for sounds beyond those of the cicadas and crickets that took over the night. Satisfied they were alone, she came inside, and let the screen door slam. She closed the heavy, hand-made door. She walked halfway across the room to her stricken visitor and stopped as she cradled the Marlin so it pointed safely at the floor. She studied him for a few seconds as he bent forward, his elbows on his knees, his face buried in his hands. Then she moved into the kitchen.

Beyond his exhaustion he heard a metallic squeak, followed by the sound of running water.

When the woman returned with a tumbler of water, Jason was asleep with his head back against the chair and his legs sprawled out in front of him.

11

*B*etty Vaslovic went to the front door at the sound of the chimes. Sarah Thompson stood under the porch light holding a baking dish covered with aluminum foil.

She walked in and set the dish down on the foyer side-table before the two women embraced awkwardly. Sarah took the food container to the kitchen, then they went tearfully to the living room and sat down knee-to-knee on the sofa.

"Oh, God, Sarah, I can't believe this is happening to me." Betty looked at Sarah through red, tear-stained eyes. "I'm sorry, I'm just thinking of myself. You have—" Her voice was barely above a whisper.

Sarah put her arms around Betty. "There, there, dear. It's alright. I know how hard it must be for you with Mel gone. I'm sure Jason's alright and will come home soon. I'm sure he has his reasons."

Betty pulled away to look into her old friend's face. "Sarah, I can't believe they think Jason killed Mel. They were boyhood friends." Her voice remained a hoarse whisper as she mouthed the dreaded words. She applied a tear-dampened handkerchief to her swollen eyes. Her lips curled again in a grimace of grief.

Sarah closed, then opened, her eyes. "It's an impossibility, Betty, an outrage to think such a thing. They're grasping at straws." She patted Betty's knee as she looked closely at the other woman.

"Oh, I just hated that gun! Mel insisted on buying it. He said it was for protection, and look what happened!" She began to cry again.

"Of course, Betty, of course. Try to calm yourself, dear."

Betty opened her eyes, red from hours of tears, looked away, then back at Sarah. "Poor Jason must be frightened half to death."

"With the FBI acting so outrageously, I'm certain he's afraid to contact me just yet."

Betty's eyes opened wide as she covered the lower part of her face with her handkerchief and nodded. "You think so?"

"Yes. But he will soon. We'll get this awful mess cleared up. They think he's responsible for everything. It's ridiculous. Some of these government agencies. And to think we're supposed to trust them." Sarah closed her eyes in confirmation and nodded her head. "Betty, dear, is Roy coming in?" She patted Betty again.

Betty took time to control herself. "Tomorrow. He had a business trip he just couldn't get out of. He felt miserable about it, but I told him there was time." She sniffed.

"He'll stay with you, then?"

"For a few days. Janie—his wife—is expecting. He'll be here a couple of days after the funeral."

"Lord, what must he think?"

"He wants me to come live with them."

"Oh, Betty, that would be so good for you. To get away from here." She patted Betty again instinctively.

Betty shook her head. "I couldn't stay for long. It would be unfair to them." She studied the floor, then looked up. "Are yours coming?"

"Yes. Flo will be here tomorrow. The boys will arrive in the next day or so." Sarah brushed at her own hair with her fingers. "They're quite concerned and feel I need them. I do, and I don't. They're so wonderful. All our kids."

"Oh, yes." Betty sniffed again, applied her hankie, then, "Sarah, where could Jason be?" She shook her head, a gesture of disbelief.

Sarah sighed. "I've been wracking my brains. I thought he might have gone to Truchas. I called some friends who live nearby, but he's not there. The police told me this afternoon they found his pickup truck out in Corrales. It was parked at the Territorial House restaurant."

"What was it doing there?"

"I just can't imagine, unless he met someone. I confess, it concerns me."

"Sarah, what happened out there? At the base?"

"I don't know. I just don't know." She shook her head and looked away. "The FBI agent said there was some sort of theft. And the awful thing is that they suspect Jason! Can you believe that!" She drew in a deep breath and released it rapidly.

Betty shook her head, her face sallow with splotches of red. "Do you think it had anything to do with that awful disaster—that explosion—out there?"

Sarah shrugged with both shoulders. "I don't know. I really don't see how it could." She paused, then asked, "Betty, did the police find anything?"

"What do you mean?" Betty's voice had decayed to a whisper.

Sarah shifted her weight and withdrew her arm and put both her hands together in her lap. She worked them together nervously. "Well, I mean, did they find any evidence—left by the person who did it—off—of anything physical?"

Betty shook her head, slow to respond. She looked down at the floor, then up. "Not that I know of." She tilted her head at Sarah.

"I mean—did they go through the house looking for—oh—fingerprints? A weapon of some sort? Other than Mel's gun?"

Betty looked away as she searched her memory. "I don't know. When I returned, there were a lot of policemen here. They took photographs of everything and searched everywhere—but they didn't say anything to me about it."

"Nothing?"

"They said they might have to come back." Betty shrugged. "Then today more detectives came. They said they were from—from homicide. They didn't find anything, either. I guess . . ."

Sarah nodded her head, her face lined with deep concern. "I'm sorry, dear." She hesitated, then went on. "Betty, did *you* find anything different when you came back?"

Betty's eyes had dried measurably. She shook her head as she studied the carpet again for guidance. "No. Mel was as neat as ever. He even made the bed before he—before he—"

"Oh, dear Betty." Sarah wrapped her arms around the grief-stricken woman as she sobbed anew.

After several minutes, Betty gained her composure. "There must have been a burglar."

"Of course, dear. Of course." Sarah stared off into space.

Betty thanked Sarah for the dish as she saw her to the door and promised to come over on the weekend. Before turning out the lights, she went through the house, checked all the locks, set the alarm system and wound the grandfather clock in the hall. She brushed her teeth, put on her nightgown and got into bed. She lay on her side for a time, looking tearfully at a framed photograph of Mel she had moved from the piano, then tried to read a magazine. Finally, exhausted, she turned out the light, rolled over onto her back and began to sob quietly, her hands over her eyes in the dark, as the tears rolled down her cheeks and onto the damp pillow.

Outside, half a block away in a darkened part of the street near a clump of bushes, a man in dark clothing stood watching the Vaslovic house. He saw a woman leave the house, get into a Mercedes parked in the driveway, and depart. As lights extinguished throughout the house, he remained patiently still in the shadows.

Confident that no lights would come on in the house again, he checked his surroundings, looked at his watch, then walked quickly along the street, past the house, then across to the other side. He stopped next to a large tree which stood in a front yard two houses away from the Vaslovic place. There he remained for a full minute and watched the Vaslovic house. He moved again, this time straight to the Vaslovic yard, then along the fence that marked the boundary of the driveway shared with the neighboring property. Without hesitation, he made for the gate that led to the back yard, opened, then closed it quietly.

Once in the rear yard of the Vaslovic house, he stood and waited in deep shadows between the house and the fence for any sound or movement. Satisfied he had not been detected, he reached inside his black jacket, pulled out a stocking mask and put it on over his head and face. He moved his head around, up and down, high and low. He looked up at the power poles in the alley and at the assemblage of wires between there and the house. He took a pair of small diagonal cutters from a compartmentalized leather tool belt strapped to his body just above the waist and felt along the dark wall, and traced a wire that dropped to a small box near the gas meter. He squatted, severed the wire with the cutters, then waited.

Satisfied there was no change in or around the house, he put the cutters back. He stood and moved slowly to the corner of the building. Again, he listened carefully. In a few seconds, he was at the French doors that connected the patio with the living room. He looked at the doors, then turned and scanned the rear yard and the ragged edge of light created by lights on the fences, houses and trees that surrounded the yard.

He turned back to the doors and reached for the tool belt. With precision, he removed a small, rolled cloth packet. He knelt down and laid the packet on the patio floor. He spread it open and extracted a tiny pinpoint flashlight. He shown the light at the top of the door, moved it back and forth, and peered closely. He extinguished the light and put it into his jacket pocket, then pulled a small drill motor from the packet. He then fit the motor with a bit and drilled a diagonal hole in the wood door frame just above the upper outside pane of the left French door. With the drill put away, he removed a small cylindrical magnet and pressed it into the fresh hole. With the flashlight in his hand again, he cupped his hand over the light, better to find a thin piece of steel from the packet. With the light off, he crouched in front of the door knob and picked the lock. In eight seconds, the door was unlocked and open. He rolled the tools up and returned them to his waist holder. He waited ten seconds as he listened and watched. From his pants pocket, he took a handkerchief and wiped the glass and the door knob. Then he put on a pair of thin black gloves, entered the house and carefully, silently, closed the door.

He made his way quickly and quietly to the bedroom hall. He moved with stealth and care, and felt along the wall as he went. He came to an open door and looked in. He moved across the dark hall to a second door. It was also open. He barely made out the big bed in the dark.

The man reached into an inside jacket pocket and retrieved a small, sealed plastic bag. He opened the bag and took out a small sponge, which he held away from his face. Then he walked into the room and straight for the bed.

"Who's there!?" Betty shrieked as she sat straight up. "Who's there!?" She shrieked again.

The man leapt at the bed and grabbed the hysterical woman around her neck. As she struggled frantically and kicked her legs, he held the sponge to her face. In three seconds, she collapsed. He laid her gently on her back, covered her and adjusted the pillow under her head.

He put the sponge back into the plastic bag and re-sealed it. He pulled the flashlight out and began shining it around the room, pointing it here and there, but took care not to let its beam cross a window. He moved efficiently from room to room, careful not to disturb anything, as he inspected every piece of furniture and every closet. If he moved something, he returned it to its place.

Five minutes later with his hand to his head in puzzlement, he stood in the living room. He scanned the room with the tiny light, then carefully felt along and behind each picture frame. One of them, a small oil, was flat against the wall and would not swing from the bottom. He pulled at the left side, and it hinged away. He felt the surface behind and found a ten-inch diameter, circular safe.

The man reached into his tool belt again and came up with an ear plug and a small black box. He placed the earplug into one ear. The wire from the plug he inserted into the little box, then stuck the magnetized box to the safe door and turned the dial with his gloved right hand.

The safe door was open in a little more than one minute. With the flashlight held in his teeth, he searched through a bundle of insurance policies, currency, and a small jewelry box. He rifled through the items once more, then returned everything to its place, closed the door and closed the painting door. After he took the stocking mask off, he left the house through the French doors, and was on the street and a block away in another forty-five seconds.

12

*J*ason was recalled from the edge of dreams by the sound of a fly circling the room in preparation for its tweny-first attack on the sun-drenched window set deep into the outside wall.

Flat on his back, he opened his eyes, then panicked at the unfamiliar surroundings. Above him was a ceiling composed of ancient pieces of painted, decoratively-stamped tin sheet nailed to an even older set of thick, square beams. The metal was coming loose here and there, the nails pulling out—in a couple of places entirely—such that he saw the water-stained pine slabs comprising the roof above.

He licked his dry lips and turned his head to the left to look at the object of the busy insect's passion. Through the warped glass panes of the wooden sash, the sun's intense rays slanted into the room at a shallow angle that indicated early morning. He blinked his eyes in an attempt to clear them, then checked the rest of the room.

The crude, unpainted Z-frame plank door was closed. Chips and cracks here and there in the old plaster that covered the odd, stone-and adobe walls revealed dark earth behind the painted gypsum. A single ladder-back chair and a mirrored dresser stood across the room. Hung on the wall in an oval frame, the sole decoration in the room, was a retouched photographic portrait of a bearded, balding man dressed in a nineteenth-century era suit, his cheeks grotesquely and falsely pink.

When he thought about the fact that he was flat on his back with a blanket over him, he bolted upright, an action which brought instant pain and soreness to his neck, back, thighs and forearms. The bed squeaked and bounced as he swung his legs clumsily over the edge of the bed and pushed the blanket aside. Dizzy, he sat for a moment and looked down at the old, thin mattress and the edge of the black wire bedsprings beneath.

A small table stood next to the bed. His watch lay on its surface next to a kerosene lamp with a blackened chimney, its wick draped into a transparent glass tank, half -filled with amber kerosene. Next to that was a simple, inexpensive electric lamp with a light brown, stained paper shade. The envelope he had taken from Cuzco's shirt pocket was near his watch. He stared at the things from his pockets, then stirred himself to look for his shoes which he found aligned carefully under the bed.

His socks were still on his feet. He ran a hand through his unkempt, thinning hair, then realized there were small bandages on his cheek, his right forearm, and the back of his right hand. The cuts and bruises on his hands, face and stomach throbbed as he awakened.

The fly had given up and was walking across one of the window panes.

His shoes on, loosely tied, Jason made his way past an armoire to the door and opened it. The room he stepped into was barely familiar. Straight ahead was a window and to its left an outside door, open, with a crooked screen door covering it. To his right was a fireplace with a rock mantel. Several pieces of furniture were scattered around the room. An old sofa and an overstuffed chair were covered in cracked, black leather. A floor-model reading lamp with a tasseled shade, straight out of the nineteen-twenties, stood next to the overstuffed chair. Between the sofa and the fireplace was a crude bookcase with what he quickly estimated must be close to a hundred books, mostly paperback. More, some hardbacks, were scattered here and there on the chairs, the sofa and on table tops. Several were propped up on the mantle. A poorly-rendered oil painting of a pastoral scene hung over the sofa, while a small pencil portrait of a woman decorated the wall opposite. The old wood floor was covered near the center of the room with a worn and faded eight-by-ten foot rug. To his left another open door through the foot-thick wall led to the kitchen. He heard not the slightest sound.

He walked to the front door and looked out through the ratty screen and beyond the shade of the porch. Two horses, a roan and a bay, grazed in a field beyond a barbed wire fence, their tails whipping occasionally at insects. In the distance rose the sharp escarpment of a rough-hewn mesa, its sides striated with alternate horizontal bands of dark and buff rock.

Thirst outstripped his curiosity, so he moved away from the outside door and into the kitchen. The sink and drainboard were to his right as he entered, beneath a long, narrow window that looked out onto the porch. Cabinets reached to the ceiling on either side of the sink above the drainboard, which was comprised of well-weathered tongue-and-groove pine boards. In the center of the room was a round, antique oak table with massive, but delicately-turned legs. It was covered with red, checkered oilcloth, torn in places and patched with curling tape in others. Three chairs of the same make and vintage as the table stood at angles near, or under the table. On the table top was a collection of half-full jelly and peanut butter jars, condiment bottles and a disparate salt and pepper set. A clean, empty bowl sat near the edge of the table, a teaspoon next to it. Offset from center on the table was an old, well-used kerosene oil lamp, its resevoir half-full, its wick and glass chimney blackened from use. A partially open box of kitchen, or stick, matches lay next to the lamp.

Jason took in the rest of the room, including a huge wood stove beyond the table. To the left of that was an outside door. Opposite the sink, set against the wall, was a massive chopping block on stout, piano-like legs, its top surface worn from use. Next to that was an old, single-door refrigerator. A lamp with a single incandescent lamp hung from the stamped metal decorated ceiling by its own electrical cord.

He went to the cabinets and looked for a glass. When he opened the faucet, he heard a pump start somewhere, and felt and heard the pulsing through the pipe. A substantial splash of clear, cold water surged into the glass a few seconds later.

He drained the glass twice, set it down, empty, on the drainboard, then subconsciously rubbed his sore places as he continued to inspect the premises. He moved slowly to the leaning screen door and looked out past the shade of the porch. The woman was outside, working in a garden, well away from the house. He exited onto the porch, and blinked against the morning sun. He walked over to her.

As she pushed on a long-handled shovel with her booted foot, she heard the screen door slam and turned to look toward the house. She stopped, stood straight, and held the shovel handle erect with both gloved hands. With her foot still on the shovel, she watched from under the brim of her wide straw hat as Jason approached.

"Morning," she said. Her greeting carried a tentative tone.

Jason smiled and cleared his throat. "Good morning." With the sun behind her, he found her difficult to see.

"Sleep all right?" she squinted at him.

"Yes, thank you. I hope I didn't take your bed." Jason shaded his eyes against the sunlight.

"Put you up in the spare room. Looked pretty beat up. You tender?"

Jason grimaced and touched the bandage on his face. He nodded. "Yes, I am." He paused. "Thank you for the nursing."

"You're welcome. Couldn't let you suffer." She made a wry face.

They walked back into the house where she fixed breakfast with what Jason decided was a smooth, easy manner. At her invitation, he sat on one of the oak chairs at the round kitchen table and rubbed his legs.

She did not seem much like his recollection of her from the night before. She was a slight woman, whom Jason decided was probably in her mid-fifties. Her face was pleasant, hardened in a way he couldn't fathom, but amazingly free of age lines, with almost luminescent skin. Faded, but mildly flattering dungarees and a red plaid shirt, hid what he suspected was a good figure. Her relatively new hat, which rested on the table, had before hidden thick brown hair tied off in two braids that fell down her back.

He looked around and thought of the rifle. It was nowhere to be seen, although there was a rack for one over the fireplace.

When she went to the firewood box, Jason got up stiffly and moved to her side and took the pieces she had lifted from it. She looked at him in a matter-of-fact way, and let him put the wood in the stove and attempt to start a fire, while she moved off to put the food together. He tried in vain to get the fire going. In the end, her experience triumphed over his gallantry, much to his chagrin.

After turning the bacon, she looked at him. "I went up to look at your plane this morning."

"You climbed up there?" Jason's eyes were wide with surprise. He sat and looked up at her.

"Horseback. There's a trail, but only went part way. I could see. Pretty rugged. You were lucky." She sat down across from him.

Jason shook his head and rubbed his forehead with the palm of his hand. "Yes," he said. "But how did you manage to get me onto that bed? I'm bigger than you."

"If you'd hauled as many grain sacks and hay bales as I have, Mister, you'd know." A sardonic smile creased her pleasant face, then evaporated as she occupied the other chair across the table. "Matter of knowing how to throw dead weight around."

He studied her features, amazed. "My name's—" He hesitated, contemplating a lie, then continued. "Thompson. Jason Thompson."

She nodded. "Vera. Tyler."

He smiled.

Without responding, she rose to poke at the bacon with the two-pronged fork she wielded. "What happened?"

She wasn't facing him, but he felt as though she had eyes in the back of her head.

"Got lost. I was looking for an airport I thought I knew about down here and ran out of fuel. From up high, the rocks looked like a road in the half-light." Jason watched her from the corners of his eyes.

"You got some ailment, don't you?"

Jason furrowed his brow. "How do you figure that?"

"Found some pills in your pocket. Looked like some my husband used to take regular." Vera turned and folded her arms across her plaid shirt and looked at him with clear, hazel eyes. Jason shifted his gaze to gauge the shape of her breasts as she moved her arms, and suffered a rush of guilt.

She recognized what he was doing and looked away and pretended not to notice.

"Do you live here alone?"

"My husband died a few years back. Been keepin' this place up myself." She looked sad as she stared at the bare one-by-six pine floor of the kitchen. "'Fraid I've let it go some." She tilted her head, raised her eyebrows and smiled.

Jason gave in to his sore legs, stood up, limped slowly to the sink, and looked out the window. He noticed a pair of power lines that led to the house. "You have electricity."

"Twenty years. No phone."

"You still burn wood for heat. No gas?"

"Could get propane, but it's expensive to install. And to burn. I've had plenty wood. Although it's getting in short supply."

"How far from town are you?" He peered at the horses grazing in the distance.

"Town, twenty-three miles. Gas station an' short supplies about ten."

"Is there an airport near here?"

"Nearest I know of is more like sixty. At least the type that'll take a big plane. Some ranchers have strips."

"Sixty miles," he repeated. "I was off."

Vera laughed.

Jason turned away from the window at the sound, charmed.

"I'm a long way from anybody or anything," she said in a matter-of-fact tone.

He smiled again and leaned with his back against the drainboard. A strange wave of well-being swept over him. "How do you survive? I mean, way out here like this? What's here?"

"Les—my husband's dad—homesteaded this place a long time ago. Couple a' sections. Might not look it, but good grazing. Most of it. Up the canyon and on the mesas. I run two, three hundred head of beef cattle—depending. And I garden." She looked around as though she could see through the walls.

"Depending?"

"Weather. Rain and snow. Affects the grazing."

"Surely, you don't manage all that cattle by yourself?"

"Nope. Certain times of the year, the boys come up from Deming and Mexico and give me a hand. They drive 'em for me. Part of the land is good for sheep. When I run 'em, I have some Mexican kids. They're good. I don't make a lot. Then, I don't need a lot." She shifted her body to face him. "Right now, I got a few yearlings, some mama cows and a couple 'a bulls. I'll have more next season. Depends on the price 'a beef."

For him, the hardness he had felt from her the night before seemed to have melted away. It was more likely, he reasoned, something he had invented for her because of the series of problems he had encountered over the past few days. He watched her with a new light as she rose and moved to the stove, tended the bacon, then busied herself with eggs and toast, and what looked and smelled like red chile. Her back was to him again. He returned to the table and sat.

Vera continued to move her arms rhythmically, working the food on the stove. "You one 'o them drug runners?"

"What?! Why would you think that?" He was shocked at her question and felt his heart rate quicken.

"You don't look like one, but then, I've never seen one. This area gets 'em now and then. They sometimes crash their planes." She squinted out the window over the sink toward the mesa where the plane teetered. "Up from Mexico." She carried two plates to the table.

"And you think I might be one of them." He looked straight at her, the inkling of a grin on his whiskered face.

Vera went back to the stove for the toast and the chile. "Can't be too sure of anything these days." She sat and started to eat without looking at him. She motioned to the small pot with the dark red chile sauce. "Grow it here myself. Like it on eggs."

Jason grinned and picked up his fork. "It just so happens I do, too."

They ate in silence for a while. Jason's voracious appetite made him forget everything else. Vera got up for more toast, and they finished with more coffee.

"Have anything with you? Clothes?" She asked.

Jason shook his head. "I couldn't get them out. I was dangling almost on my side. The plane's hanging by a couple of branches up there. I was afraid it was going to fall down the cliff with me in it. I don't even have my wallet." He hoped she hadn't detected the lie about his clothes.

"Got a razor you can use." She looked at him as though she had never said a word about drugs. "We can get you a toothbrush later."

"Thank you. Would it be possible to get to a phone?"

"Sure. Nearest one's at a gas station about ten miles from here."

"Can you help me get there?"

"We'll go after you get cleaned up."

They finished, saying little more. She drained her coffee cup, got up and clattered the dirty dishes into the sink.

Jason thought Vera handled her Ford pickup truck like a man, then as quickly, mentally flogged himself for a ridiculous, sexist thought. He always had confidence in Sarah's driving, but then she never drove a three-quarter ton pickup truck over dirt roads at speeds of up to forty miles per hour. Vera had her straw on, her braids half way down her back and a pair of dark glasses over her eyes against the intense sun that glared against the windshield. The road was dry and relatively smooth. Behind them, dust roiled up and powdered the bed of the truck where the remnants of two green hay bales swam around the worn steel bed as the vehicle swayed along at a speed greater than Jason thought advisable.

They were on a paved secondary road after traveling more than eight miles. They then turned west, away from the mid-morning high sun.

As they approached their destination, Jason noted from his window that the altitude was still high enough for small evergreens to grow on the side of a nearby slope. He scanned the black humps of the Gila Wilderness to the north. Then he looked south, where the land dropped, flattened and stretched away, beyond the last of the evergreens, in dun and black-green silence toward northern Mexico. The heat rose in a mass from the barrens.

Vera pulled up to one of the three pumps. "Phone's inside. I gotta gas up."

Jason got out of the truck, stopped and put his hand in his pants' pockets to feel for coins. He came back to the pickup as Vera got out and began to open the gas filler cap just behind the cab. "I'm embarrassed, Vera. No change." He grimaced at her across the truck bed.

With no outward reaction, she pulled a small leather coin purse from her Levi's jacket pocket, opened it and handed him some coins.

"Thanks," he said.

"You'll just have to owe me." She grinned and tilted her head in a friendly gesture.

He was amused and delighted with the ancient gas station. It was an old concrete block building sporting a rock fascia and a wood canopy supported by weathered steel poles with chipped paint. It was a combination curio store and café with a four-stool counter and two rickety tables of chromed steel and plastic. The tables sported salt and pepper shakers and napkin dispensers, as did the counter, set out in front of each stool.

The pay phone, surrounded by grubby handprints and dozens of notes and crazy sketches in pencil and ballpoint pen, all at odd angles to each other, was bolted to a wall of the station immediately inside the dirty glass door. A girlie calendar, an imitation of Vargas, six years out of date, hung to the left of it, and a small, tattered phone book with a missing cover dangled from a dirty string.

"This is Benjamin. It's important I get through to Mr. Adams. Right. My engine conked out again, and I'm a long way from home. Right. Away from home. Stranded." Jason cupped his hand over the mouthpiece and looked around. "Take down this number. When he finds the phone, tell him to ask for the Tyler ranch. Tyler. Ten miles. From this phone. Tell him I'm waiting."

When Jason hung up, Vera was behind him, sitting on a stool at the other end of the café counter, talking to a wizened old man who stood behind the register. He walked over to her.

"Get through?" She asked.

"Not much luck. I'll have to call later." He sighed and looked out through the dirty, fly-blown window at a car that pulled in under the canopy.

"Well, we'll get you a toothbrush and you can come on back with me. You can call later. But we ought to let the law know how you happened by my place."

He started to say something, then hesitated and took a different approach. "I'd appreciate that. I'm still pretty sore. And I'd really like to have a look at the wreck."

"Sure."

He sighed, "But can we wait awhile on the law?"

She sobered. "Why?"

Jason looked around, ensuring no one overheard. The old man had moved off into the garage, leaving them alone in the shabby room. "Don't get me wrong,

Vera, but I haven't been entirely honest with you. Listen, can we go? I'll tell you about it on the way."

Vera pinched up her mouth and looked at one of her slim rough-out boots. She raised her head to look him in the eye. "Okay. Let's go. Better not be drugs."

13

*T*he Thompson living room was large and airy, as wide as the entire front of the house. Jason had torn out dividing walls years before, making two rooms and a hall into one. Windows with low sills swept along three sides, allowing outside light to flood in from all but one outer wall. Two large Navajo rugs graced the polished hardwood floor. An old black upright piano upon which the children had practiced to little avail nestled in a corner near the stair that led to the upper, bedroom story. Tastefully subdued furniture was arranged into two living sections; one side for the television set and piano, the other for conversation and guests.

Sarah sat at one end of the couch that faced the piano and television. She thought Betty Vaslovic looked small and frail sitting at the other end, facing her. Then there came one of those thoughts that make one feel guilty at such times to Sarah, "What a difficult feat for an overweight woman." A younger woman, taller than Sarah, who resembled her around the eyes and chin, stood near one of the windows that looked out onto the front of the house and the porch.

"Mother, it looks like we have company," the woman said.

Sarah rose and moved to the window. "Oh, it's that Grayson, the FBI man. And Lucero." She turned away with a frown. "Why do they come now? It's nearly lunch time."

The three women each reacted to the ringing of the door chimes; Betty Vaslovic with a nervous twitch and turn of her head, Sarah with her frown, and the young woman by answering and showing the government agents into the living room.

Grayson spoke to Sarah, while Lucero stood apart, his hands clasped together across his belt line. "I'm sorry for this intrusion, Mrs. Thompson, but we need to talk to you." He looked at Betty, who had turned to face them. "I'm glad you're here, Mrs. Vaslovic. We'd like to have a few words with you, too."

"What could you possibly want with my mother and Betty? Grayson, is it?" The young woman, arms folded across her chest, spoke sharply to the FBI man.

"This is my daughter, Florence, Mr. Grayson. Flo, this is Mr. Grayson—Peter? Of the FBI." Sarah moved back to the sofa with Betty and sat.

Grayson introduced Lucero and spent a minute trying to make small talk with Flo about her place of residence, but found her unreceptive and distant, so he turned to the two women on the sofa. He asked permission to sit, then did so without waiting for an answer. "Mrs. Vaslovic, do you mind if we begin with you?"

Betty looked wide-eyed at the FBI agent and spoke with a meek voice. "No."

"Mrs. Thompson, I hope you don't mind." He looked at Sarah, then concentrated on Betty. "We understand you had a prowler last night. Actually, a break-in. Even though there's no physical evidence of a break-in, that's what the police are calling it."

Betty nodded, barely able to speak.

"Mrs. Vaslovic, I'm truly sorry to have to speak to you about this, but it's very important."

Betty looked puzzled as she touched a handkerchief to her face.

"Really, Mr. Grayson," Flo cut in, "must you do this now?"

Grayson turned to Flo. "Mrs.—Florence—it is extremely important we gather as much information as we can as early as possible after an incident like this. It not only helps our case, but could help to clear your father."

Flo turned and strolled away, fuming, her arms still folded across her chest.

"Now, Mrs. Vaslovic—" Grayson threw Lucero, who remained impassive, a frustrated glance, before he focused on the distraught woman. "Mrs. Vaslovic, you told the police you were drugged?"

"Yes."

"He—it was a man—he knocked you out with drugs?"

"Yes. He put something over my mouth. I don't remember anything after that."

"What time did you wake up?"

Betty shook her head and furrowed her brow. "It was around nine. I always get up earlier than that." She fiddled frantically with her handkerchief.

"You're sure it was a man?"

Betty looked up at Grayson, surprised. "Why, yes."

Grayson hesitated. "Forgive me, Mrs. Vaslovic, but why are you so sure?"

Betty looked at Sarah as though frightened, then back at the FBI agent. "Well, he was strong. His arms—and the smell."

"Smell?" Grayson asked.

"Yes. It was a tobacco smell. Faint, but I could tell."

Grayson shot Lucero a glance, then back. "Tobacco? Cigarette smoke?"

"No. Pipe smoke."

Grayson nodded his head, a tiny curl of satisfaction appearing on his lips. "Mrs. Vaslovic, could you identify the brand? The tobacco brand?"

She shook her head. "I know it was pipe smoke, because my father always smoked a pipe, but I don't know the brands. It's different from cigarettes." She closed her eyes, lowered her head, and put her hand that held her handkerchief over her face.

"Okay," Grayson said. He took a notebook from his inside jacket pocket. "Was there anything missing—anything at all?"

Betty shook her head, eyes still closed. She began to twist the handkerchief, her knuckles white.

Grayson jotted in his notebook. "I told you earlier the police said there was no sign of forced entry. Are you sure you heard nothing?"

"No. All of a sudden, he was in my room—oh, God—"

She leaned toward Sarah and began to cry, and Sarah moved next to her to put her arm around Betty. Flo crossed the room to the rear of the couch, put her hand on Betty's shoulder and patted it. She glared at Grayson, who looked up at her, then ducked his head in frustration.

"Mr. Grayson, why are you asking all these questions when the police already have?" Flo glared at Grayson as she continued to sooth the distraught Betty Vaslovic.

"Mrs.—"

"D'Angelo."

"Mrs. D'Angelo, we are investigating the theft of government property, and we have reason to believe there is a strong connection between that theft and the incidents at the Vaslovic house, including Mr. Vaslovic's mur—death."

Flo straightened her back, but continued to glare at Grayson.

"Further, Mrs. D'Angelo, we are trying very hard not to disturb the lives of your mother or Mrs. Vaslovic in this investigation, but we do have to investigate. It's critical." He stopped and looked at the two older women on the sofa, then continued. "The fact is, Mrs. D'Angelo, we are well within our legal rights to have both your mother and Mrs. Vaslovic downtown in the Federal Building talking to us in our offices." He hesitated for effect, then went on in a more subdued tone. "I don't think you want that, anymore than we do. I don't think your mother or Mrs. Vaslovic want that either."

The room was quiet as Flo, her mouth in a grim line, her eyes about to brim with tears, turned and moved slowly back to the front windows. She looked out with her arms again folded against her chest in a sign of frustration and anger. Her mother put her hand on Betty's knee and lowered her head, while Betty dabbed at her red eyes. Lucero moved closer to the windows on the other side of the room and looked out.

Grayson turned the page in his notebook. "Mrs. Vaslovic, the police report states that your house has an alarm system. Is that true?"

"Yes."

"Did the alarm sound?"

"No, it didn't."

"Was it on?"

"Yes, I turned it on before I went to bed."

Grayson took care of an itch in his left ear with his finger, and Lucero came back to the center of the room. "So someone came into the house without disturbing anything and without tripping the alarm?" He looked up.

Betty nodded her head almost imperceptibly. Then she twitched. "No! No, the phone was dead!" She worked her mouth and looked at Sarah as though for permission, then back at Grayson. "I couldn't use the phone to call the police, so I went next door and called the police. They found the line cut."

Grayson studied her reaction with his brow furrowed. "When did you discover the phone was dead?"

"This morning. When I tried to call the police." She sniffed into her handkerchief.

Grayson watched her, then wrote in his notebook. He stood up, excused himself, turned his back to the women, and went to Lucero. He spoke in a low tone. "Get with APD and suggest they have another look at the alarm system. Tell 'em what we've heard here. Maybe do another search. There's something missing. This smells like a professional. Something they're probably not used to. Tell 'em we want to avoid a Federal warrant." He hesitated, his strong gaze still on his partner. He shrugged. "Who knows?"

Lucero nodded and left the house.

Grayson pondered and was slow to return to the women on the sofa as he studied patterns in the floor coverings. "Mrs. Thompson, the police told us you also had a break-in last night. Is that true?"

"Yes." Sarah thrust out her jaw, waiting for the rain of questions from the FBI man.

"Can you tell me about it?"

"Yes. It was around two. I haven't been sleeping well at all. I had been reading, and had just turned out the light. I heard a noise. From outside. We have a room—well, you know about it—the studio—over the garage. I looked out, but couldn't see anything at first. Then I saw a light from one of the windows. It was just an instant. Like a flashlight. I called the police."

"They found nothing?"

"The door was broken." Sarah looked at Grayson, wide-eyed and grim.

Grayson flipped several pages and read from his notes. "Police report shows that the frame on the latch side was jimmied. Correct? Is that building alarmed?"

"We had one. It wasn't working, and we had so few problems, we just stopped worrying about it." She cast a brief smile at Betty, shot Flo a look, then concentrated on Grayson again.

Grayson walked to the window near Flo and looked out. He slapped his leg with his notebook. "I find it very strange that both your houses were penetrated on the same night, and nothing was bothered or taken. Don't you find that odd?"

He turned and looked from Sarah to Betty and back. His tone had taken on a more serious demeanor.

"Just what are you driving at, Mr. Grayson?" Flo asked. She had returned from her self-imposed exile at the window to stand at one end of the sofa. Her arms were at her sides.

"What I think is that somebody is looking for something special. They think something could be either place, and they haven't found it. Or if they have, we have yet to realize it."

"What would they be looking for?" Sarah wrinkled her brow at Grayson. She shook her head in a short, jerky motion.

Betty, confused, looked at everybody in the room in turn.

Grayson made a quick, negative gesture with his head. "Your husband, Mrs. Thompson, and yours, Mrs. Vaslovic, both worked at the Labs. Classified items were taken from the Labs. Perhaps someone thinks these items—or copies of same—are in one of your two houses."

Betty dropped her head and dabbed at her eyes once again.

Sarah shook her head back and forth in a slow, wide arc, both hands in her lap. "That's ridiculous. Absolutely ridiculous." She looked up at Grayson.

Flo had moved close the front door. She stared at Grayson, her mouth agape. "That's utterly preposterous!" She advanced on him, as he studied reactions carefully. "My father and Mel Vaslovic are—were—loyal Americans. You owe my mother and Betty—Mrs. Vaslovic—an apology!" She pointed with enphasis.

Grayson looked at Flo directly. "Mrs. D'Angelo, tell me what you think. Your father and Mr. Vaslovic have been life-long friends. They worked together for many years, closely, sometimes on the same projects. The security breach occurred within your father's organization. Soon after, his close friend is dead, and your father disappears. Now these incidents—" He jabbed his finger at her in his frustration.

Flo looked at him, let out a sigh and turned so as not to look directly at him. She moderated her voice. "I don't know, Mr. Grayson. All I know is my father and Mel are—were—patriotic men. You have nothing. All of this is coincidence. Pure coincidence." Her chin went up in defiance.

Grayson hesitated, then spoke in a low voice. "Mrs. D'Angelo, two things: Your father is missing, in effect a fugitive, and we have evidence pointing to his involvement."

"What?! What are you saying!?" Flo whipped around and flared at Grayson, eyes wide, face flushed, then turned toward the sofa. "Mother! Do you know what he's talking about?!"

Sarah started to speak, but Grayson cut her off. "Your mother doesn't know what that evidence is, Mrs. D'Angelo, and we're not required to tell you what it is. And the Federal Government is not stating with any certainty that your father is guilty of any wrong-doing. But we have evidence and we need to speak to him. Do you know where he is?" Grayson raised his eyebrows at her.

Flo, furious, gasped, "Mr. Grayson, if I did know my father's whereabouts, I certainly wouldn't tell you!" She turned away again.

Grayson, his mouth set in frustration, nodded and looked away.

Sarah, alerted to distant sounds, turned to peer out the front window, and rose from the sofa. "Oh, my God!"

"What is it, mother?" Flo asked, then spun around to follow her gaze.

All but Betty Vaslovic moved to the windows that fronted the porch and looked out. A small crowd was gathering on the sidewalk in front of the house. Cars were arriving in twos and threes, parked sloppily in the street, and a large white van with a variety of antennae on its roof, including a small satellite dish, was in the process of parking against the curb. Nearly all had news emblems painted on their sides.

People on the sidewalk talked loudly to each other. Some wore headphones and ran cables from the van to cameras carried on the shoulders of big men just beyond the Thompson's outer fence. Then a group of men and women followed by cameramen began to surge toward the front porch. Across the street, two black-and-white APD cars rolled up, and four uniformed officers jumped out to effect crowd and traffic control.

As the sound of footfalls on the porch and banging on the door began, Sarah took Betty by the arm and guided her toward the stairs. Flo followed and spoke to her mother so Grayson couldn't hear. Betty continued up the stairs, and Sarah turned and followed Flo. Flo went up to Grayson, who wore a surprised, concerned look as he watched the melee outside.

"How did this happen, Mr. Grayson? Why are these news people here? We thought this was being kept quiet."

"Frankly, I don't know any more than you do, Mrs. D'Angelo. But I can't prevent them from coming." He looked at Sarah. "Mrs. Thompson, only you have the authority to tell them to leave."

Sarah wrung her hands nervously, and turned away from Grayson. She was transfixed by the sight on her front porch. One of the news people she saw was the man who had been there before. He had worn a dark blue sport jacket, and said he was from Reuters. She wracked her brains for his name. It was like a French city, she remembered.

She turned back to Grayson. "Please, if you do nothing else, tell those people to go away, or ask the police to send them away. I really can't bear this today." With that, she crossed the room and mounted the stairs. Then she stopped and returned to the front woindow. She watched Grayson and Lucero leave, and continued her vigil as Grayson approached an APD officer and spoke with him, then turned and moved slowly away.

Grayson followed Lucero to their car and got into the passenger seat. Lucero did not start the engine.

Grayson stared out the windshield. "We're getting nowhere fast." He glanced at his partner, then faced forward again.

Lucero scratched a place on his head. "So it would seem. What's the plan?"

"I really don't know," Grayson replied. "Hell, we've interviewed everyone. Even taken potential evidence from their goddamn studio, but until we get some forensics back—"

"There's gotta' be something. The Vaslovic death, break-ins, the breach. Where does it lead?" Lucero stared at Grayson's left side.

"Mm," Grayson murmured. "That old fox, Thompson's got something going. Where the hell is he?" He waved his hand. "These women don't know anything. And we gotta leave 'em alone, or we'll be facing a harrassment charge." He looked at Lucero as he nodded. He sighed, "Home, James."

Lucero cranked the engine to life, and the car slid away from the chaotic scene behind them.

14

*V*era Tyler and Jason went to the combination service station, café and general store which sold such delicacies as stale doughnuts and overly-priced candy bars, plus dusty little boxes of automotive fuses for cars, long since out of production, and packets of Watkins aspirin, a brand which disappeared shortly after World War II. In one corner of the room were a few clothes and body-care products. Vera treated Jason to a new toothbrush and offered to buy him some underwear and other items, but Jason demurred on anything but the toothbrush. He was embarrassed, though, so he promised to wash his dirty clothes on their return to the ranch.

As they walked back to the pickup in the bright midday sun, Jason sensed that Vera was turning over in her mind his request to delay notification of his wreck to the authorities. He put his hand on her arm to stop her as she moved past the pickup tailgate for the driver's side.

"I know you're worried. I could send a telegram." He glanced back toward the station.

She stopped and looked at him with the first frown he had seen. "Have to go to town for that, but I've got a sick colt to look after."

"Tomorrow, then." He had difficulty concealing his relief.

Nothing more was said until they reached the secondary road that led north to the ranch. The pavement gave out a quarter-mile past the highway, just where the first barbed wire fence line marked "Private Ranch Property" and the land began to rise into the evergreen-covered foothills of the Gila country.

He knew Vera was waiting for his promised explanation. "There are no clothes in the plane," he said. He didn't look at her as they rocked along. He wished he had his dark glasses, which were most likely still in his windbreaker pocket aboard the crippled Cherokee.

"What?" Vera's voice betrayed no excitement as she kept her eyes on the road.

"No clothes. I didn't bring anything with me."

She cast him a glance, still with no sign of alarm.

"You're going to find this hard to believe, but I was kidnaped. I was taken at gunpoint near Albuquerque. I was being flown somewhere—I don't know where—and when we stopped near St. John's, I got away. I knocked the pilot out. The guy who captured—kidnaped—me. I took the plane."

Vera drove with her eyes straight ahead, her face calm, although Jason noticed she was chewing on the inside of her lip.

Jason sighed deeply and continued. "I hit him on the head with a wrench. When I pulled him out of the plane—I guess it was—the fuel transfer valve broke. He must have hit it with his foot. I ran out of gas. It's been years since I flew. I thought I knew where I was going. That's it. Come to think of it, I was damned lucky the plane didn't catch on fire because it's still got one full tank."

Vera remained silent for another minute, then pointed off to the left. "Deer. See it?"

"No. You don't believe me." He took in a deep breath, looked out his side window, wiped his whole face with his hand in frustration, then released the volume of air in one rush.

Vera took her hat off and put it on the seat, then ran the fingers of her right hand forcefully through her hair, tight as it was with the braids. "I don't see many people the way I live, but for some reason I'm able to tell whether they're honest or not. You may be lying, but I don't think so. For one thing, you're too old to get here the way you did and be too far from the truth."

"Vera, I'd be very grateful to you if you'd let me stay until my friend comes without calling in the authorities." He studied her profile.

"The one you called?"

"Yes."

"You have to go back and call?"

"No. I lied about that, too. I left a message, but I don't know when he'll come."

"Why didn't you call someone else? Are you married?"

Jason snapped his head around to look at her, then away. "Yes. But I can't call her. There are reasons."

"Reasons?" Vera peered at him for an instant.

"Yes. For one thing, I'm sure our phone is tapped."

The only sound in the cab was the roar of the pickup's tires and the squeaking of plastic on metal as it raced along the uneven dirt road.

"Why would somebody tap your phone?"

He closed his eyes, scratched his forehead, then looked at her. "Vera, you're very kind to help me. You don't have any reason to do so. Anyone else would have notified the sheriff or the state police by now. I can't tell you anything more. If you want to turn this truck around and take me to the sheriff, I won't resist."

A long moment ensued while the noise of the vehicle took over again.

"You can wash your clothes in the machine. It's old, but it does the trick." She put her hat on again, as though she needed it to navigate.

Relieved, but puzzled by Vera's reaction to his story, Jason was able to relax a bit and enjoy the scenery the rest of the way to the ranch house. He spotted a deer and pointed it out to her as they crossed through a mountain pass in a heavily forested area.

Peter Grayson left the Thompson house after convincing most of the news people that Sarah would not come to the door and enlisting the aid of the city police to help send them away. After his impromptu conference with Lucero in the car, they drove away. As they did, he used the radio, then, with a change of plans, had Lucero return to the Thompson's by a different route. They parked one street away, out of sight of the house.

Grayson got out of the car, walked to where he could see the house, and stopped. He scanned the place and the surrounding yard and street for a few seconds before he continued to the corner. From there, he strode to the carpet cleaning van parked at the curb, and rapped on a window. The side door of the vehicle opened, he stepped in and closed it.

The cramped interior was dark, lighted only by a glowing computer screen; yellow, green and red indicators on an array of electronics panels, and two high-intensity lamps over a pair of small pull-out tables. All of this complex gear was fastened to one side of the van's interior, with the other side open for maneuvering.

The man who opened the door wore a pair of headphones at the end of a long, spiral cord, and returned to his swivel chair in front of an expensive, burnished steel and black-trimmed reel-to-reel tape recorder. Another man, who also wore a pair of headphones, sat in front of the computer screen. To the right of the computer was a printer. Above it was an active color television monitor, the picture of the Thompson house in its center. To the right of that was a vertical rack of exotic radio gear. Behind the second man a powerful monocular scope was fixed to a tripod. Both men pulled off one ear of their headphones. Grayson sat in the third chair and faced them.

"What you got?" He asked. He looked from man to man.

The man at the recorder spoke first as he shook his head. "A few phone calls since we started the tap. Nothing much."

"What? Personal? Describe."

The first man turned to the other who handed him a printout. The man scanned the fold-out, pin-feed paper. "Friends. Two or three from a Justin Thompson and another Thompson. Male."

"The sons," Grayson offered.

"This guy, Manning, Jason's boss at the Labs called. Talked about fifteen minutes. Wrong number for a Benjamin. More calls from friends. Some woman called about a watercolor field trip. A Florence D'Angelo made two calls out of state. Then another call from the same woman about the watercolor trip. Mrs. Thompson called the grocery store and the drug store. Something for the Vaslovic woman. That's it so far." He looked up.

The other man said, "Only people in and out have been the Vaslovic woman, you guys and all those news people."

Grayson remained quiet and immobile for ten seconds, then spoke. "Play me the wrong number and the ones about the watercolor trip."

The recorder man sighed, consulted the printout and keyed some numbers into a console beneath the recorder. The reels spun at high speed for a few seconds, then stopped. He pushed another button, and the reels moved forward slowly. A speaker above the big tape machine hissed to life. They heard the sound of the telephone ringing twice, then Sarah's voice.

"Hello?"

A man's voice replied, "Hello. Is Benjamin there?"

"Who? Benjamin? I'm sorry, you have the wrong number."

"Oh, I'm sorry."

"Alright. Goodbye."

A click, then a second click when Sarah hung up.

The van technician keyed more numbers, the reel moved and parked, then ran slowly again.

"Hello?"

"Is this Mrs. Thompson?" A woman's voice.

"Yes. Who's calling?"

"Mrs. Thompson, I'm calling for the Watercolor Club. So far, the plans for our next watercolor trip to Arizona are on schedule."

"Good. Thank you so much for letting me know. Goodbye."

"'Bye."

Again the tape fast-forwarded, stopped, then rotated slowly.

"Hello?"

"Mrs. Thompson?"

"Yes?"

"There's been a change in plans for the upcoming Arizona watercolor trip. It's been canceled."

Pause.

"Is there a problem?"

"The guide can't make it."

"That's unfortunate. Do you think it will be re-scheduled?"

"I don't know."

"I was really looking forward to that trip. Would you please see what can be done to put it back on the calendar?"

"Certainly."

"Thank you."

"You're welcome."

"Is it possible for you to let me know as soon as you have word when the trip will be re-scheduled?"

"Of course. I'll call right away."

"Thank you."

The click of the caller's phone, then a pause before Sarah's hang-up.

The operator fast-forwarded the tape, again entered numbers into the console before he turned to Grayson.

Grayson stared first at the man, then past him. "When were those two calls from the club?"

The operator looked at the computer-generated log. "Yesterday. Both of 'em. First in the morning around eleven; second around four."

"I guess they're not traceable."

The man shook his head. "Impossible. Too short. And on tape. You think something's fishy about them?"

"I don't know. We don't have much to go on." He took a deep breath and blew it out forcefully. "No trace of Thompson, and that old broad is so unflappable." He shook his head and paused. "Strange she'd be worried about a goddamn watercolor trip at this time."

"The woman caller had an accent," the man at the computer said.

Grayson looked at him. "I noticed. Spanish, maybe. Lot of that around here."

"What's new with the Labs?" the man at the tape recorder asked.

"Nothing. All we have is some possible evidence from Thompson studio. Doesn't make sense. Nothing more right now. You guys keep up the good work and let me know if anything breaks."

The two men glanced at each other, nodded in concert, then at Grayson, before they re-fit their headsets.

Grayson sat at his desk, Lucero across from him. His coat was off and his tie loosened. The small, spartan office was lined with framed certificates and photographs of smiling men shaking hands or displaying weapons.

"So what did you find out at the Vaslovic place? Anything?"

Lucero re-adjusted his big frame. "APD was cooperative. We know why the break-in was silent. The guy was a pro. He drilled a hole in the French door frame and buried a stick magnet next to the magnetic door switch. The switch is part of the alarm system. That kept the alarm from going off. Also found a wall safe. If it had been opened, we couldn't tell. A guy that professional? He may have gotten inside without leaving a sign."

"Anything in the safe?"

"Nothing. I mean, beyond your normal stuff. A little cash, insurance policies. You know." He shrugged and raised his eyebrows.

"And Mrs. Vaslovic verified that the contents were intact?"

Lucero nodded emphatically. "Yep." He compressed his lips.

Grayson swivelled away in his chair to look out through his fifth-story window. "Was a camera ever found?"

"Yeah. One of those little one-shot deals."

Grayson swivelled back. "No thirty-five or nine millimeter? Digital?"

Lucero shook his head slowly.

"Shit." Grayson stared at the other agent, then looked away. He tapped his left palm with his right fist in rhythm to his thoughts. "If Thompson was responsible for the theft of classified documents from his own organization, then he must have had an accomplice. If it was Vaslovic, why was he killed? And if it was Thompson, why would he be stupid enough to leave evidence around implicating himself? It doesn't add up."

"And where is he?"

"The odd thing is he was informed of the breach in the morning, goes to lunch and comes back for the rest of the day as though nothing has happened. Comes to work the next day, then disappears after calling his wife and telling her he'd be home."

"Did we record that call?"

"Nope. Too early. We weren't set up." Grayson, quiet while he collected his thoughts, slapped his left palm with his right fist, then continued. "Then his truck is found out there in Corrales. People at the restaurant don't remember much, except that he met with a man. Nothing after he left."

"He left alone?"

"According to the girl on the cash register, he walked out fifteen minutes or so after the other guy left."

"Doesn't prove anything. Did they remember the other man?"

"All we got out of them was that he wore a dark jacket. No one noticed a car."

"Do we sit this one out?"

"No way. That data has been passed or is about to be passed. The director is under the gun from the White House, Congress and the press to shore up the technology drain."

"Right." Lucero squirmed.

"At first I wouldn't have given you a plug nickel for suspecting Thompson, but now—" Grayson pulled at his nose and studied the desktop. "Lucero, what do you have?"

"'Kay." Lucero nodded and hauled a one-inch-thick manila file up onto the desk and opened it. "This was put together by P.R. Branch. A quickie. Okay. Thompson and Vaslovic—the men—go way back. You knew that. They both went to Penn State, then their separate ways for awhile. Before they finished graduate school, Vaslovic had a flirtation with the left. Socialist Youth League, later on the Attorney General's list as a Communist front outfit. He got Thompson involved." Lucero stopped to look up briefly at the attentive Grayson, who failed to react.

"According to both clearance forms, they became disenchanted and disavowed any further association. Periodic five-year brush-ups have turned up nothing to implicate them in anything anti-American or pro-Communist or otherwise subversive. I seem to remember a place in Thompson's file where he remarked that he had made a youthful indiscretion.

"Vaslovic was first-generation. Folks from Eastern Europe. His mother died of breast cancer when he was in high school. References say he was a good kid and a hard worker, but had some bitterness about treatment his parents received. Claimed his mother would have lived if they had had money. Apparently was embarrassed about his parents. Their problems with English. The old man was a janitor. Attended Penn State with Thompson. Both with advanced degrees in physics. Vaslovic had a financial struggle; had to work during those years, but his personal history shows his dad helped the best he could.

"Thompson has a file that reads like an Andy Hardy movie. His dad died in some sort of laboratory explosion. Chemist. The mother raised Thompson and helped him through school with the death bennies. They were pretty close to the Vaslovics from the time they were in grammar school. Became kind of a surrogate family after Mrs. Vaslovic—the mother—died. Thompson has had a pretty strong influence over Vaslovic down through the years. Helped him get almost every job he ever held."

"Including the one at the Labs?" Grayson asked.

"Yes. Brought in from G.E. Uh, Vaslovic was Catholic; Thompson is Episcopalian. Both have voted Republican since Eisenhower."

Grayson got up, stretched and looked out the window. "Sound pretty damned normal, don't they?" He turned around. "This is crazy." He tapped the surface of his desk with his finger. "If one of them decided to cop classified data—or had been doing it for years—then why? Ideology? Money? Revenge? Blackmail?"

Lucero looked up at Grayson as he stood behind his chair and shook his head. "As you might expect, this Socialist League had so-called friendship ties with the Soviets. Loose, but—"

"Naturally." Grayson returned to his seat. "What about the women?"

Lucero sat and flipped pages. "Betty Anderson Vaslovic. Born in Minnesota. Third in a family of five. Dad was a failed farmer who had to move to the city. Routine. Secretary at one of the places where Vaslovic interned during graduate school. Weren't married right away. Vaslovic came back for her after several years." He looked up and spread his hands in a gesture of futility.

Grayson nodded.

"Sarah Louise Boyden Thompson. Born in Massachusetts, although the original birth records were lost and she had to petition for substitutes. Family well-to-do. Thread, yarn and cloth manufacturing. Entire family—except for Sarah—two sisters, the mother and father—killed in a boating accident off the Maine coast. Business taken over by partners and Sarah became a ward of the bank. Chemical Trust, New York. Attended Wellesley; degree in fine arts. Met Jason Thompson during his post-graduate days at Penn State."

"What circumstances? After Thompson was messing with the lefties or before?"

Lucero read from the report, then said, "Not entirely clear, but looks like right about that time. No reports of her involvement."

"Strange. Thompson comes from the old middle class, attends Communist-leaning meetings, then meets and marries a woman from the upper classes. She had money, right?"

"Yeah. Plenty of it. She supported them until he could earn enough to support them."

"Hm. Of course, there have been examples of rich liberals. But most of them never actually get actively involved. How soon after they met did Thompson stop with the meetings?"

Lucero went back to his file. "Started right about the time they met, attended on and off for about a year then dropped out. Graduated the following Spring, got his first job that Fall. They were married shortly after that."

"Her politics?"

"Strictly conservative. If she was liberal in the early days, she dropped it. She was even a national Republican delegate during one presidential campaign. The only thing we can't trace with her is an occasional trip to Canada. Seeing a relative."

Grayson shook his head and changed his position in his chair, then wiped his face roughly with both his hands. "This doesn't fit standard profile for spies." He was silent while Lucero closed the file and removed it from the desk. "When were they first cleared?"

Lucero opened the file on his lap, flipped through several pages and pointed at a place on one of them. "Uh, okay; Thompson was first with a Secret about three years after graduate school. Vaslovic one year after that when he joined him at Blakely Research."

"I know it's too goddamn late, but I think we should have these people cleared all over again."

"Re-cleared? Are you serious?"

"We have to do something. We're going to be crucified if we don't. At least this way we're doing something. Fill out a request for a complete investigation. I'll sign it and get the old man to go along with it."

"From when?"

"The beginning." Grayson swept his arms out wide.

Lucero sucked in a mouthful of air, blew it out forcefully, picked up the file and started for the door.

"Listen; one other thing." Grayson frowned as he stared at the floor.

"Yeah?"

Grayson scratched his head. "Check into this watercolor club that Sarah Thompson belongs to." He looked up. "Okay?"

Lucero nodded, turned and left.

Vera gave Jason a towel to wear, took his clothes and threw them into the old, high-ringer Maytag that stood just outside the kitchen door under a protective lean-to.

At first, he felt silly and awkward, but then relaxed as he sat in a living room chair with the towel around his lower extremities, reading a book from Vera's small library, while he waited for his clothes to dry.

He fell asleep but was awakened when Vera came in through the squeaky screen door with his clothes off the line. They had dried quickly in the high, dry air. Refreshed, he went outside and strolled around the grounds, looking at the colt in its stall, the outbuildings and Vera's efficient little kitchen garden. The smell of the raw earth, sage, *piñon* and animal ordure made him relax to an extent he had not felt in years. He grabbed a hoe and took after some weeds in the garden while Vera tended the colt.

Vera fixed beef steak and potatoes for dinner, along with home-grown vegetables and her fresh bread. She spirited some bottled beer from the rear of the refrigerator to round out the meal. After dinner, they sat on the porch on two old straight-back chairs and looked at the stars above the dim, dark line of the mesa to the west.

Perhaps it was the dark of night, he thought, but Vera began to talk about herself at his gentle prodding. The words came slowly and calmly, as though she were relating a story about someone else.

"I was born in Waco, Texas. My folks were poor. My daddy was killed in a truck accident, and my ma got sick. She didn't have any money, so they put her in a state hospital, and I was made ward of the state. She died a few months later. I lived with a foster family for awhile, then was adopted by some others when I was five."

She paused, stared at nothing, then continued. "My foster father molested me from almost the first day until I was thirteen, so I ran away. Ended up in Hobbs. Oil fields." She chuckled. "Mexican woman took me in. Had a steam laundry. Gave me a job, food, place to stay. Place burned down when I was seventeen. I hitched a ride to Millard."

Vera slapped at a bug on her arm. "Les—my husband's father—saw me wandering along the sidewalk. You could see my socks through the soles of my shoes, and I was real hungry." She laughed lightly. "He asked me if I could cook for him and some ranch hands. I lied. Said I could. He brought me here."

"Weren't you frightened? I mean, after what happened to you earlier?" Jason peered at her outline in the dark.

"By that time, I was so hungry and tired, I didn't care. I'd determined that, if anyone so much as touched me, I'd kill 'em." She chuckled. Vera spoke with a calm that shocked, yet fascinated, him.

"I'm sorry," he said, his voice close to a whisper.

"Why? Turned out good. He was a good man. He let me learn how to cook without a whimper. I cooked some real bad meals at first. Gradually, though, I got better at it. Besides, that woman in Hobbs—Flora—showed me some good Mexican recipes I remembered. So we traded. They taught me about beef and potatoes; I taught them about good Mexican."

There was a spate of silence while both he and Vera thought about what had been said, then she continued. "Les taught me to read. He loved books. That's the greatest thing he did. He taught me to read. And he bought me more books. I know I sound pretty "hickey" to you, but I've learned a few things."

"I didn't—"

Vera continued to look into the distance. "Then his son came back. He was so handsome. I didn't realize it, but I'd fallen in love with the old man. But I went crazy for his son. He liked me, too."

She fell silent, looked at him for a moment, then looked away in the gathering gloom.

"And you married him."

Her silence continued another five seconds, she faced forward, then, "That I did. I took care 'o Les when he come feeble. I took care of my husband when he got sick. Now I have the ranch to myself."

Jason sensed that Vera couldn't bring herself to mention her dead husband's name. "No children?"

"No. He couldn't."

"And you got the ranch?"

"I was his wife. Sheriff and lawyers told me it was mine. I got the deed." She sighed. After a few more seconds of silence, she asked, "What about your wife?"

Jason fidgeted and took a deep breath. "Sarah. We've been married a long time." He hesitated. "Three children. Grown and married. Four grandchildren. She's an artist. Not good enough to sell for big money, but okay."

Vera listened for more. "You're troubled about it." She paused. "None of my affair. Didn't mean to pry."

"It's okay. I don't mind. It's just been difficult the past few days."

"Don't think it's gonna rain tomorrow."

He looked at her in the dark. "Was it supposed to?"

"I follow the Farmer's Almanac. Says it's supposed to. Don't believe it. Sky's wrong." She didn't return his look as she continued to face straight ahead.

They spent the rest of the time before bed sitting in the dark, watching the stars as they wheeled past, disappearing one by one behind the mesa ridge to the west.

15

*D*espite Jason's confession, they made the trip the following morning to Millard, in the opposite direction from the filling station and farther away, another thirteen miles. Vera told him she had to buy some groceries, anyway, plus some tack and sacked oats for the horses. He was nervous, not absolutely convinced Vera wouldn't go to the sheriff.

She parked the Ford pickup at an angle along the wide street with its high concrete sidewalks and old horse rings, directly in front of the post office. She invited him to go with her, but he declined, saying he felt uncomfortable; that she might run into somebody she knew and have to explain him away. She said "okay," got out and walked down the same side of the street toward a row of old buildings with porches that extended out over the sidewalk. She disappeared into one of them.

He sat in the truck for three minutes watching the main street of the little town, too nervous to get out. He finally left the truck after deciding to go to the post office. He studied the collection of FBI wanted posters, knowing full well it would be too early for one with his blurry photograph. Again on the sidewalk, he looked up and down the quiet street.

Directly across the boulevard he saw a building with an indented front of plate glass. It was the sign above which caught his attention. It advertised insurance, notary service and a travel agency. He stared at it for a few seconds, then checked in the direction Vera had gone, before he stepped into the nearly empty street.

He tried the door, then peered through the dirty picture-window at the dark, empty office. He instinctively looked at the place on his wrist where his watch would be, then realized it was Sunday. He turned and walked back across the street to the public telephone outside the post office.

He flipped through the worn pages of the thin, tattered directory that hung from the coin table, then found what he wanted. He picked up the receiver and dialed an 800 number.

"Yes. For flights from Washington to Albuquerque. Arrival times." He waited, then said, "No, Washington, D.C. That's right." He waited again and listened. "How about other airlines? Can you help me? You're sure those are the only times? Okay, thanks." He hung up and stared at the instrument, deep in thought. Then he walked away.

Five minutes after Jason got back to the truck, Vera returned. She carried two grocery sacks and a large brown bag which she threw onto the seat. "For you." She started the engine.

He looked inside the sack and saw two solid-color, long sleeved shirts and a package of underwear shorts.

"You can pay me back later. There's a couple 'a pair of Levi's my husband wore at the house. They're clean. I think they'd fit you." She looked at him, gauged his torso, then away.

"Vera, you didn't have to do this, but I really appreciate it."

"Can't go around in the same clothes all the time." She backed up, drove forward half a block, then made a sharp left turn into an alley leading to the side door of a feed store.

A teenaged boy waited with several heavy dun-colored sacks and an open cardboard box, all of which he wrestled onto the bed of the pickup.

Once they were on the highway out of town, Jason spoke. "Those places were open on Sunday."

"Small town, but it serves a wide area. They've got the business. Used to be they didn't."

"Were you tempted to turn me in?"

"No, but sooner or later that plane's gonna be spotted, and they're gonna ask questions."

"What will you say?"

"Don't know. Maybe I didn't hear it, or I couldn't go up there. I don't know."

"Think anybody saw me with you?"

Vera shook her head. "If they did, you could be a ranch hand. That's common here."

"I'll be gone soon."

As the Ford rounded the last dusty bend into the wide, flat area that constituted the ranch headquarters, Jason scanned the long, straight lines of the mesas at the base of the piedmont to the east and the plateau to the west. The sky was a severe blue, with only a few distant clouds to the north. To his left, he noticed a black dot that seemed to grow out of the sky. It became a high-winged, single-engine airplane which lowered in altitude, ran along the ridge of the mesa, circled and flew by again.

Jason craned his head around to follow the flight path of the plane. "Jesus Christ! I should have known!"

"Who you think it is?" Vera shot him a concerned look, then ducked her head, trying to see the circling plane in her outside rearview mirror.

"One of three things: a passing pilot has spotted the wreckage, it's someone official, or it's the people who took me!"

Vera maintained her normal speed, pulled into the yard, then into the garage alongside the barn. She shut the engine down in the cool shade of the outbuilding, then opened her door. "Stay put until I come get you. He can't stay up there forever."

Jason's face and eyes showed strain. "Is there any place for him to land?"

"Like I told you, not near here. He's a long way to go for that. If he tried to land on my road he'd more'n likely run into something. Clip his wings." She shut the door and spoke through the open window. "Stay put."

Vera left the garage, with the grocery sacks and walked calmly to the house. Jason ran to the front of the small building and peered through a crack. He saw Vera take only a passing interest in the aircraft, then disappear into the house through the kitchen door. In a few minutes, the sound of the plane faded and was gone. Vera came back for him, and he met her half-way across the yard. She carried the brown bag with his new clothes.

"Looks like he's gone," she said. She squinted at the southern horizon.

Jason shook his head as his gaze followed hers. "I don't like this. Listen, is there a way I could get up there? The one thing I did have is still up there.

There's a jacket with my wallet in it. I could pay you back."

Vera turned to study the high escarpment. "We can take the horses. There's a trail along the top, but I don't know how close to the ridge. Trail starts over there." She pointed.

Jason rubbed his left arm and stared blankly as his head throbbed dully for the first time since the crash.

Vera turned back. "Feelin' woozy? Better rest."

"It's time for my pill, anyway." He patted his shirt pocket with the little white envelope. "I'll be okay. We can go."

He took a pill with water. Vera brought out a pair of the promised Levi's and an old, but serviceable, straw hat, and they saddled two horses.

He had little reason to believe he would ever ride a horse again, but found he enjoyed it, even though it made him feel vulnerable, as though he would lose control and fall. They rode across the narrow valley floor to the base of the mesa. He worried as they approached the red and dun rock that rose abruptly, unsure there was a way, but Vera's horse went unerringly to a narrow trail that was suddenly clear to him, and his horse followed dutifully. It took more than half an hour to thread their way to the top. Jason avoided looking down as they wound back and forth at steep angles among sagebrush, small *amole* plants, prickly pear and *piñon*.

When they reached the top, they stopped. Jason turned in his saddle, thrilled at the wide vista. The ranch house and outbuildings below looked puny against the backdrop of the marching mesas, the sweeping plains, the rolling piedmont and the blue-black mountains, with the desert to the south. He had mistaken the outcropping of light rock for a road that stretched away toward the south, parallel to the mesa ridge bordered by stands of evergreens. As he looked down the steep side of the mesa, he found it difficult to understand how he had made it down by himself. Vera started off again, and his horse followed without his command.

The going was rough and slow, so the horses were deliberate in their approach to the rocky terrain. Soon tree branches slapped at them, and he ducked with his hand out protectively.

"There it is." Vera, ten yards in front of him, pointed at the wreckage.

He came up to her, dismounted and looked around. "I can't believe I wasn't killed."

"I brought this along for a safety." She held out a length of yellow nylon rope.

They looped the horses' reins to a gnarled, half-dead *piñon*, made their way to the edge, and stopped. The left wing of the Cherokee was bent near the fuselage, so that it stuck up and away from the rocky ground. The tail section was intact, but there was a severe wrinkle in the fuselage halfway to the main wing. The body slanted down and hung precariously over the mesa edge. The right wing, only nicked and scratched by tree branches, was in better shape than the left, but had a small hole in one part of the riveted aluminum, and three feet of the tip was torn away.

Jason tied one end of the rope around his middle, took off his hat, and, with the other end of the rope around a tree trunk and Vera holding it tight, lowered himself to the wing and the cabin. As he put one foot on the wing root, the plane groaned and moved a couple of inches. The small tree which held it in check waved its branches. He backed off, looked up at Vera, then approached it again. He steadied himself on the wing and leaned through the broken pilot's window into the cabin.

He leaned farther and managed to reach his jacket on the rear seat. The smells of the plane's interior washed over him. He recalled the odd, mechanical smell of all airplanes; hot plastics, high-grade oils, aluminum. He smelled something else, too. It was gasoline.

Vera took up the slack as he backed out of the cabin. His shirt caught on the broken window plastic, and he suddenly felt trapped. He held his jacket in one hand and pushed on the side of the fuselage with his hands, then on the wing root with his right foot. The aluminum of the plane cried out with a metallic screech, and the plane lurched downward, snapping branches as it moved. He shouted instinctively and Vera pulled hard on the rope. He lost his purchase on the plane, and it dropped onto the rocks below. The Cherokee came to rest again when the right side slipped from the grip of one small ponderosa, hit the trunk of another, and caused its branches to whip wildly.

After he caught his breath and scrambled to the top, he sat and stared into the distance. He panted, more from fright than from exhaustion. Vera coiled the rope and came over to him. She quatted down next to him and rubbed his shoulder.

Her hand was warm and firm, and he realized in that moment that Vera wore no perfume. What he smelled when he was so close was her clean, natural self, something with which few women were comfortable. He looked at her face closely, then averted his eyes toward the distant Gila, as he allowed a set of conflicting feelings to play themselves out.

16

*J*ason and Vera rode down the steep trail more slowly than they had gone up. Jason looked down nnervously at his horse's hooves until they were almost on flat terrain.

Grateful to be back on flatter ground, he helped Vera put the horses away with a new verve. When Vera went inside to fix a green chile beef stew, he remained in the horse barn to scatter hay in the stalls and collect his thoughts.

He found himself being more formal with Vera, partly, he reasoned, because of the nervousness he felt over seeing the plane, and partly because of his attraction to her. He strained to hear every sound, and wished there were a television set. The ranch was too far away for either broadcast or cable, and he assumed she couldn't afford either or satellite. Vera's ancient radio, was inoperable. She went to bed early that night, but Jason stayed out on the dark porch where he watched and listened, alert, fearing the worst.

After breakfast next morning, he and Vera sat drinking coffee.

"What happened to the rifle?" He asked.

She paused, looking at him openly. "Keep it in the bedroom. Want to go hunting?"

He smiled down at his cup. "No."

He spent the morning helping with chores. He watched the road in and scanned the sky. Vera went about her business, but kept a concerned eye on him. After lunch, Jason, tired from a sleepless night, took a nap. Vera went outside.

He fell asleep within a few minutes, and later dreamed about an uncontrollable, cold truck he was driving. Suddenly colors flashed across his vision and his eyes popped open.

"You're a tough one to hold onto, Mr. Thompson." Antonio Cuzco stood over him. He grinned and prodded Jason's shoulder with his Beretta. His mouth was close to Jason's ear, and Jason felt his hot breath. Cuzco's voice was low and controlled.

Jason lay on his back, and when he tried to rise, lost his balance and fell on his side. He gasped for air, and covered both eyes with his hand. When he removed it, he stared, wide-eyed, at Cuzco. "How—how did you get in here?!"

"Through the front door." Cuzco gestured insolently with his Beretta.

Jason, his face ashen, stared wildly at the man. "But—!"

"Did you think I would just drive up here and knock on the door? I don't think so." Cuzco pulled the semiautomatic away, walked to the window and looked out. "No, I stopped the car around the bend, out of sight. Then I came along the bottom of that mesa there, behind those buildings." He pointed through the glass with a proud smile. "I came to the house. There was nobody here. Except you." He turned and looked at Jason with a sardonic grin and waved the pistol.

Jason gathered himself together and sat on the edge of the bed. He felt dizzy and his head began to pound along with his heart. "Why are you here?! Why don't you leave me alone?!" He put both hands over his face and shook his head.

"Why am I here? Why don't I leave you alone?" With Cuzco's mocking words, his smile decayed into something which betrayed anger and cruelty. "Mr. Thompson, there are those who worry about you. I worry about you. You gave me a lump and a bad headache. You wrecked a good airplane. You're lucky you weren't hurt." He stopped, moved toward the door, then wheeled. "Mr. Thompson, you are not safe. Even here. I found you. Others could find you." Cuzco's voice became almost saccharin.

Jason dropped his hands from his face, looked up at Cuzco again, then covered his face again. "What are you going to do?" He spoke through his splayed fingers.

Cuzco peered through the open door into the next room. "We are going to leave. Get your shoes on. Let's go." He gestured with the pistol.

Jason put on his jacket and walked in front of Cuzco, who stopped him just before he got to the outside door to the porch.

"Wait. Where are they?"

Jason turned, anxious about the pistol. "Who?"

"The people who live here." Cuzco showed annoyance, which Jason recognized as a component of the man's fear.

"I don't know. Gone." He looked through the screen into the sunny yard, hoping not to see Vera.

"You're lying." Cuzco turned and looked back, left and right. "Listen, you stay close to me. If we see them, you tell them I'm a friend who came to get you. Understand?"

"Yes; okay." Jason shook, and tried to control it.

Cuzco moved close to Jason. He held the muzzle of the pistol against his back. They were halfway to the grazing fence when they heard the sound of a rifle being cocked behind them.

"Hold it there, mister." Vera stood on the porch, her Marlin leveled at Cuzco.

Cuzco spun around, as did Jason, only slower. Vera saw the gun in Cuzco's hand. She raised the rifle to her shoulder and took aim at Cuzco's chest.

"Hey, lady, what's the matter?! This is my friend!" Cuzco shouted, as he held both hands, the Beretta in his right, out high and wide. He tried to smile.

"Then why the pistol?! Get away from him and drop it!" Vera insisted.

In a sudden move, Cuzco took cover behind Jason and jammed the Beretta into his back again. "Try to shoot me, lady, you'll hit him! Fire at me, I'll kill him!" He grabbed Jason's right arm near the small of his back and side-stepped him along the edge of the pasture fence.

Confused, Vera dropped the rifle's muzzle six inches, and her eyes darted between the two men in front of her.

"Vera! I don't want you hurt! Take it easy! It's okay!" Jason's voice was raspy and quavering. His head hurt.

Cuzco crabbed Jason along the fence line toward the base of the mesa where the plane teetered at its top. He walked backward as he watched Vera with feral eyes while she kept the rifle aimed roughly in their direction. As they got closer to the boundary of untamed sage that rose away from the flat earth of the ranch proper, Cuzco pushed his captive faster, and the two of them staggered between the rugged, fragrant plants over increasingly rough, rocky soil. Jason stumbled and swivelled to look back at Vera who was at the edge of the porch with the Marlin lowered. He was forced forward again as Cuzco pushed at his ribs with his semiautomatic.

"Why are we going this way?!" Jason asked. His voice trembled. "Your car's the other direction!"

"Shut up! I want the log from the plane." Cuzco's voice came in excited bursts.

"Why?! What the hell?! This is the wrong way! There's a trail—!" Jason's eyes blazed with panic, and his head pounded more heavily.

Vera, with the long weapon held in both her hands and pointed roughly ahead of her, stepped off the porch to follow. "Stop!" She shouted. "Where are you going?!" Her heart raced, and her face was peppered with perspiration. She swiped at her hatless head to control wisps of errant hair that had pulled loose from the sweep back to her braids.

"Stay back, lady! Stay out of this and you won't get hurt!" Cuzco faced Jason and pulled him along while looking over his shoulder at Vera below.

From Vera's point of view, Jason and the interloper were almost lost in the jumble of pastel rocks, beige dirt and grey-green flora as they climbed the side of the mesa, zig-zagging back and forth against the steep incline, nowhere near the trail.

Vera caught motion out of the corner of her eye. To her left, she saw a light-colored sedan coming up the road, with a swirl of dust climbing behind it. She looked up the side of the mesa again, but lost sight of the two men. She spotted them again, then turned to watch the approaching car. She pointed the Marlin at the car as it approached, close to the porch. She confirmed her hunch that a man was at the wheel. Vera stepped off the porch and walked around to the driver's side. She pointed the rifle at the man's face. "Who are you?!"

"Hey! What's going on?! Lower the rifle, okay?!"

"What do you want?!" Vera kept the muzzle of the Marlin pointed at his head.

"FBI, Lady! You the owner here? Why are you pointing that thing at me?!"

Vera backed up, looked at the car, then pointed the gun with increased resolve. "Don't look like FBI. And why would the FBI be here?!" She snarled.

The man opened his door a crack. "Listen, you're—"

"Hold it!" Vera shouted. She glanced toward the mesa, then back again.

The man, halfway out of the car, followed her look. "What's going on?!"

"Mister, you better tell me who you are and say why you're here, or by God, I'll shoot you! I'm personal friends with the sheriff here, and he won't have any sympathy for your side of the story!"

"Okay! Take it easy! My name is Nantes. I'm here for Jason Thompson. Is that him?" He pointed toward the mesa.

Vera peered at Nantes fiercely, swung her head to look at the mesa again, then back. She relaxed her grip on the Marlin slightly. "Who—? How did you know he was here?!"

Nantes got out, closed the door and stood against the car with his arms high, palms out. First he pointed to his chest with his right index finger, then reached inside his windbreaker jacket and produced a small leather-bound identification folder. She looked at it, he snapped it closed and put it back in his pocket. "Thompson called for me. Indicated he was in trouble. Looks like he is. Who's with him?"

"I don't know, but he's got a gun. He's trying to take him away." Vera's look of suspicion had not completely died away, but she let the Marlin's muzzle point at the ground.

"Look, I need to go after them, and all I've got is this pistol." He opened his coat to reveal a shoulder holster with a nine millimeter semiautomatic. "I need your rifle."

"You think I'm gonna hand over this gun to you, mister?" Vera raised the rifle again.

Nantes held his palms out at face level. "Look, lady, I'll trade you. Reach inside and get my gun. Hold it on me if you want, but those two up there are getting harder to see, and I've got to go after them. Please!"

Vera looked toward the mesa again, unable to fix her eyes on the distant figures moving between the rocks. She looked hard at Nantes. "How do I know you're not with the other fellow?"

Nantes drew in a breath and let it out slowly. His thoughts swirled as he looked at the hardpan beneath his feet. He looked up. "Look, if I were with him—whoever he is—I would attack you and signal him that it's safe. I'm here to help Thompson. How did he get here, anyway?"

Vera indicated the mesa with a move of her head. "Plane up there. Crashed it. Couple 'a nights ago."

Nantes looked up at the mesa. "Up there? A plane?"

"Yes."

"Alone?"

She nodded.

"How the—?! Listen, lady, I don't know what's happened, but I do know I've got to go after him! Please!"

"Shit!" She transferred the rifle to her left hand and reached out to remove the weapon from under Nantes' armpit as he held his arms high, his eyes fixed on the mesa slope. With the heavy pistol in her possession, he lowered his hands and she handed him the .30-.30 long gun.

"How much ammunition?" He leaned the rifle against the side of the car, removed his coat and threw it through the open car window.

"Full. One in the chamber and four in the magazine." She took in a deep breath, then released it.

Nantes looked down at the lever-action rifle in his hands with a wince at the news of the number of rounds. He then took off at a lope without another word, while Vera stood near the car, Nantes's pistol drooping from her hand.

As though in a trance, Vera did not watch where she was going, but moved slowly toward the house. She saw Nantes run through the sage at the base of the mesa, then slow as he struggled against the ever steeper incline. Finally able to identify Jason and the other man above Nantes, she watched them move slowly as they neared the sheer cliff at the top. The aluminum of the airplane glinted in the sunlight above them and to their left. Motivated, she took off at a run for the house and returned shortly with an old pair of binoculars.

Nantes puffed madly as he struggled against the sudden hard work at high altitude. He stopped every twenty feet to catch his breath and peer up the slope with one hand on one knee and the other gripping the Marlin, butt-down on the ground as though it were a crutch. For Vera, Jason and Cuzco were no more than shifting patches of color. Just above them was a band of rose-colored sandstone. Nantes braced himself and tried to relax. He took several deep breaths, raised the rifle and fired a shot at the band of stone above their heads.

Vera had the glasses trained on the area where Jason and Cuzco were fighting scraggly juniper amid boulders of volcanic tufa and sandstone. A puff of what looked like smoke appeared above their heads, then she heard the crack and thundering echo of the .30-.30 report as it bounced off the mesa wall and across the narrow valley. She moved the glasses down and around to find Nantes with the rifle still at his shoulder. She re-focused on Jason and Cuzco, in time to see both men stop and turn to look down the slope at the new threat. Vera heard another report, and saw a puff of dust near Nantes, who ducked. Cuzco had fired back. She tried to focus on Cuzco but couldn't and looked for Nantes again. She spotted him and watched as he moved up the steep slope.

Vera saw Nantes close on the kidnapper and Jason, who she assumed probably suffered. Nantes moved fast, and was more than halfway up the slope, since he decided to attack the mesa straight on, despite the difficult terrain. She saw Cuzco and Jason look down periodically as they moved closer to the plane. Vera watched Jason fall and roll away a few feet as Nantes fired at their pursuer again. She saw a puff of rock dust as the shot hit very near the stricken plane's left wing which hung down over the side of the rocky mesa. An instant later, the small ponderosa which held the Piper in check gave way at the same time the sound of the shot reached her ears.

She lowered the binoculars and watched the Cherokee heave over and tumble toward the ledge where she last saw Jason and the man with the pistol. Then an orange ball of flame and a cloud of dense, black smoke grew out of the plane near the wing root.

Vera looked first without the glasses, then with them, searching for Nantes, the man who claimed to be an FBI agent. She saw him bring the rifle down and watch as the plane was engulfed in fire. Then Nantes rallied, and half-ran, half-stumbled, toward the inferno. Vera, who still clutched the binoculars, dropped the pistol onto the porch floor and ran toward the base of the mesa.

Nantes felt the heat from the ball of flame that bloomed from the side of the mesa above him. For several seconds, he stopped, confused. Then he pushed on, and tried desperately to run, but was frustrated by his shortness of breath, as well as by the small rocks and loose soil which acted more like ball bearings under his feet than solid ground. He couldn't make out which of the figures ahead, silhouetted against the bright orange light, was Jason.

Nantes changed to a zig-zag route up the slope, his breath coming in gasps against his quick expenditure of energy. The rifle dangled from his right hand as he pulled himself along, and used his left to grab rocks and bushes for leverage. He looked up and made out one of the figures who fought to move away from the inferno. He moved closer.

Vera watched through the glasses as Nantes struggled with somebody among the rocks. Because of the smoke, long minutes passed before she saw clearly. She watched as Nantes finally worked his way down the talus slope, to where he appeared out of the pall created by the fire. She saw him cradle one of the apparently unconscious men under his arms as the man dragged his feet along behind. The Marlin was caught awkwardly under one of Nantes's arms. It was slow going as the man, who claimed to be an FBI agent, struggled down the steep incline. She couldn't tell whether the limp form was alive or dead. Nantes stopped every few feet, then placed the man carefully in the shade of a small juniper tree. Vera watched as she saw him stand and wipe his brow, then turn again to the task of picking his way down the treacherous slope, alone. Toward the bottom, where the land began to level out, Nantes ran before stumbling, then righting himself. Vera ran to meet him as he made his way past the last of the sage.

"God! What happened!" She demanded.

Nantes, his brow furrowed, shook his head. His words came in bursts between gulps of air. "Sorry. The plane—must have—had a lot of—fuel—aboard. That last—shot—knocked it loose—from its perch. I guess—a spark—set it on fire." His pants were torn near the left front pocket, and his shirt, as well as his face and hands, were blackened and dirty. He leaned over, resting the bulk of his weight on one knee. He used the Marlin to steady himself.

"But—but where are they?!"

"I think one of 'em's dead. The other needs a doctor." Nantes made a jerky, negative movement with his head. His eyes were sad, then he closed them in pain.

Vera's hand flew to her mouth. "Which one? Which one?!"

"Sorry. I think it's Thompson." Nantes looked up, then lowered his head.

Vera turned away and stared up the slope at the area of blackened rock and twisted, melted aluminum, then walked slowly back toward the house.

Nantes followed. He stooped to pick up his pistol which lay on the porch, and returned it to his shoulder holster. "Ma'am, I'm sorry, but I need your help."

Vera's shoulders sagged. She sat down on the edge of the porch floor and buried her head in her hands. She raised her reddened, tearing eyes to Nantes. "What?"

Nantes handed her the Marlin. "You don't have a phone, do you? I don't see a line."

"No."

"You have to go for help. I've got to get back up there with some water. I need someone to help set a splint and get that guy down here."

Vera stared at him. "I'll go." Her voice was dead.

"Soon. Please."

Vera disappeared inside the house and returned with a Mason jar full of water. "First aid things are in the kitchen cupboard. Left of the sink. Be back soon as I can."

Nantes nodded, took the water, then walked back toward the mesa and struggled up the slope as she went to the garage, got into the pickup and drove away.

When Vera returned, followed by two men in a white pickup truck fitted with a special ambulance body, Nantes's car was gone. Puzzled and anxious, she stopped in front of the porch, got out to look for the FBI agent's car, what she soon realized was a futile gesture. She then climbed part way up the side of the mesa where the fire still smouldered. She saw nothing but the burn damage and the barely discernable skeletal remains of the Cherokee.

The EMT driver parked his vehicle behind Vera's truck and emerged along with his partner. They walked over to her, studied her face, then looked up the side of the mesa. She ignored them. She turned and went to the front door. There, she pulled a piece of paper from behind the screen door cross bar. It read,

ABLE TO GET MAN DOWN. TAKING HIM TO DOC. BACK ASAP
FOR THOMPSON. PLZ TOUCH NOTHING—FEDERAL MATTER
THNKS, V.N.

Vera, too upset to eat anything else, ate a bowl of soup and two saltines for supper and collapsed into bed soon after. She tossed and turned until close to 3:00 a.m., when she drifted into a dreamless sleep. Shortly after five, she entered a REM sleep, during which her subconscious mind conjured up a stew of disconnected, violent events, interrupted by noises from the outside.

She popped awake as a streak of light flashed across the wall of her bedroom opposite the south-facing window. She sat up with the realization that she had heard the sounds of cars or trucks. She leaped from bed and staggered to the window but saw nothing. She threw on her robe and raced for the front door. Three vehicles had passed the porch and pulled up near the base of the steep-sided mesa. Two were black sedans, the third a boxy ambulance-cum-rescue van. All three sported white, U.S. government license plates.

Even from that distance, she recognized the FBI man who called himself Nantes as he emerged from the passenger side of the lead car. She watched him bark orders to several other men, who were clad in either blue jackets or white jumpsuits, as he pointed up the side of the mesa.

17

*M*emorial services for Jason Thompson were held at one of the three largest churches in the city, the Episcopal Cathedral in downtown Albuquerque. The Cathedral was a beautiful building, built in the European Gothic tradition with a four-story ceiling and marble flooring.

Outside, it was midday and very warm; inside, it was cool and serene with muted sunlight streaming at a high angle through stained glass depictions of the saints to create patches of bright colors on the floor near the outer reaches of the rows of padded wood benches.

Sarah Thompson sat in the second row right, close to the center of the pew, her back straight, her head high. She wore a light blue suit with a simple matching hat and veil. Seated to her left was her daughter, Florence; to her right was her older son Charles, who resembled his father, and beside him was Justin Thompson, younger and closer to his mother in appearance.

Sarah was assailed by the strong odor of flowers that wafted from the altar to the rafters, as she stared at the immense pipe organ that rose to the rafters. Her mind drifted away to the bizarre thought that it was strange that the woman seated at the keyboard, sending somber notes to reverberate in the huge cavity, was barely visible.

Dressed in black, Betty Vaslovic sat on the other side of Florence, her face puffy and sallow, with red splotches on her cheeks and forehead. To Betty's left was a somewhat puggie Roy Vaslovic, her only child.

Flo and Charles held their mother's blue-gloved hands. Sarah's eyes, though dry, betrayed red above dark circles, and the lines on her face were deeply etched. She had applied some makeup in a half-hearted manner, and it showed.

Florence's face was marked with sadness and her mouth was fixed in a tepid, bitter-sweet smile. Her light and tasteful makeup efforts worked well despite her feelings. She, too, sat ramrod straight. Charles Thompson and his younger brother showed no outward signs of weeping, but both their faces were set in grief. Roy Vaslovic, whose face was soft like his mother's, his head and hair more like his father's, sat quietly with his hands in his lap.

Jason's secretary Angie, Dave Manning and Vicky Torres sat together two rows behind the Thompson family. A scattering of other people from the Labs sat in pews across the aisle and at least four rows back. More than a dozen people straggled in, some of whom nodded to Manning or others from the Labs, before being seated variously throughout the cavernous room.

Across the aisle from where the Thompsons and Vaslovics sat, in the row immediately back, was another woman, older and larger than Sarah, with her head down. She raised it ocassionally to look over at Sarah, and shook her head. No one knew the old woman in a poor coat and a nondescript hat, who sat at the rear, near the entrance. She sniffled occasionally and applied a dainty lavender handkerchief to her nose.

The Thompsons and Vaslovics avoided eye contact with anyone behind them or to the sides. They stared variously at the altar with its trappings and the shiny pipes of the organ, or at their hands.

The heavy, dark Gothic door that led to the street opened and Peter Grayson, dressed in a dark suit, entered. He stopped to remove a pair of dark glasses, looked around briefly, then selected a seat in the last row against the inner aisle.

The service was brief. Aside from the eulogy given by a priest in a white robe and purple sash, nothing was said on Jason Thompson's behalf. When the service ended, the priest came down in front of the pew where Sarah sat, took her hand and whispered his condolences. He then nodded at the others in the family pew and walked to the front of the church. The organ music waxed again, and the room echoed with the rustle of people taking their leave.

Florence craned her neck to look at the big front door and saw that the cathedral was virtually empty. She patted her mother's knee, smiled wanly at her, and gave her the signal to leave. The Thompson and Vaslovic families all stood slowly.

Sarah and her daughter led the procession of the two families out of the church. As they reached the outside door, Angie, who had been standing in the shadows behind a pillar near the front, stepped up to Sarah and hugged her tearfully, and nearly knocked the older woman off balance. She then turned away and walked into the brilliant sunlight without a word. Dave Manning spoke to Sarah and Florence and nodded to the two young Thompson men at the door. He went to shake their hands in turn, then he, too, departed. Vicky Torres smiled and whispered some comforting words to Sarah and her children. As she crossed herself, she spoke to Betty, then left as well. Betty, unable to bring herself to greet people, stood apart, holding onto her son Roy's hand.

Grayson stood on the concrete steps and leaned against the steel railing that edged them. His eyes were hidden by the aviator type dark glasses he had put on against the bright sunlight when he exited the church. He had waited for Sarah and her family to emerge as he watched the open door where the priest now stood.

Sarah smiled weakly, on and off, as the priest attempted to console her in brief conversation immediately outside the door. He held her hand and patted it several times as he spoke in a low tone. Her three children shook the priest's hand, and, as a group, waited to descend the steps onto the nearly vacant sidewalk behind their mother. Flo joined her mother.

Grayson watched Sarah as she came down the steps, her arm in her daughter's. He pushed away from the railing. "Mrs. Thompson," he said. He removed the dark glasses.

Sarah stopped and looked at him silently, her eyes distant.

Justin followed behind Flo. Charles, who was two inches taller than his brother, was a step behind. Both men looked at Grayson with surprise.

"Mrs. Thompson—Sarah—I wonder if I might have a word?"

"Good God, Grayson, have you no sense of decency?!" Flo growled. "What is this about?!" Her voice was full of menace.

Grayson looked hard at Florence D'Angelo. His voice conveyed conviction. "My sympathies, Mrs. D'Angelo, but government business." With his temper softened, he looked at Sarah. "I'm sorry it turned out this way."

Sarah searched the FBI man's face. "How kind of you, Mr. Grayson." Her words were tinged with sarcasm, a sense that did not escape those who heard her.

Charles came down two steps and circled his mother to confront Grayson. He spoke in a low, growling voice. "Who are you and why are you bothering my mother?!"

Justin Thompson watched his brother and the federal agent as he stood next to Florence.

Grayson, as he reached inside his jacket to retrieve his identification, fixed his eyes on Charles. "I'm Peter Grayson, Charles. Special agent, FBI, Albuquerque office." He flipped his ID wallet closed and returned it to his jacket pocket. "It's not my intention to harass or embarrass your mother or any of you, but we do have an on-going investigation, and I have a duty to perform. I'm sorry it has to be today and now, but I have little choice." He paused. "I'm sure your mother would prefer a few minutes here rather than her home."

Florence asked, "You're still investigating, Mr. Grayson?"

Grayson looked at Florence with steady eyes. "I also came out of respect. You may not believe that, but it's the truth. I met with your father twice. I liked and respected him—but the investigation is still open. It's unfortunate, but the facts of the case point to your father, however not conclusively. There are many unanswered questions. Believe me, I would be delighted to clear your father."

Betty moved close to Sarah, tapped her gloved hand and whispered, "Sarah, I'm going on to the car. I hope you don't mind."

Sarah looked at her intently and patted her arm. "No, dear, of course not. You go on. We'll be right there." She smiled and nodded at Roy, who moved off with his mother.

Sarah changed her demeanor as she returned her gaze to Grayson. "Anybody would think my husband had been tried and convicted. At least that's the way some of his former friends and associates see it." Her voice quavered for the first time as she looked up at Charles.

He took her hand.

Grayson inhaled deeply, looked at his shoes, scanned the front of the church and the parking area, then back at Sarah. "It looks as though your husband didn't lose all his support, Mrs. Thompson. Do you understand the need for haste in a case such this?"

"Of course. Why?"

"I need to ask you a couple of questions."

"This is outrageous!" With her voice under control, Florence cut in.

"What questions, Grayson?" Justin asked with anger in his voice. "What could my mother possibly know that would help you?" He held out both his hands in a question.

Sarah put her hand on Florence's arm and looked at her younger son. "It's alright. At least it's here and not in our living room." She looked up at Grayson. "What is it?"

Grayson put his hand on the black steel railing. "Sarah, why do you think your husband went to southern New Mexico? Why was he there?"

"I don't know, Mr. Grayson. I really have no idea." Sarah pursed her lips in overt annoyance.

"Did he have friends or associates there?"

"Why do you persist, Grayson?!" Charles, angry, cut in. "My mother just told you—she doesn't know, goddamnit!"

A pause ensued while Charles Thompson and Peter Grayson stared at each other.

"Jason had no friends or associates in southern New Mexico that I am aware of." Sarah closed her eyes and made an impatient hand gesture.

"And you have no contacts there?"

"Of course not." Sarah snapped her answer and stuck her chin out at the FBI man.

Grayson paused. "Sarah, how long have you been a member of the water-color club?"

Florence's mouth dropped open, and she looked from Grayson to her two brothers in turn, then back at Grayson. She shook her head in disbelief.

Sarah stared at Grayson for several seconds before answering. "More than ten years. What possible business of the FBI could that be?" Her voice was close to a whisper.

Grayson shifted his weight from one foot to the other. "Does the club have a regular management? I mean, is there someone there who maintains records and schedules trips, or is it ad hoc?"

Again Sarah hesitated before answering. "I have the feeling, Mr. Grayson, that you already know the answer to the question."

Charles turned and took a step away in frustration and anger.

Grayson shook his head. "We've looked into the club, but not deeply enough to know how it's organized. I thought you could help me out." He studied her eyes.

"What has this to do with the theft of government property or my husband, Mr. Grayson?" Deep annoyance shaded Sarah's question as her heart and respiration rate rose.

"Look, Sarah, in the course of our investigation, we have come across conversations between you and members of the club which, frankly, don't jibe with what other members have told us."

"God! You people!" Florence spat, her voice an angry whisper. "You have my mother's phone tapped!"

Grayson glanced at Florence, then returned his focus to Sarah, his eyes glaring. "Can you help me out?"

"How can I help you, Mr. Grayson, if I don't know what you're referring to?"

"Specifically, a conversation you had with a woman about a trip to Arizona."

"Oh, that." Sarah looked away briefly, then brought her eyes back to meet his.

"What can you tell me about it? No one we spoke to had any knowledge of such a planned trip."

"You were correct, Mr. Grayson, when you said something about ad hoc. The fact of the matter is, members often set about discussing possible trips but not saying anything to other members until they have been fully planned. In this particular case, I was concocting a surprise for the other members. I'm chair of the Arrangements Committee this year. It has not gone well."

Grayson took out his notebook. "I find it a bit odd, Sarah, your arranging a watercolor trip with your husband missing, and under a cloud of suspicion. What is the name of the lady helping you with the trip?"

Sarah released Florence's hand and moved slowly past her son Justin, across the steps to the opposite railing. She put her hand on the top rail, then turned to face the federal agent. "I am a person, Mr. Grayson, who has seen tragedy. From an early age. Part of the way I maintain my sanity is to keep on with my life. Part of the way—in my own, quirky way—I could bring Jason back was to pretend that nothing was wrong. Making plans for a painting trip to Arizona—well, he would have come back, you see. I was wrong." She paused, then moved back to stand next to Justin and put her hand on his arm. She looked down, then up. "Cynthia Sanchez is her name. I can't recall her number. I'll have to look it up for you."

Grayson wrote, then looked at her, his face calmer. "Thank you."

"Now you can answer a question or two for me, Mr. Grayson." Sarah's voice rose in strength.

"Of course." Grayson put the notebook away, turned briefly to squint at the sun, then put his dark glasses on. He returned his gaze to Sarah.

"Who found Jason?"

Grayson reached for his notebook and flipped through it. "Our information is that the downed plane was spotted by a local pilot. He notified the FAA and our people were called in."

Sarah shook her head, frowning. "How did they know it was Jason?"

"Your husband's wallet was found near the burned-out wreckage. As we explained, the case forensic team also obtained dental records."

"And you think he was alone?"

Grayson nodded his head as he put the notebook away. "Strong evidence. Forensics was pretty thorough."

"Will I get his personal things back?"

"There wasn't much, Sarah—just the items in the wallet. Of course. You received the jacket and briefcase from his office? And I believe his truck was returned yesterday." Grayson stood away from the railing.

"Yes," Sarah answered.

"Did he fly the plane, Mr. Grayson?" Florence asked.

"We have to assume that, Florence. His file indicates he trained for single engine rating. The report shows no evidence of others at the crash scene. Other human remains would have been close." He tried to smile at Flo, but couldn't muster the sincerity.

"Jason hadn't flown for a long time, Mr. Grayson. He gave it up as a favor to me. I doubt if he could have after that much time," Sarah said.

Grayson shrugged with obvious impatience. "Well, I've kept you too long. If there's anything I can do for you, please let me know." He backed down a step as he spoke.

"There is one thing," Sarah said.

"Yes?"

"Exactly what evidence did you find in the studio? I think I have a right to know."

Grayson sighed. "I'm sorry, Sarah, I'm not at liberty to say. The government's case isn't concluded, and there is Title Eighteen secrecy involved. Sorry."

Sarah looked hard at the FBI man, then lovingly took Florence's and Justin's hands in each of hers and walked down the remaining steps and away. Grayson stared after them and wiped his brow, then looked at the bit of moisture which came off on his hand.

18

*T*he Mercedes, with the rear doors, trunk and hood open, was parked in the up-slanted concrete driveway alongside the Thompson house. In front of the car was the garage—open—with Jason's rebuilt pickup truck parked inside.

Gracie, the older woman who sat across the aisle from the Thompson and Vaslovic families at the memorial service, was leaning into the back seat on the driver's side, arranging a pile of pillows and blankets. With his shirt sleeves rolled up, Justin Thompson, leaned under the hood of the car. Florence came through the kitchen door with a small suitcase in her hand. Behind her, Charles carried a larger suitcase and a portable television set.

To the left of the door frame, on the stucco, a poorly executed, elongated swastika had been sprayed on sloppily with black paint. The late afternoon sun cast mottled light past sharp shadows from nearby houses and yard walls, and filtered through the leaves of trees across the street.

Sarah emerged from the house still in her blue suit, without the hat and veil. Her skirt had new creases from her napping in it, and her blouse collar was unbuttoned. She carried a small overnight case. When she got to the open car trunk, she stopped and looked across and up the street to the empty stretch of curb where the carpet van had been until late the day before.

Florence and Gracie watched her while Charles loaded another suitcase into the trunk. Sarah then moved slowly for the front of the car where Justin had emerged with dirty hands. Charles closed the trunk while Gracie walked around the car to close both rear doors.

Justin lowered and latched the hood, then wiped his hands on a rag as he smiled at his mother. "Checked the oil, Mom. Guess Dad had it changed last month. Belts and other fluids okay."

"Thank you, Justin." Sarah ignored the possibility of getting grease on her clothes as she hugged her younger son hard. She turned and walked to the driver's door. She stopped and looked up at Charles as she put her arms around him. "Thank you for coming, Charles."

"I'm sorry Beth couldn't be here, mother. We want you to come out for awhile. Soon." He patted her back.

"Of course, son. I'd love it." She kissed his cheek.

"Oh, mom," Charles said.

"Yes, son?"

"Dad's ashes—"

Sarah looked away, then back at her eldest son. She nodded first, then shook her head. "I don't know, Charles. Can we discuss it later?"

Charles nodded with his mouth pinched and stared at the concrete of the driveway. They then stood and rocked gently to and fro as Flo put her arm around Justin and started to cry. Tears streamed down Gracie's cheeks.

Charles opened the driver's door as Gracie, her face twisted in grief, approached Sarah, and they embraced.

"Thanks for being such a good friend, Gracie." Sarah fought back tears.

They broke as Gracie covered her face with her hands and started to sob. Florence moved to comfort her while Sarah got behind the wheel of the Mercedes and Charles clicked it shut.

Gracie calmed and said, "I can't watch you go, Sarah. I'm going home now."

"All right, Gracie. I understand." Sarah patted her hand which lay on the window sill.

Florence hugged Gracie goodbye, then turned to Sarah. She leaned over to talk to her through the open window as Charles and Justin stood behind her. "Mother, please don't stay up there too long. I worry about you."

Sarah put her hand on the window sill. "I'll be all right, Flo, dear. I've got to get away by myself for awhile. You know how I am." She smiled sweetly at all three of her children. "I'll come and visit all of you soon. You and Charles should get back to your families."

"I will, Mother. I'll stay the night and leave tomorrow." Flo straightened and looked away.

Charles bent down to look at his mother. "Justin and I will be here for a couple of days, mom. We'll look after things. Anything in particular you want done?"

"No, dear, nothing. Just relax. I'll call and let you know I'm okay. I won't be able to stay up there long."

Justin said, "Chuck has to get back in a few days, but I can stay for a couple of weeks." He looked at his brother.

"Mother, are you sure you're in the proper frame of mind to drive up by yourself?" Flo asked as she turned and moved next to the car window. "Why don't I—?"

"Flo, I need to take my frustrations out on something. It might as well be a steering wheel." She smiled wanly.

"That could be dangerous, Mom," Justin said.

"Really, children, I'll be fine. Please don't worry. I do need to be by myself for awhile, and you know I'm a good driver."

"Alright, Mother," Flo said.

One by one, all three leaned through the open window to kiss their mother.

North of Bernalillo, where the traffic on I-25 thinned out, the sun choked on the horizon of plateaus to the west of the broad, shallow Rio Grande Valley. To her right and behind her, Sarah turned momentarily to look at the last light turn the Sandia mountains into its namesake, a watermelon; a striped, purple giant in a brown field. She looked north and west as the dying sun painted the edges of fast-moving storm clouds vermillion.

She sat back to listen to the smooth humming of the car's tires against the blacktop, correcting its track now and then with a deft hand. From the time she left the house, she checked the inside rearview mirror every few seconds to see if anyone was following. If a car stayed too long behind her, after making a mental note of the vehicle and the people in it, she slowed to let it pass, and tried to commit the license plate number to memory. By the time she passed Algodones she was reasonably satisfied she was not being tailed.

With the gathering dusk, she clicked the head lamps on, then dimmed them. She reached out and flicked the radio on and punched a button but, dissatisfied, punched another. Finally happy with her choicie of station, she adjusted the volume.

At Budaghers, no more than a wide spot in the road with its own off ramp, she pulled off the Interstate and parked in the dusty yard outside the ratty combination general store, service station and bar. A lone neon beer sign, garish in the cool evening air, flickered through the dirty window of the bar. She sat for a minute to watch the cars pass to see if another car pulled in behind her. Satisfied she was not being watched, she got out and went to the single phone booth which stood outside one corner of the decrepit building.

She listened for a tone, keyed a number and deposited coins after the computerized voice told her the cost. After ten rings she hung up to return to her car and rejoin the northbound highw ay.

As she pushed the Mercedes up the steep *La Bajada, The Descent*, a steep section of the highway that climbed out of the Rio Grande valley onto the Santa Fé plain, large splats of rain began to beat on the surface of the windshield. The splats then cascaded into a rush as the storm she had seen earlier greeted her in full force. With the greenish lights of the sleek dash reflecting off her face, she activated the windshield wipers. They clopped back and forth noisily at first, struggling to wipe the entire wet surface of the glass. A flash of blue-white lightning flickered, then rose to brighten, then die in the sky ahead to her left.

She managed the car through Santa Fé's highway by-pass and encountered a gentler rain north of the city. Occasional flashes of lightning signaled the storm's center as it moved west to east across the river valley to the Sangre de Cristo range from the Jemez Mountains.

At an all-night Allsup's on the highway north of Santa Fé, she stopped and bought enough groceries for her dinner that night and food for the following day. She put the bag of victuals on the rear floor of the car and used the phone once again to no avail. Then it was back to the car to drive on.

Her radio station had long faded, causing her to tune and re-tune, trying to find something that didn't assail her ears. In frustration and relief, she killed the hissing thing and settled back into her own thoughts.

A mile before the turn off, the rain picked up in intensity again. The lonely highway glistened warmly in the reflection of the Mercedes's head lights. Sarah hardly saw the fading white line that indicated the center of the crowned asphalt road. The weather turned colder with the hour and the altitude, so she was forced to fight back with the heater, making the car somewhat stuffy.

Tired and hungry, she dug into the big, soft leather bag at her side and fished around for a package of cigarettes. She shook one out with her other hand on the wheel, then managed it into her mouth inexpertly. Smoking was a habit she had been trying to kick, one that Jason had abhorred. She pushed on the cigarette lighter, waited for it to pop, then brought it out and up to her mouth. The front of the car glowed red for five seconds, then returned to black and green.

The final winding miles into the village of Truchas were not as hazardous as she had feared. The Mercedes was more surefooted than she had remembered, but Jason had always driven this part. Ahead, past a curve in the road and a thin line of darkened wet trees, she saw the lights of the poor village.

She thought of the name of this place, Truchas, plural for "trout" in Spanish, named after the glorious spotted fish found in nearby mountain streams and the people, descended from Spanish soldiers, priests and merchants who had come with, and after, Coronado. They had not found gold,, so they had to settle for dirt; but from the soil came houses of adobe like those of the Indians and of their own Spanish forebears. There was wood, fruit, meat, wool, leather, grapes and more. She reminisced about how she and Jason had both liked the Spanish. It was because, for the most part, as with most mountain peoples, they were religious and suspicious of foreigners, but loyal to a fault if befriended. She had read about them; and how, being principally Catholic, some adhered to the ways of the *Penitentes*, a secret breakaway order of flagellants.

Sarah was warmed by the fact that many of the people of Truchas had learned to respect, and even like, the *Gringo* Thompsons, partly because they had showed them respect by trying to speak their language, partly because they chose to live in an adobe as they did, and partly because they gave a few of them employment from time to time.

As the car came into the outskirts of the town, the head lights revealed a bar of slick, brown mud athwart the narrow, patched pavement. A ditch had been cut but not re-paved. Sarah slowed and bumped the Mercedes across it.

The low, soft adobes of the town crowded against the road, with their darkened windows, seemed to slumber in the night. They looked to her as though they had grown from the earth. She peered at the black rectangles that marked the windows and doors as she passed. The buildings, ghostly shadows of earth and wood in the blackness of a cold, wet night, seemed forlorn and dead to her. Sarah was cheered when she found two houses that showed signs of life with yellowish light that filtered through white, lacy curtains, and fell across the wet, deserted road, so silent and unrevealing of the life in this little mountain town.

She shivered as she tried to see someone inside one of the houses through the rain-streaked windows of the car. Even an outline would have been comforting. She slowed before she came to her road then turned the wheel to guide the Mercedes down a dirt lane running with shimmering rain water turning to mud as it wound along a path laid out by the practicalities of animal husbandry. She turned right. There was the house, straight ahead. But she must have made a mistake. Light poured from one of the windows, making the slanting rain drops shimmer.

She stopped the car and looked about. No, there was the low wall on the left, leading to Garcia's place. To the right of the house was the rock wall bordering the tiny orchard. It was the right house. In the dark, hard against the wall left of the window was a nondescript sedan. Her expression froze as she tried to think past the anxiety that rose within her. She sat and stared at the large window to the left of the front door, its panes set into an old refurbished frame and sunk into the bull-nosed roundness of the adobe wall. Oddly, her mind wandered away from the reality of the moment.

She and Jason had discovered and purchased the old place a dozen years before;, and the two of them, hiring local help to make it livable, had come up summers and weekends to work on it. It had been a place to retreat from the imported crassness of Albuquerque and the increasing phoniness of Santa Fé. It was high in the mountains, with people who knew of little but the struggle against the elements and the harshness of their mountain fastness as a guide.

But the light was on.

Sarah's heart beat faster and her breath came in short, shallow bursts.

Then her anxiety turned to anger and resentment at the intrusion on her privacy.

She gunned the car forward. It jolted and slid to a stop before she set the hand brake. She switched the engine off first, then the lights. Sarah grabbed her handbag and placed it in her lap. She then sat for ten seconds before opening the door. She heard ticking sounds coming from the engine as it cooled along with the patter of the gentle rain on the steel of the roof and hood.

Trance-like, as though she watched herself from another position, she went through the motions of opening the door and getting out with her handbag securely in her hand before slamming the door—partly in anger, partly in fear—as though to warn whomever might be there. Had she or Jason simply left a lamp on the last time they were here? But there was the odd car.

Sarah guessed she wouldn't need the key. She was correct. The knob turned easily in her hand, and she pushed the heavy tongue-and-groove door open.

To her left, a sofa, whose back was to the area immediately around the front door, faced a small fireplace with a wood mantle. Left of the sofa was an end table with a shaded lamp. It was on, and, aside from the fire, the only source of light in the room—the same light she had seen from the car.

Between the sofa and the open area near the door was a large Mexican Indian rug, much like the one that lay between the sofa and the fireplace. Behind the sofa and against it was a small, plain wood desk with a chair under it and with a table lamp that sat on its surface. Across the room from the front door was another white-curtained window, its sill, as with the one by the door, close to the floor. In several places around the room on the earth-brown walls were framed paintings and drawings, some by Sarah herself. Eerie light and shadow danced across the ceiling of open beams and rough-hewn boards caused by the flaming wood.

She stood near the door, still open, and stared in disbelief at the back of a man's head silhouetted above the line of the sofa back. The smell of aromatic pipe tobacco filled the room and created a filmy layer of bluish smoke that hung below the ceiling beams. Droplets from Sarah's handbag created a small, shiny puddle on the basket-weave pattern of the red-brick floor near her shoes.

The man turned, then stood as he pulled the pipe from his mouth. It was the man who had claimed to be from the Reuters news agency. He smiled knowingly.

Sarah took a step forward as a wave of relief mixed with incredible curiosity surged through her. "What—what are you doing here?!" She was about to drop her purse, but recovered.

Victor Nantes came around the sofa, then stopped, as he slipped his right hand into an outer pocket of his unbuttoned jacket. Sarah noticed that his coat was the same cut and color as the one he wore the last time she saw him.

"Mrs. Thompson. So good to see you." His eyes twinkled as he took a pull on his pipe.

Sarah was agape, and her voice rose an octave. "I demand to know the meaning of this! How did you get in here?! How—?!" Sarah stopped as her eyes narrowed and her brain raced. She studied the man's face.

"Please come and sit down, Mrs. Thompson." He held out his hand. "It's late, and I'm sure you're tired after your long trip. Allow me to close the door. It's cold out, and it's taken a long time to build up the heat in here."

He moved past her casually, as though in residence, and gestured toward the fireplace. He closed the door gently, turned to face her, then walked around the sofa to the lamp end.

Sarah stared angrily at him, wide-eyed in disbelief after she moved to stand rigidly near the fireplace. "I don't remember your name." Her tone was icy.

The light from both the table lamp and the fire, as it struck him from below, played monster tricks with Nantes's features. The room was silent except for the crackling of the fire. Only the windows in the thick earthen walls allowed any of the sound of the rain to pass into the room.

"Nantes. Victor Nantes."

"Yes. Newsman."

Nantes looked around the half-dark room. "I can certainly understand why you and Jason come up here. Charming. Absolutely charming." He faced Sarah again, then, after a pause, said, "I suggest you sit, Mrs. Thompson. Do you mind if I smoke?" He held his pipe in his right hand.

"It hardly matters now, does it?" Sarah hesitated, glanced down at the haze, then studied the intruder's face. She moved slowly to the dark end of the sofa and sat, keeping her eyes on Nantes all the time, her handbag held tightly in her lap as though waiting demurely in a bus depot. Nantes ignored Sarah's reference to the smoke in the room, and re-clamped the pipe between his teeth, then moved in front of her to the fireplace where he stooped to poke at the burning wood. He took a small log from a pile near the hearth and placed it in the flames. He straightened, leaned against the wall with his arm up on the mantel, and looked at her. He began to speak, but was interrupted.

"I find all this quite tiresome, Mr. Nantes." Sarah's voice quavered slightly. Although her hunger had passed, her stomach ached with tension. "Extremely rude. I—I'm speechless. Here I come to my private retreat to rest, my husband gone, and find you, of all people, trespassing. Ensconced in my home." She paused for two breaths, then she cocked her head at him. "How did you find this place? And why are you here? Is this part of your duty as a reporter?" Her eyes belied the fast pace of her heart, and became glaring slits.

"Mrs. Thompson, I understand your feelings, but my presence here—which I intend to explain—is very important; very relevant to you." Nantes looked at the glowing pipe bowl in the half-dark room. "You have been through a very trying time, Mrs. Thompson. You have been shocked, buffeted and re-shocked in a sordid mess. But I have another shock for you. A surprise. Now please relax. Sit back."

Sarah hesitated, but followed his suggestion and sat back, away from the edge of the sofa, where she had been perched, her eyes riveted on the intruder.

"That's it." Nantes looked down at his shoes for inspiration and continued. "You see, Mrs. Thompson, sometimes, in cases such as this, things are not precisely what they seem. Sometimes, something is done—or created—for the effect it will have. Uh, because of this, people are sometimes duped or misled; taken down the garden path as it were."

"Please get to the point! I want you to leave so I can retire. I'm exhausted." Her voice was sharp and unforgiving, and she shook her head violently as she glared at him.

He looked at her severely for a moment, then down and away. As Sarah Thompson watched, dumbfounded, Nantes took the pipe from his mouth, walked to a narrow door to the right of, and in the same wall as, the fireplace. He opened the door and pushed it inward. He stepped back.

Sarah, transfixed, turned her head and body to watch the man. Muted light fell into the room from beyond the door. In another instant the sound of footfalls reached her ears as a shadow filled the doorway and Jason Thompson walked slowly into the room.

19

*S*arah rose like a shot, her body bent as she pushed away from the sofa. "Jason! My God! Oh, Jason! You're alive! What happened!? Why—?! How?!" Her nearly breathless sounds became muffled as she rushed to her husband, and she almost knocked him down as she buried her face against his chest.

"It's alright, dear. Everything's okay, now," Jason whispered as he stroked his wife's hair with one hand while he held her tightly with his other arm. He closed his eyes and rocked with her. When he opened them, as he continued to comfort her, he searched the room. His eyes were dry. He settled his unemotional gaze on Nantes, then looked away.

Nantes moved slowly toward the area behind the sofa near the front door as he chewed fiercely on the stem of his pipe, both his hands in his pants pockets. He moved close to the outside door, where he wheeled to look at the couple across the room. He caught Jason's eyes for a moment, then searched the room before he settled on a spot on the round beams that supported the ceiling. "You see, Mrs. Thompson, I did have something for you."

Nantes's voice was barely audible, but Sarah pulled away from her husband's embrace and looked across the room at him, her face full of wonder. She looked back at her husband. "Oh, Jason, are you all right? You look so bad—so tired." She stepped back to arm's length, both her hands still touching his waist. "Do you feel well? You look ill, dear. But—how can this be?! The memorial service—they said you were dead, Jason! What's going on?! Have you eaten?" She moved against him, pushed away again to look at him, then hugged him once more.

"Yes. Please, dear, sit down." He spoke quietly. "You need to listen." He took her hands in his and gently removed them from his sides.

Sarah took her hands slowly from his, looked up at him, then at Nantes, then back. "Jason dear, but—your blood pressure—I've been so worried." She calmed, but continued to peer at Jason with deep concern. She shook her head in disbelief.

"I'm fine." Jason closed his eyes and nodded. "Really. I am."

Nantes returned to stand in front of the fireplace.

Jason also moved to the mantel to face Sarah. He wore a loose cardigan, and he buried both his hands in its pockets for warmth. Sarah sat on the corner of the sofa nearest her husband, her feet on the floor in such a way that she could trade looks with both men.

Nantes moved to the end of the mantel opposite Jason. He rested his left arm on the wood piece, his pipe cradled in his right hand. His happy expression was tinged with triumph.

She smiled at Nantes. "I apologize for doubting you, Mr. Nantes. I must confess I am bewildered, though—breathless."

"No apology necessary, Mrs. Thompson."

Sarah felt his demeanor had become a bit smug—an emotion she gladly granted him. She looked from Nantes's face to her husband's, then back. "I don't understand—I mean, the FBI and—"

Nantes shifted his weight. "Well, Mrs. Thompson, we have a bit more freedom than the FBI."

"I think Sarah deserves an explanation." Jason stared at the brick floor. His tone was crisp.

Jason's tone of voice triggered something in Sarah. She felt it was cool, almost brittle. She scrutinized his face in the low light.

"Yes, of course. We've taken too long to get down to cases." Nantes pushed away from the mantel. He paced in a small area around his end of the sofa. "Alright, Mrs. Thompson, first off—"

"I think you've earned the right to address me by my first name, Mr. Nantes. It's Sarah."

He smiled and dipped his head. "Thank you. Sarah. First, I must ask you to swear that what you are about to hear will never pass beyond this room. Not even to your children. It is essential. Do you understand?"

"Yes. Yes, I suppose so, Mr. Nantes." She shifted nervously, her hands folded in her lap.

"Very well." Nantes continued, "Now, Sarah, I told you I was with Reuters. The news agency. That's true, but it's a cover. I'm an agent of the Central Intelligence Agency. CIA." He stopped long enough to study Sarah's face and gauge the effect of his words. "So is Jason." Nantes fell quiet while Sarah absorbed his words.

She stared at Nantes, then slowly pivoted her head to look at Jason, whose glance was darting back and forth between her and the other man. Her mouth went slack. "Jason? The CIA?" She shook her head slowly, her face in a deep frown. "No, no. Why, dear?"

Nantes looked at the charred tobacco in the bowl of his pipe. "Jason has been running a mole for us."

"What?!"

"A mole. A deep-cover foreign agent," Nantes said.

"I don't understand, Jason." Sarah's expression was twisted with incredulity.

Jason spoke, his voice low, almost inaudible, with barely-hidden tension, "The end of my undergraduate days. Dean Munson, my old physics teacher. You didn't know him, and I probably didn't talk about him."

He moved away from the end of the mantle, looked at the ceiling, then stepped back, re-living the past with his eyes. "Mel wanted me to get involved with that Communist youth group. I went out of curiosity and as a favor to him. You remember. Munson knew about it. He came to see me. He knew I was fundamentally opposed to Communism and the group." He shrugged. "I was against his plan at first, but became intrigued with the idea. I didn't even associate it with patriotism, or danger, or whatever. It just happened."

Nantes, his head lowered, studied Jason hard from underneath his eyebrows, then looked down at Sarah. "He—Dean Munson—wanted Jason there, alongside Mel, from the beginning. To watch him. To control him, if possible, since it appeared Mel was seriously involved." He jerked a thumb in Jason's direction.

"Mel!? No! Jason !" Sarah insisted. Her frown returned.

Jason barely nodded his head as he looked at the bricks in the floor.

Nantes went on as he paced toward the outside wall so his back was to both of them. "Yes, Mel Vaslovic. Jason was introduced to a friend of Munson's who had connections with the CIA. He was brought in under tight wraps and trained in short doses so as not to raise any suspicion. He's been undercover ever since. The FBI would go crazy if they knew any of this. That's their turf." He waved his hand nonchalantly.

Sarah, a pained exression on her face, turned from watching Nantes to look at her husband. "But Jason, dear, why didn't you tell me?"

"I couldn't. How could I?" He frowned, close to annoyance. "It was absolutely essential nobody know. Not even you." He spoke quietly, but with a trace of irritation.

"Now I remember. Those weekend trips you made to Washington. Supposedly for the company you worked for."

Jason nodded and raised his eyes to the ceiling.

Nantes moved to the center of the fireplace to face his audience. "Sarah, Hoover was uncontrollable. He made terrible blunders during the war. Elements within the Central Intelligence Agency decided to do something. A special counter espionage unit was formed. Jason was an early recruit."

Sarah shook her head. "Espionage." She said the word reflectively as she turned away from Nantes to gaze at her husband, who had wandered away from the fireplace to study the Indian rug that lay between the sofa and the rear wall.

"Yes, counter espionage," Nantes said. "Their fears were not directed solely at the Soviet Union, either. They saw that regime and its agents as a threat, to be sure. What they also realized were the possibilities of other espionage besides military. Industrial, political and so forth."

"And so, this group within the CIA was to—" Sarah looked at Nantes, who leaned against the mantel again.

"As I indicated, perform counter espionage, as it were. To burrow from within the implanted foreign cells formed here. They began with the Socialist Youth League."

"Counter espionage." Sarah said in a near whisper.

Nantes nodded. "With our people in place within these organizations, we could feed them disinformation. And keep track of where the data went at the same time." Nantes looked at the two Thompsons in turn.

"You mean to say, Mr. Nantes, that this CIA group actually helps these—these foreign agents?"

Nantes leaned forward from the waist. "Please, call me Victor, Sarah. Turn-about is fair play." He gestured with his pipe.

"Victor," she smiled.

Nantes straightened his posture. "Well, I'm not so sure I would go so far as to say we help them. It would be more like fooling them, you see." He managed a wry grin.

"Incredible," Sarah whispered. She moved her eyes about, fathoming Nantes's words.

"Yes. We've pulled off a few coups. There are several mysteries the FBI and British MI6 would like cleared up. Even the Mossad. Shin Bet. Israelis." He smiled, warming his palm with the pipe bowl.

Sarah looked up at her husband, who watched Nantes carefully. "My lord, Jason, you mean you've been spying all these years? Then what the FBI says is true?" She spoke lightly.

He returned her gaze with his own sober look, then looked at Nantes, whom he expected to carry on.

Nantes broke away from the fireplace mantel, agitated with the feeling he had not been getting through to Sarah Thompson. "No, no, Sarah. Jason has not been spying. No. Just the opposite. But he has been controlling someone who has. A real, live foreign agent." Nantes watched for the impact of his words, and kept his narrowed eyes riveted on her.

Jason, with his eyes intense, looked at Nantes, then Sarah.

The room was silent while Nantes and Jason waited for Sarah to understand the implications of Nantes's words.

"Mel?! You can't be serious. My God—" She looked away and stared at nothing.

"It's true, Sarah." Jason pulled his hand out of his sweater pocket and brushed it impatiently across his hair.

None of the three said anything for several long seconds.

Sarah stared at her husband. "My God. Mel," she gasped as the revelation sunk in. "I can't believe it!" Her words were whispered, but perfectly audible to the two men above the crackling.

The room was otherwise quiet.

Jason, unmoved, continued to examine her face.

"Yes," Nantes said, "Mel Vaslovic. Long time friend of the family." Nantes finally could contain himself no longer and paced away from the fireplace to the lamp end of the sofa, then to the dark window that looked out onto the muddy lane where the Mercedes sat, cooling in the wet night. Without turning to face them, he continued. "He's been working the other side. The buzz word is mole. Deep-cover mole. And Jason has been his control for years. Feeding him doctored information. Up until a few days ago." He turned around with the pipe in his teeth and his hands behind his back, the satisfied professor, ramming a point home to an awed class.

"I find this frightening and disturbing, Mr. Nantes. Victor." Sarah hesitated, then looked up at Jason. "Did you kill him, dear?" Her eyes were wide, her brow furrowed.

"I was under the impression Mel killed himself," Jason said. He looked at her directly.

Nantes, his brow creased by a frown, cleared his throat and moved away from the window. "No, Jason, not true. It was made to look that way." Nantes took the dying pipe from his mouth and tapped it against his palm before he leaned over toward the hearth to patiently guide all the flecks of unburned tobacco and charred remains onto it.

Jason, stock still, showed no surprise, but his eyes darted about for a few seconds.

Nantes said, "The APD lab report, confirmed by FBI forensics, shows that Mel actually died of poisoning. Apparently administered by a dart. Several minutes before the bullet wound to the head. Definitely not suicide." He blew through the empty stem. He looked at Sarah in the low light of the room.

"I see," she sighed.

Nantes continued his attention to his pipe for another ten seconds, then continued. "But then, you knew the police and FBI suspected murder, Sarah."

"Yes. But the police will arrest Jason for Mel's murder when they find that he's alive." Sarah, her hands in her lap, leaned forward and furrowed her brow at Nantes.

Nantes refilled the pipe. He slowly dipped the bowl into a tobacco pouch and tamped it with his thumb, then ritualistically held a liquid petroleum lighter to it. He crossed his eyes to watch the bowl as he sucked the stem to start the embers. He looked down at the woman on the sofa. "I don't think so, Sarah. Your husband is officially dead. They're no longer looking for him. He'll receive a new identity and a safe place to live out his life with a reasonably carefree future." The pipe lit, his hands went into his jacket pockets, and he raised his chin high to blow a huge cloud of smoke free. "Both of you will."

"But—how did you manage this? And why?" Sarah looked at both men in turn, then stared at Nantes.

"Excellent question. You see, we believe Mel realized Jason had been feeding him rigged data to pass on to his contacts. Contacts, incidentally, we've been aware of. At any rate, he stole some information from the Labs and set Jason up to take the fall. He was followed, or intercepted, and whoever did, decided he was redundant, and worse, a problem. They eliminated him." Nantes had created a luxurious cloud around his head. He peered through it as he held the pipe out reflectively.

"So you arranged for Jason's 'death'?"

"Not really. A fortuitous accident. Someone did die, but not Jason."

"Who?!" Sarah frowned.

Jason looked first at Nantes, then his wife. He spoke slowly, in a low, controlled tone. "My kidnapper. He told me his name was Cuzco." He walked to the window past the little door from which he had emerged and looked out into the wet night.

Sarah watched him. "Who? Cuzco? Who was he? What happened to you, dear? Where did he take you?"

Jason continued to look out at the rain through the moisture condensing on the window, and patiently explained the events leading up to his faked death.

"My God, Jason!" Sarah stared at his back, then twisted back toward Nantes as she looked for an answer.

Jason remained turned away and quiet, his hands folded behind his back.

"Although it doesn't make sense, most likely someone associated with Mel," Nantes offered. He paced away from the mantel toward the open area behind the sofa and studied the patterns in the brick. He turned and looked at Jason, still at the window, his hands now in his sweater pockets. "Jason, how do you figure Mel got onto you? And how was he able to breach the files? You've not explained that."

Jason continued to look out the window. He took in a deep breath, then, without turning, said, "Mel knew a lot about me. He knew I have a poor memory for numbers I don't need all the time. Like for lock codes." He stopped, turned his head briefly to glance at his wife, then resumed his vigil. "I made the little Ojo de Dios things—the god's eyes made with colored yarn. I keep—kept—one in my office with the numbers for the security room and our file cabinets coded in colors. The RMA code. Resistor Manufacturer's Code. Ten colors make up ten numbers. Known to electronic technicians and electrical engineers."

He stopped, turned slowly and crossed the room to the fireplace, where he held out his hands to warm them, his back to the others. "I use—used—the god's eye to remind me of the codes when I needed them, which was seldom. When Bob Parsons got argumentative at the retirement party, he let slip that Geronimo Queen was an on-going, productive project. I had led Mel to believe it was dead. That was the official line. Mel must have put two and two together. My theory is he went to my office the Monday after the party while I was out, on the pretext of wanting to see me. I know that much, because Angie told me. He must have copied the colors off the god's eye. Sometime after that and before three A.M. on Tuesday morning, he went into the security room and helped himself to the classified files. Using the codes woven into the God's eye. Probably hid somewhere in the building and waited for the right time." He turned and looked at his wife and Nantes, then strolled to a dark part of the room. "I'm sure he left the file drawer unlocked so the guard would discover it." He cocked his head to one side.

"Jason—how clever—and how terrible!" Sarah exclaimed. She shook her head slowly.

"I think he was the one who called the news people," Jason added.

Nantes walked back in the direction of the fireplace. He rubbed his chin with his right hand while the other carried his ever-present pipe. "To hurry along his plan to frame you. Of course."

"Makes sense to me." Jason turned and faced Sarah, who had angled herself around to see him. He took a deep breath and released it. "After the FBI interviewed me, showed an interest in Mel and he didn't show up to work Wednesday, I began to worry and knew I had to talk to him. I went to his house. I found his body."

Nantes said, "So you suspected Mel right away. Why didn't you tell me that at the restaurant?"

"By that time I didn't know who to trust." Jason gazed at Nantes steadily.

"I see—" Nantes frowned. "What happened to the file?"

"The file?" Jason asked.

"The file Mel stole." There was a trace of impatience in Nantes's voice.

Jason strolled away toward the front door, his head down. "Yes, of course. The file. He found the file he wanted—or thought he wanted—and managed to smuggle it out past the guards, probably in his briefcase, or hidden inside his shirt. It was easy, since there was no general alarm." He shrugged. "Then on Tuesday he went to our studio to photograph the pages in my darkroom. He knew Sarah had an extended watercolor trip that day. He told me he'd been to the doctor's. He let himself into the studio. He photographed the pages, then reduced them to microfilm using my equipment. Something that had been my job. He planted evidence to implicate me and took what he wanted."

Sarah turned her head to watch her husband as he paced. "But Jason, how do you know all this?"

"When I heard the FBI had evidence, I remembered seeing a chalky substance under one of Mel's fingernails. I went to the studio after I found him. I figured he'd gone there. The studio was unlocked. He knew where the keys were. The pot you were throwing had been tampered with."

"Pot?" Nantes asked. His pipe had gone out and he sucked on the stem.

"Yes, Victor, a pot. Mel buried a frame of the film in the fresh clay. I guess he figured with lack of oxygen baking wouldn't hurt it, or that the FBI would find it before it could be fired, which they did. You needn't worry about the rest of the data. I doubt if it ever got passed. In retrospect, it was stupid of me to leave the film or the pot there. It never occurred to me that the FBI would look there." Jason stared at Nantes.

Nantes, his mouth firm, glared at Jason.

Sarah, aware of something between them, looked from man to man.

Jason directed his gaze at his wife. "You see, Sarah, Mr. Nantes here wants the film. The film or films Mel made of the file he stole." He looked at Nantes, then back down at Sarah. "He told me things after saving me from Cuzco he should have kept to himself. Like the reports of break-ins at the Vaslovic house and our place. He was the burglar, you see. Weren't you, Victor?" He looked up at the CIA man again.

"That's goddamn ridiculous! Why would I break into your's or Mel's house?!" Nantes, his face a mask of anger, waved his pipe violently, as he leaned forward, tense.

Sarah, her mouth agape and eyes wide and the color draining from her face, again looked from man to man.

Jason broke into a wry grin, the first sign of mirth Sarah had seen. "Because you figured there had to be film—there always was, since you're control, Victor—and you wanted it. Because Mel tipped you that he had something special. That's why you were in Albuquerque so fast. I checked the flights. Because you didn't know where it was, and figuring you had a chance of finding it, you risked breaking and entering; and because you were Mel's conduit. You were turned somewhere along the way. That's why." His voice remained low and calm.

"You're crazy, you know that?! Out of your mind! You've gone demented in your old age!" Nantes stalked across the room to the window where Jason had been and looked out.

"I don't think so, Victor. The real reason you responded so fast to my call was that Mel had called you earlier. You were already in Albuquerque. Things went wrong for you after I told you he was dead. You didn't dare go near his house—yet. You had our mailbox all set up, knowing I'd be calling for help. But you panicked and went in later, after I disappeared."

Sarah gasped, and looked frantically from one man to the other.

"And when you came to get me at the ranch. Cuzco didn't have to die. You thought I was unconscious, but I wasn't, and I saw you drag him into the flames. It was the perfect opportunity. As a good CIA operative, you would want to find out who he was and who he was with, if not bring him in. At least you would have disappeared after notifying the FBI or locals anonymously."

Jason stood stock still and watched Nantes' back. "And there's your report of only one crash victim. Me. The forensic people will eventually find out that the body found there was not mine, they'll interview the woman at the ranch and know there were two of us, and I'll become a fugitive all over again. No, fact of the matter is, if you'd found the film, you would never have shown up. You figured I'd lead you to it by coming to get me."

Sarah gasped for the second time.

Nantes bobbed his head insolently, listening with his back still turned. "I have news for you, Mr. Thompson." With his head lowered menacingly and a grin on his features, he turned to face Jason. "You were out like a light. Unconscious. I dragged you off that mesa and got you to a safe house. I came back with a team and we sanitized the place. The FBI was satisfied. They won't talk to the woman. It's over. You're not a fugitive. You're dead. The other body is ashes!" He nodded, his whole body involved. "And why the hell did the two of you go for the plane? Why not straight for his car?!"

"Cuzco wanted his log book. I told him there was an easier way up, but he wouldn't listen." Jason rubbed his face with his hands, but remained calm. "What about the plane? The FAA and NTSB. They'll investigate. They'll chase—" He stared at the crazed Nantes. "Okay. You've covered that angle, too. Don't tell me. Right?"

"Jeezuz. What fools . . ." Nantes wheezed the words out between teeth clamped hard on the pipe stem. He shook his head silently, then turned around slowly. The semiautomatic from his shoulder holster was in his right hand.

"Oh, my God!" Sarah whispered.

"You're a bright man, Jason, but not bright enough. Why not let well-enough alone? Here you are, on top of retirement, and now it's all over." Nantes put the dead cold pipe in the left side pocket of his jacket, transferred the pistol to his left hand, and kept it trained on Jason while he pulled a long, black suppressor from his right-hand jacket pocket. He screwed it onto the pistol barrel. "You're right, you know. Money looked a lot better than duty . . . even to poor, old Mel. It's amazing what living in the capitalist world can do to your ideals." He shook his head.

20

*T*he rain had stopped.

Jason began to feel dizzy and his headache crept back. He moved to the front window nearest the Mercedes and looked out. He clasped his hands tightly together behind his back in an effort to control his anxiety. "So, who killed Mel Vaslovic?" He asked.

Nantes, still across the room, answered. "Well, that's one thing you can't pin on me, Jason, old man." He had finished screwing the suppressor onto the barrel of his semiautomatic.

"Hm," Jason reflected.

Sarah remained transfixed on the sofa.

"I'd like to know. Cuzco?" Nantes asked. He raised his head and looked down his nose in a gesture of arrogance.

Jason shook his head slowly. "I don't think so."

"Well, I don't really care," Nantes said.

"Maybe you do," Jason said. "What do you think, dear?" He turned his head and shoulders enough to look at Sarah.

She was tensed on the edge of the sofa, her purse pulled against one leg. Her eyes danced between the two men. "This is hardly the time, Jason." Her voice had become a growl.

"Sure, it is." He turned around fully. His face was loose and haggard. "It may interest you to know, Nantes, that I think Sarah knows who Cuzco was and who killed Mel." He stared briefly at Nantes, then down at his wife from his standing position across the room.

Nantes unconsciously began to swing the muzzle of the pistol between Jason and Sarah as he looked from one to the other and shook his head. He frowned first at Sarah, then at Jason. "What the hell are you talking about?" His eyes became slits and his brow furrowed.

Jason colored slightly as he smiled in a half-hearted way. He glanced around the room, pressed both his hands against his head and looked at the ceiling beams. Then, as he worked his palms against each other, he strolled to the little desk set against the back of the sofa. He crouched over the desk top and stared at his wife. "When you were up that Monday morning early, and when you were so curious about whether I had lunch with Mel on a day you knew I never had lunch with him, I didn't think much about it, Sarah, but it made sense later. It made a lot of sense after I needed a pill and took one from the envelope Cuzco had so thoughtfully brought along on our little jaunt."

Sarah, her body turned to follow him, frowned. "What pill, dear?"

"Verapamil, Sarah! Verapamil! My blood pressure pills! Why else would Cuzco be carrying Verapamil?!" His hands came apart and he jerked his fist in the air to make a point before he shot her a severe look, then stood up straight and turned away to avoid further eye contact.

"Jason—he—this man was carrying your blood pressure pills?! How do you know they weren't for him?" Sarah whined.

"Sarah, oh, Sarah, please. Too much of a coincidence. Verapamil is only one of several specifics for blood pressure. Please." He paused. "Hell, he didn't take them!"

"Someone at the base, perhaps? Mel knew." Sarah stared after her husband, but darted glances at the armed man to her left.

"Hey, what's going on?! You mean to say Cuzco had your blood pressure pills on him?!" Nantes' face was screwed up in a question, his pistol pointed at nothing in particular.

Jason arched his back in an attempt to cure the ache in his hunched shoulders. He faced the blank wall opposite the long room from the flickering fireplace. His hands were deep in his pants pockets. He nodded. "That's right. He had them. If they had been from someone connected with the Labs, they wouldn't have been packaged that way. That was a commercial envelope. It didn't have the name of our pharmacy on it, but it was definitely a commercial envelope used by retail pharmacies. The Labs use a different style. I know. I was treated on a field trip once. They're brown. Special markings. Besides, who at the Labs? The Division doctor?"

"Jesus—!" Nantes exclaimed. His face became feral.

"Mel knew I had hypertension, yes; but he didn't know what I took. He had only a passing interest, and never asked. Besides, he was dead."

"Jason, dear, what are you getting at?"

Jason, eyes closed, smiled to himself and shook his head. "Oh, God, Sarah, please." He held both arms out wide, then let them drop noisily against his sides as he shook his head widely from side to side. "I should have realized. It's amazing. I've been racked with the notion ever since I took that envelope off of Cuzco at St. John's."

He stopped, turned and looked at the two people across the room from him. "It's funny. The FBI came to me years ago about you, Sarah, and I was furious. They were worried about your background. They could never find a decent paper trail. Your parents' and sister's deaths, the replacement birth certificate. You show up just at the time Mel and I are starting with the Commies. And all the money from the bank. Why the bank, I asked?" He put his finger to his head.

Sarah, her head lowered and her mouth puckered in concentration, turned slowly away and stared at the fire.

Nantes stood with his mouth open and eyes slitted again. "Hey! What's going on here?" He swung his concentrated gaze between the two other people in the room.

Jason ignored Nantes as he continued to look away in his recitation. "Then all the concentration on the Vaslovics. I mean everything. The kids, the parties, the trips, the constant concern over every aspect of their lives. And those emergency trips to Canada to see a cousin who I suspect didn't exist." He stopped pacing and pointed a finger at the ceiling. "Then I thought back. Yes. Up early. You worried about the fiasco at the party, afraid Mel, hot-headed as he could be sometimes, might pull something. You came back from the watercolor trip Tuesday and you saw Mel leaving the studio, right? You didn't follow him then, but you thought it over, realized what he was probably up to, then confronted him Wednesday morning. Right? He hadn't left the house. His car was cold. You killed him—somehow—then shot him with his own gun."

There was a deadly silence in the room while he hesitated, then continued. "When you heard that things were coming apart at the Labs, you didn't have time to comb the studio and were faced with the FBI, you had Cuzco follow me to what turned out to be my meeting with this fellow here, Nantes." Jason stopped moving and stared at the dark floor. "But, I'm troubled. There must have been a second film frame. Or more. There were four missing pages."

Sarah remained frozen, her eyes fixed on the fire.

Nantes, his eyes ablaze with curiosity, took two steps toward the other man in the semi-darkness. "Why?"

"There was a bead." He wheeled to look at Nantes. "You know, the ones we sometimes used to conceal and move the microdots. One of them was under the bed in Mel's bedroom. Sarah missed it. He must have taken it when he was at the studio. That means the frame in the pot was not the only film; that he had a copy. I broke it open, but there was no dot."

Nantes stared at Jason, then turned to look at Sarah. "Is what he's saying true?"

Sarah continued to stare into the fire. She sighed heavily. "Oh, my. You're right, dear. I found three frames he had and destroyed them. I didn't see the bead. I should have known he'd try to move them using beads. But I didn't think he'd try to frame you."

"I wonder why he didn't take four beads? Four frames, four beads." Puzzled, Jason looked at the ceiling. "And the one he had empty . . . " He paused. "Probably dropped it onto the floor . . . " His voice trailed off.

Both Sarah and Victor Nantes stared at him, waiting.

He stiffened. "What happened to the paper file? Did you get that, too?" Jason asked.

"No." Sarah shook her head slowly, her eyes dreamy. "I couldn't find it."

"He got rid of it," Jason said. Feeling very cold and exposed, he moved slowly, bent and defeated, toward the front door, both hands in his pockets again, his arms against his body. He stopped a few inches from the door and studied the grain in the wood. Tears began to well up in his eyes.

Nantes held the semiautomatic high, pointed at the ceiling before he turned back toward the window out of which he had been looking. His face was a mask of wonderment, his mouth slack.

Sarah sighed again as she turned away from the fire. She gave her husband a pitying look, then smoothed her skirt with her hand. "They put me in early. It was ideal. I was to watch the two of you. You and Mel. Report everything, especially any deviation from routine. I was to blend in. Family, friends, church, voting patterns. I believed. I really did. It died after a time. You were right, Victor, about being in a free, democratic capitalist society. It was more than that, of course. The children, mostly." She got up wearily and went to stare into the fireplace. "I didn't know Mel had been turned and was using his role as a way of making money. There was no Canadian cousin. Those were meetings with my control." She paused. "I love you, Jason. I have from the beginning." She returned to the sofa and hugged her purse.

Jason stared at the door, his head tilted in pain. He wiped at a tear.

Nantes watched Sarah with the muzzle of his pistol now trained on her. "What was Cuzco's role? Who was he?"

Sarah folded her arms across her chest. "Rank and file. Good man. A separatist from Puerto Rico. Loyal to me. He was a courier and doubled at anything else that was needed. I'll miss him. It got so mixed up." She chuckled ruefully. She cast Jason a glance, then turned back to the flames. "He was to get you out of the way until things could be worked out. I needed time. There was going to be some sort of message from a dissident group. Like the Symbianese Liberation Army. I could have fixed the evidence. I don't know—something like that. I was very angry with Mel. He was furious with you, Jason." Her voice trailed off.

She rose slowly and walked to the window that looked out onto the car, her arms still protecting her chest. "I knew something was wrong at the party. I can understand his anger. He thought you were with him all along. He told me he decided not to let you in on his becoming an industrial spy, figuring you would be opposed. But for a different reason. You're so idealistic. Far more than the rest of us, really." She sniffed a little laugh. "The odd thing is, we were both wrong about you. He would be devastated."

Nantes advanced a step on Sarah. "How did you kill him?"

"Dart gun. Specialty of the old KGB." Her voice was low.

"From Cuzco?" Nantes asked.

"No. Cynthia Sanchez. She's the armorer." Sarah turned away from the window and walked slowly to the sofa, where she again sat with her purse against her leg.

Nantes watched Sarah with admiration and awe. When she sat down, he looked over at her husband. He was leaning with his back against the door staring into space with his hands still in his pants pockets.

Neither he nor Nantes saw her move. It was slow and subtle, much like a woman planning a demure assault on her mouth with a favorite lipstick buried in her purse. It was a pistol she pulled out instead. By the time Nantes was aware of it, Sarah had the weapon up and leveled at him. Before his hand muscles began to clench the blue steel of the semiautomatic, she pulled the trigger twice in rapid succession, firing two tiny poison-laced titanium needle darts into his body. The first pierced his jacket and shirt, and penetrated the left side of his rib cage. The second burrowed deep into in his neck.

Nantes jerked and swung around, brought the heavy semiautomatic around to point at her, and pulled the trigger. The pistol coughed and the bullet took Sarah in the chest, just above and to the left of her heart. She threw the dart gun involuntarily. It thudded onto the desk behind the sofa, then clattered to the hard brick floor. She sat, mouth open and glassy-eyed for two seconds, then collapsed onto the floor next to the hearth.

Nantes jerked and twitched, lost control of his pistol, which clattered onto the floor, and fell back against the wall. He was dead before he hit the floor.

Jason hardly realized what had happened at first, and watched helplessly as he watched Sarah and Nantes shoot each other. He took a tentative step toward Sarah, then hurried around the sofa to kneel down beside her. She was dead.

He stood up and looked down at Nantes's crumpled body. He lingered for a few seconds, then walked out through the heavy door into the damp, cold night. He left the door open.

Oddly, he thought, his dizziness and headache had left him. Over his left shoulder, the three-quarter moon was breaking through the clouds and bathing Truchas and the traces of snow on the caps of the pristine Sangre de Cristo mountains above it in a clear, blue glow.

21

*V*era walked through the front door of her house, across the porch, and onto the hardpan in front of it. She stopped for an instant to squint against the fresh morning sun to her left from under her broad-brimmed straw hat, then up to the side of the mesa to her right. The recent rains had gone a long way toward erasing the blackened area left by the fire and the scars where the wrecked Cherokee had lain crumpled and melted into globs of aluminum.

She looked down at the softening tracks where the government truck had come to carry off what was left of the plane. They had destroyed some of the sage; but they would grow back in a few months.

She turned away and walked toward the barn as she whistled at the roan in the pasture. The horse snorted and shook its great head, threw up its tail and raced along the fence, then stopped to graze again.

A glint of light caught Vera's attention, so she turned her head. Something shiny from the sunlight bouncing off it was coming toward her along the road from the south. It looked like a pickup truck. She stopped to watch with a sense of dread and took a deep breath against the feeling. As the truck came closer, she searched for a memory of it, but there was none. It was too shiny. Old, but renewed. There was a man at the wheel. Nothing unusual. She stopped in her tracks and waited, deeply curious, because there was something familiar beginning to well up. The man wore dark glasses; yet in the dark of the cab against the light of the rear window, she felt there was a familiar shape to his head. Then she knew who it should be but could not. She smiled and frowned at the same time at the ridiculousness of her surmise.

She walked toward the pickup as it moved slowly along the final stretch of road into the ranch.

Jason rolled the window down as he stopped the truck alongside her. His smile was compressed, wry, and mixed with triumph. "Think you could use an extra hand?"

Vera's mouth dropped open, and she lost her composure for the first time in a long while. She stared wildly, shook her head and flapped her arms against her sides. "But, you—!"

He nodded dramatically. "I know. I'm supposed to be dead. Officially, I am, but I may not be much longer. I repeat my question. Can you?"

"Just might. We can talk about it over lunch. Got some fresh beef steak." Her heart jumped and her eyes were bright.

Jason saw tears well up. "Good." His face split in a wide grin, then he sobered. "I'd like to park this where it can't be seen."

※

Peter Grayson sat perusing reports at his desk in the federal building in Albuquerque, when Lucero entered and rapped on the door frame. Grayson looked up. "Yeah. What's up?"

Lucero carried a manilla folder. He advanced and stood in front of Grayson's desk. "The Geronimo Queen case?"

"Yes?" He wore a pained expression.

"Something peculiar. Thought you better have a look." He held the folder out.

Grayson continued to stare at Lucero as he took the folder with measured trepidation, hesitated, spread it open and looked inside. "What am I gonna find in here?"

"Well, remember the guy who filed the report on the Thompson plane crash? Agent named Nantes? Can't find any record of him on the bureau roster."

Grayson stopped reading and looked up. "No?"

"No. But here's the kicker. New Mexico State Police and the Rio Arriba County Sheriff's office reported finding the bodies of two people, a man and a woman, in a house in Truchas. The woman was Sarah Thompson and the man, one Victor Nantes." Lucero shrugged broadly with his shoulders and arms, his eyes wide.

Grayson, his mouth agape, stared at the other FBI agent.